PRETENSE

More by John Di Frances

Achieving Sustainable Growth & Profitability: The Practical Application of Strategic Innovation in Business (2016)

Minding The Giraffes: The People Side of Innovation (2012)

Reclaiming The Ethical High Ground: Developing Organizations of Character (2002)

JackBilt™ A Company: Of Happy, Successful People (2001)

UPCOMING

Fiction:

IMBROGLIO TRILOGY: The BAIT! — Book Two
REVELATIONS — Book Three

Non Fiction:

REAL Strategic Planning: A CEO's Guide - Release 2019

Radical Leadership—Release 2020

IMBROGLIO TRILOGY

PRETENSE

IMBROGLIO TRILOGY

JOHN DI FRANCES

RELIANCE BOOKS PUBLISHING

Cover Design by eclipsedesign

RELIANCE BOOKS PUBLISHING, LLC
www.RelianceBooks.com   Contact@RelianceBooks.com

PRETENSE is the first book of the IMBROGLIO TRILOGY
http://www.ImbroglioTrilogy.com

Author: John Di Frances—Author, BusinessConsultant & Speaker
www.StrategicInnovation.Consulting   www.difrances.com

Names: Di Frances, John
Title: Pretense /by John Di Frances
        p. cm.

Hardcover	ISBN: 978-0-9709908-6-0
Paperback	ISBN: 978-0-9709908-7-7
Large Print Paperback	ISBN: 978-1-7321578-0-4
eBook	ISBN:978-1-7321578-2-8
Audiobook*	ISBN: 978-1-7321578-1-1

1.Thrillers 2. Action & Adventure 3. Suspense 4. Realistic Fiction

*AudioBook formats—Downloadable Audio files, PlayAway® & CD

The people and events in this book are fictional … but could happen.

Plot, character development, realism, and believability are critical to me in developing these stories. The places described are real, including street names as well as hotels, restaurants, airports and train stations … and depicted as closely as practicable to the actual locations.

I write for those who enjoy an intricate, yet believable plot with enough twists, turns, and action to keep the suspense flowing. At the same time, I believe that action should not dominate, much less overwhelm the storyline.

PRETENSE is dedicated to fiction lovers everywhere.

John Di Frances

IMBROGLIO TRILOGY

With heartfelt thanks to all of those who read through some rather **rough** early drafts and provided constructive criticism which made for a better story. And with special thanks to my tireless editors Sarah Anne Webber and Christy Di Frances, PhD., whose input through many months and five long edits helped me to craft a far richer and more fluid novel.

And special thanks to Tara Hurley, for the great service she rendered to us.

And lastly, to my wife Sally, who encouraged me to write fiction.

IMBROGLIOTRILOGY.com

IMBROLIO DEFINED

im·bro·glio

noun: imbroglio; plural noun: imbroglios
an extremely confused, or complicated situation.

synonyms: complicated situation, complication, problem,
difficulty, predicament, trouble, confusion, quandary,
entanglement, muddle, mess, quagmire, morass, sticky
situation, bind, jam, pickle, fix, corner, hole, scrape,
a confused heap.

IMBROGLIO TRILOGY

"The strong man is the one who is able to intercept at will the communication between the senses and the mind."

Napoléon Bonaparte

IMBROGLIO TRILOGY

Chapter 1:

A Trendy Couple

March 11th, Bratislava, Slovak Republic

It was an unusually warm day for March, and the abundance of sunlight made one feel as though spring had actually arrived. The sunshine, with its inviting warmth, gave the illusion that on such a day, nothing bad could possibly happen. The day was simply too perfect.

Passing the front desk, the couple paused momentarily for Bruce Pearce to pass the ornate brass room key, tethered by a long gold and crimson braided cord, into the upturned palm of the Front Desk Manager. Marrol's Boutique Hotel was in every way a match for the trendy Irish couple, Bruce and Sarah Pearce, who both enjoyed the privilege of dual British and American citizenship. As they stepped out from under the the luxury hotel's imposing edifice with its Neo-Baroque architecture and opulent interior, it seemed as though the stylish pair was simply an extension of the hotel itself. Yes, elegance personified.

Sarah Pearce's Irish ancestry was clearly evident. Her creamy complexion, delicate hint of freckles, penetrating blue eyes and fiery red hair were only the beginning of this beguiling woman. She was stunning! Though only five foot five, four-inch heels afforded her a statuesque five foot nine inch height. Sarah flaunted a perfect figure and had the poise of a woman who may have once modeled professionally. A small rectangular black purse in her left hand held vertically at the hip, further accentuated her height.

Sarah certainly knew how to dress, although today she clearly wasn't seeking public attention. A black, floppy wide-brimmed hat covered much of her face while her red, wavy hair cascaded from beneath. Designer sunglasses further shielded her from inquiring eyes. But that's where any attempt at concealment ended. Her snug black dress did nothing to hide the exquisite proportions of an athletic physique. It's mid-calf length, together with her stiletto heels, directed attention to a pair of beautifully toned legs. At thirty-five, heads would turn, and conversations stop when Sarah walked into a room.

At her side, her husband Bruce cut an equally striking figure with his muscular six foot two inch frame and self-confidant bearing. He wore dark sunglasses, a tailored white shirt, a black sports jacket and jeans completed by handmade Italian loafers. His fair skin and jet-black hair provided the perfect counterpart for Sarah. Bruce also gave the unmistakable impression of a heightened physical prowess and with it … the capacity to instantly respond to any circumstance—without hesitation.

Outside the Marrol, on the street side, two bellmen had already brought up the couple's vehicles. Without a word or, in fact, any form of acknowledgment, Bruce handed each a crisp U.S. $100 bill. Slipping into the driver's seat of the second car, Sarah started the engine and waited for Bruce to do likewise in the lead car. As the pair of black Mercedes

E300s pulled away from Marrol's Boutique Hotel, the bellmen grinned at each other. One commented, "Now that's what I call living!" The other nodded in agreement.

The two cars proceeded in tandem to the popular Sky Bar & Restaurant, a short distance away. On approaching, they turned right off Paulinho onto Rigehleo Street. Just before intersecting with Hviezdoslavovo na´mestie, the parking lane ended, replaced by a large stone planter containing shrubs and flowering trees. Slowing to a stop beside the last parking space, Bruce emerged from the car and deftly collected up the safety cones which had been blocking the parking space while Sarah drove on turning right onto Hviezdoslavovo na´mestie. After depositing the cones behind the planter, he returned to the Mercedes and backed into the now available parking spot screened by foliage from oncoming traffic.

Having parked their cars in opposite directions from Sky Bar, the two walked down the street towards one other. Meeting Sarah just in front of the bar, Bruce took her right hand, in which she held the car keys, in his left as they entered the building together and rode the elevator to the top floor for a late lunch. The Sky Bar is a rooftop glass sunroom offering a breathtaking panoramic view of the Bratislava. The maître d' was quick to confirm the 'Pearce' reservation and show them to their requested table along the glass wall overlooking the city and street below.

Whether as a fashion statement or to shield her face from inquisitive eyes, Sarah removed neither her hat nor her dark glasses. Likewise, Bruce elected not to take off his sunglasses. Normally, this may have appeared strange in a restaurant, but the bright sunshine streaming in through the overhead glass resulted in other patrons doing the same. The sparse conversation between the couple progressed from the art in Bratislava to their upcoming beach vacation in the Greek Isles. Bruce ordered wine, an appetizer, and lunch for two.

It wasn't long before Miroslav Cagacikova, the Slovakian Prime Minister, arrived in a party of four accompanied by two bodyguards. The maître d' seated them at their usual table, which was near enough to Bruce and Sarah that they could have overheard the conversation. That is if they had cared to do so, but they showed even less interest in the Prime Minister's table conversation than in their own.

However at nearby tables, several other heads nodded periodically in agreement as patrons overheard the Prime Minister and his deputies discuss their growing concern with what they considered the EU's heavy-handed tactics in seeking more power and control over individual countries' internal affairs. In recent months, many Slovakians had come to view the Brussels-based EU leadership with growing unease and distrust.

Following a leisurely lunch, Bruce summoned the waiter. "I am ready for the check."

"Can I not interest you and the lady in one of our chef's amazing desserts? He is widely renowned in Bratislava for his masterful creations. They are indeed superb."

"No," Bruce responded curtly, his voice lacking any emotion whatsoever.

The waiter quickly disappeared, returning a few minutes later with the check. Bruce glanced at it and then counted out two U.S. $100 bills. Handing these to the waiter he stated, "No change is required."

"I regret that I cannot accept U.S. dollars," the waiter replied, "especially such large bills."

As this was Slovakia, a country where hard currency is highly prized, the maître d' who had been watching the couple intently from a short distance away, promptly hurried over. He interceded, "We would be pleased to make an exception to our normal rule for you." Bruce then handed both the waiter and maître d' crisp U.S. $50 bills, an additional tip for their accommodation. Both men smiled broadly and thanked him.

"Please bring my wife another glass of wine," Bruce requested, as he rose to leave the restaurant. The waiter, having received the additional generous tip, was doubly appreciative, and cheerfully returned with an extra large glass of wine. Thereafter, he remained unusually attentive to the beautiful woman, now that she was alone, having been 'abandoned' by her husband.

Sarah lingered long over her glass of wine. It was now late afternoon, and the light was growing softer. The restaurant and bar had mostly emptied of the usual lunch customers and the after-work cocktail and evening dinner crowd had not yet begun to arrive.

Even if it had been busy, neither the waiter nor the maître d' were in any hurry for her to leave, and although neither had ever seen the attractive couple before, both secretly hoped they would frequently return These days few patrons understood the value of gracious tipping as this couple did. And, if she remained for another hour until the cocktail and dinner crowd began to arrive, having such an alluring beauty so prominently placed would benefit business. *If only she would remove the broad-brimmed hat and dark glasses,* the maître d' thought to himself. *Certainly, she must be even lovelier than he imagined—or why would she shield herself so from public view?* But 'hidden' so conspicuously, she did add an ambiance of intrigue to the establishment. Secretly, they wondered if she was a British or perhaps an American stage or movie star shying away from the paparazzi.

Sarah periodically glanced down at the street below, as if waiting for someone or something to appear. In between these glances, she mostly stared at her wine glass disregarding the few remaining patrons and the Prime Minister's table, although the Prime Minister's aide was noticeably cognizant of Sarah. The waiter returned to her as often as was polite, trying not to appear too conspicuous, but to his dismay, she offered him no encouragement and evidenced disinterest in his attentiveness.

It was nearing 4:00 pm when the Prime Minister's table finished lunch and headed for the elevator with the security detail. The discourse with his deputies had been in preparation for his meeting that evening with Aleksander Dunajewski, the Polish Prime Minister. Outside, a third member of the security detail brought up the Prime Minister's car for the short trip to the airport. Following a brief parting conversation in front of Sky Bar with his deputies and aide, Prime Minister Cagacikova and the security service detail got into the car. The driver immediately executed a U-turn and headed back down the street toward the corner.

Peering down at the street below, Sarah watched as the entourage dispersed their separate ways and the Prime Minister's car turned around. She opened her purse, removed a black cell phone and touched the home button on the phone. The display lit up, revealing a single pre-programed telephone number on speed dial.

By now, the car approached the corner, slowing to turn left onto Rigehleo Street. As the Mercedes executed the turn, Sarah pressed the speed dial number.

An instant later, as the Prime Minister's car disappeared from view, a bright flash of yellow-orange flame billowed out from behind the corner building down Rigehleo Street and onto Hviezdoslavovo na ´mestie. In that moment, it was as if lightning had struck, but uncannily, without the anticipated loud thunderclap. For a brief space of eternity, Sarah sat breathless … then the loud rumble of a powerful explosion split the air, rattling the panoramic windows of Sky Bar. Sarah gasped, the explosion had been more violent than she expected. Quickly regaining her composure, she turned off the phone and placed it back in her purse.

At first, frozen by shock, no one else in the restaurant moved at all. They seemed like marble statues, incapable of action. But after a few interminable seconds, they came back to life, first the waiter, then the maître d', and the few guests who only moments before had been enjoying lunch or relaxing over a drink and conversation, then finally, the two bartenders. Moments later, staff began streaming out from the kitchen, moving en masse to the window wall like a dazed herd, where Sarah sat motionless. No one spoke, they just stood there, gaping at the street below, eyes and mouths wide open, bewildered and wondering what could have happened. Out of the group, a voice said, "Do you think there's been a natural gas main explosion under the street?" Then someone half shouted, "Call the police! … Call the fire department … and some ambulances! There must be injured people down there."

Sarah remained seated and silent. Her gaze moved from the street below to her nearly empty wine glass. Guiding the glass to her lips in a smooth, effortless arc, she took one last sip and placed the empty glass back on the table. By now, the crowd at the window was moving in her direction along the glass wall, all straining to gain a better view of the scene below and to their left.

One of the cooks announced, "I'm going to call the police." Although nearly everyone had cell phones, no one had thought to use one for that call. But several people, cell phones in hand, were now taking photos and video of the burning debris strewn along the street near the corner. Across the street, and from the first floor below, people began pouring out of buildings, wondering what had caused the thunderous, window-rattling boom.

Sarah knew what had happened. Prime Minister Cagacikova and his security detail were dead. She slowly rose and, for the first time that afternoon, no one noticed as she walked towards the elevator. In fact, no one noticed her at all. Alone, she entered the elevator and descended to the first floor. She walked to the women's restroom, which was devoid of people, as was the restaurant's entire first floor.

She opened her purse and removed the cell phone. Wetting several paper towels, she rubbed the phone clean, wrapped it in them and deposited the phone in the trash receptacle. She then washed her hands, and after using several more paper towels to dry them, placed these in the trash atop the cell phone. Looking in the mirror, she smiled, pleased with her image.

Leaving the restroom, she passed through the deserted restaurant and out onto the street. By now, the scene was teeming with people, a very few even daring to move cautiously up the street toward the corner where debris was still burning. Most, however, stayed well back, unsure of what might happen next. Sirens wailed as emergency vehicles from all directions began arriving at the scene of the explosion.

Walking nonchalantly in the opposite direction from the carnage, Sarah passed the high chain link fence, silently defending the American Embassy entrance. Four Marines stood out front cradling their M-16 rifles and looking down the street at the billowing clouds of black smoke rising from the far end of the block. For once, the alluring lady in the broad-brimmed hat was invisible to those around her, even to the young male Marines, but not to the CCTV cameras mounted on the buildings along the street. Reaching the intersection and turning the corner, Sarah slipped into a waiting black Mercedes which then drove off, vanishing into the heart of Bratislava.

Chapter 2:

As If Nothing Had Happened

Arriving back at Marrol's Boutique Hotel, Bruce instructed the bellman to have the car ready the following morning at 10 am sharp. The couple proceeded directly to their luxury suite, pausing only momentarily at the front desk for Bruce to retrieve their room key. Sarah immediately changed into workout clothes—a smart-looking outfit she had purchased from Athleta, the fashionable U.S.-based women's casual clothing purveyor. Her scoop-necked, neon-green tank top formed a bright contrast to black workout shorts with reflective white side stripes. Tying her hair up into a ponytail and donning running shoes, Sarah was quickly off to the Marrol's Fitness Centre.

Meanwhile, Bruce arranged a private dinner from the restaurant for two that evening on the hotel's romantic Summer Terrace. Although it had been an unseasonably warm spring, Bruce knew that with the setting sun the air would cool, and he instructed the staff to have three propane heaters ready and lit at 7:45 pm sharp, in preparation for their arrival. Then he left the hotel, returning thirty minutes later with a single parcel under his arm.

Sarah began her workout with stretches, then weights and finally twenty minutes on the treadmill, running at a fast pace. She didn't enjoy public gyms, but fortunately this evening the Fitness Centre was deserted. Finishing at 6:30 pm, Sarah had timed her workout routine to perfectly coincide with her appointment at the Jasmine Spa, located within the hotel. At 7:20 pm she returned to the room where Bruce waited. She showered and dressed for dinner. They left the room at precisely 8:05 pm.

Bruce wore formal Black Tie attire, and Sarah was resplendent in a strapless, shimmering azure dress, which brilliantly contrasted with her brilliant red hair and accentuated her figure. Framed by a pearl choker and matching drop earrings, her hair flowed dramatically down her back in cascading waves.

At the Marrol Hotel, the Restaurant Houdini's motto: *The Magic of Wine, The Art of Taste* is manifested by an extraordinary wine list and sumptuous cuisine. The dinner, which had been pre-selected by Bruce, began with oyster soup as the first of five courses. Three different wines graced the successive dishes, with a lemon sorbet palette cleanser preceding the fish-plate third course. The round table was romantically lit by six candles in hurricane sconces; a broad swan-shaped Waterford lead-crystal vase playfully reflected the candles' dancing flames. Brimming with fresh flowers, the arrangement furnished a riot of color amid the soft candlelight, filling the night air with the intoxicating allure of roses, gardenias, and ambrosial jasmine. Two waiters attended the couple as they dined privately in a secluded corner of the Summer Terrace.

Although the day's warmth had faded with the sunset, the evening remained unusually pleasant for so early in the year. This, together with the three propane heaters, kept Sarah comfortable, despite the fact that she wore only the gossamer blue dress. But as they awaited dessert, the air chilled, and she began to shiver. Rising from his chair, Bruce removed his jacket and placed it tenderly around Sarah's shoulders. As he sat down, the pieste de resitance appeared table-side with a flourish in the form of two brightly flaming Creme Brulées, complimented by steaming caffè lungos, over which they lingered long.

Sarah's thoughts turned to their upcoming vacation in the Greek Isles, only a few days hence. Again, she reminded Bruce that she just wanted this contract to be over and the two of them to get away together ... alone. And that there was nothing appealing about a luxurious beach villa on the Greek coast with an unsavory 'third-wheel' tagging along. Couldn't Bruce do something to alter this?

"No," he reminded her. They had been over this ground multiple times before. The client had carefully planned and specified every detail of the contract, and Sarah knew the terms. He reached across the table and touched her face gently. Raising her chin, he looked into her eyes, "When this is over, we'll make an unscheduled stop in Milan so that you can enjoy a bit of extra spring shopping." With that promise, Sarah's face brightened.

"Come," he said, "let's go upstairs before you catch a chill. The night air is becoming quite cool."

Rising from the table, Bruce put his arm around Sarah, and together they strolled slowly through the Summer Terrace, enjoying the early flowers and fragrant night air. Then, taking their leave, they returned to the room.

The room was spacious, the best accommodation the Marrol offered, comprising a luxurious living room, a large bedroom, and bath, all elegantly decorated with careful attention to every comfort and detail. On the round table, a Murano Italian vase overflowed with another immense bouquet. The gold embroidered bedspread had been turned down. On it, a box of world renowned Du Rhône chocolates, specially ordered by the Marrol from Geneva, Switzerland at Bruce's request. A single red rose on each pillow completed the effect. The lights throughout the room were on, but Bruce moved quickly to dim them. Sarah walked over to one of the large windows and gazed out through the sheer curtain, at the glittering city lights while Bruce moved silently around the room lighting candles.

Approaching her from behind, he removed the dinner jacket which still hung over her shoulders and placed it on the back of a chair. Lovingly, he caressed her neck and then led her away from the window. Slowly unzipping her dress, he let it glide effortlessly to the floor. She turned to face him, but he spun her around again and unhooked her bra, then let it fall, as he had done so many times during their six years of marriage.

✳ ✳ ✳

March 12th, Morning

Bruce awoke before Sarah. The early morning light was already streaming softly through the sheer curtains, creating a translucent aura. He sat up, swung his legs over the side of the bed about to stand, but then turning back, gazed at Sarah. She was in a deep sleep, her head cradled by the pillow, on her face an expression of such peace he couldn't help but lean back over her to kiss her cheek. She looked so lovely to him, almost angelic. He could only but marvel at her beauty. In fact, she seemed to him at that moment to be more beautiful than ever before, even more so than when they had first met … or the day they had married.

He rose out of bed and moving about the room silently, quickly donned his jogging suit, running shoes, baseball cap, and sunglasses. Turning to take one last fleeting look at Sarah's face, he left the room quietly, closing the door behind him. Downstairs, he strode rapidly through the front lobby and out into the sunshine for his morning run.

Sarah awoke sometime later. As sleep departed, she thought of the previous night. What a wonderful time they had enjoyed together. Then sitting up in bed, she felt her head begin to reel. The sudden dizziness made her drop back onto the pillow. Too much wine, she thought. No … way too much wine! Oh, but it was worth it. Oh yes, so very worth it!

Laying there for some minutes, Sarah dreamily reveled in her thoughts of the prior night. How she wished they could begin it all over again this morning, but she knew they had a strict timetable which needed to be kept. Yet, the bed was so warm and comfortable and, as long as she laid still, her head seemed to float softly, adrift on a tranquil sea. Slowly, she forced herself up and out of bed. She made her way to the shower, desperately needing to be revived.

About 8 am, Bruce returned to the Marrol. Stopping at the front desk, he requested his bill. Reviewing it, he inquired, "Has this morning's breakfast, which I pre-ordered from room service yesterday, been included?" The front desk manager confirmed that it had and showed him the line entry. "Excellent!" Bruce replied. He told the manager to close out his bill as he would be leaving at 10 am. "And we'll have your car out front promptly at 10," one of the bellmen added politely. Bruce did not respond.

The front desk manager handed Bruce his copy of the bill and the couple's passports. Paying the bill in U.S. dollars, Bruce then quickly moved through the lobby, up the elevator, and into the room. "Good morning!" he exclaimed exuberantly in a loud and overly cheerful voice to Sarah who, still in a fog, was trying to finish dressing.

"Not so loud!" she whispered, "I have a wee bit of a headache this morning."

"I can't imagine why?" Bruce boomed, as a wry smile spread broadly across his face. Sarah said nothing, but shook her head slowly and stuck out her tongue at him. Bruce passed by her, delivering a sharp smack of his hand against her backside.

"Hey!" she exclaimed as she jumped, "What was that for?" Bruce continued toward the shower without responding.

Breakfast was delivered promptly at 9:00 am. It included oatmeal with cinnamon and honey for Bruce and plain yogurt for Sarah, along with a medley of fresh berries to garnish both, hot croissants with jam and a pot of strong black coffee. But as they had a big day ahead, he had also ordered two omelettes, which came with whole wheat toast and a rasher of thick bacon, slightly crispy, the way he liked it.

"How many are coming for breakfast?" Sarah inquired facetiously.

"Breakfast is the power that fuels the day," he responded, using a line he had spouted frequently in the past.

"I don't feel like being fueled this morning. More like finding a hole somewhere to crawl into and hide."

"You obviously need to repent of your wild ways," Bruce replied cheerily.

"But one requires a soul in order to repent," Sarah retorted. They both laughed.

Sarah wore another of her casual Athleta outfits. It was a brand which she frequently ordered online. She loved the way their clothing fit and moved with her body, as well as the youthful, athletic look. Sarah worked hard at keeping herself in top condition and believed that her clothing should reflect that vitality. She felt empowered when she looked in the mirror. Virtually all of her workout and casual wear came from the company's website, as their clothing accentuated her form and greatly pleased Bruce as well. The arrival of each new parcel delighted Sarah. She always knew there would be compliments from Bruce and often more waiting whenever she modeled FedEx's latest delivery.

As for her other togs, almost everything originated in Italy, where she loved to shop. Milan and Rome were her favorites, although she liked the shopping in Milan best. Each year, they would take several excursions to Italy so that Sarah could shop. On fine sunny days, Bruce frequently camped out in a nearby café to read, while she flitted from one exclusive shop to another, indulging her consumeristic desires.

Bruce never said a word about the expense; in fact, he was in her mind the *perfect husband,* willingly 'aiding and abetting' these shopping sprees. If it made her happy, and Bruce did love the clothes she bought and the way she looked in them, then he was happy. She would emerge from a shop, bags, and parcels in hand

and park them on the chairs next to Bruce in the café, where he patiently awaited her return from each foray, enjoying the weather and occasionally people watching. On a particularly good shopping day, he might hail an Uber to come collect the growing heap of packages and deliver them to their hotel. He hated carrying anything unless absolutely necessary.

Their ample breakfast concluded, Bruce picked up the backpack he had acquired and filled for Sarah the previous afternoon. He lifted it onto her shoulders; she snapped the strap buckle in place around her waist. Turning, she wrapped her arms around him and kissed him as he embraced her. Holding her for a moment, he then released her. Bruce opened the door for Sarah, and she stepped out into the hallway. It was 9:50 am.

Entering the empty elevator, she descended to the lobby. Exiting, she paused along the wall of the hallway adjoining the Marrol's lobby. An elderly couple strolled arm-in-arm past a well-dressed, middle-aged businessman who appeared to be waiting for someone. Moments later, an attractive young woman rounded the corner. The businessman smiled and greeted her with a kiss on each cheek; the two headed toward the front doors. No one else seemed to be around. Sarah hesitated a moment, looking in the direction of the front desk, where a hotel manager was standing, looking back in her direction. She waited several seconds more and then, like a stealthy cat, silently slipped out of the hotel's rear entrance.

Waiting precisely ten minutes following Sarah's departure, Bruce checked his phone for the driver's progress, then left the room, with two roller suitcases in tow. Once in the lobby, he noticed a gathering of hotel employees and three policemen, two uniformed and one in plain clothes, directly across from the front desk. As far as he was concerned, plain clothes police might as well wear uniforms, as he could instantly spot them, even at a distance.

Bruce walked across the lobby straight toward them and then, turned suddenly, in a pronounced maneuver he knew would draw their attention and approached the front desk. In a voice just loud enough for the group to overhear, he asked, "Has an Uber arrived for me yet?"

One of the bellmen, standing beside the front desk responded, "An Uber driver pulled up just a moment ago and is waiting outside the front door. Is he here for you?"

"Yes," said Bruce and with a smile handed the bellman a €5 note and walked through the door into the waiting Uber BMW.

❋ ❋ ❋

The Police

The police had arrived at the hotel at 9:55 am. There were three of them, two uniformed officers and a Detective Inspector. Earlier that morning, after investigators had confirmed overnight that the blast resulted from a high explosive charge which had been placed in a Mercedes 450 automobile parked at the corner of Rigehleo Street and Hviezdoslavovo na´mestie, the police had begun fanning out across the city to canvas all of the hotels. At the Marrol, the police first questioned the manager on duty, followed by the hotel's General Manager. They explained that they were there to interview the entire guest service staff, inquiring whether anyone had seen or heard anything unusual that might shed light on the previous day's assassination of the Prime Minister and his security detail.

The General Manager said that he completely understood the need for police inquiries. He offered the total cooperation of the hotel staff if they could in anyway be of assistance in solving this horrific crime, an act which had rocked the nation. "Such a nefarious deed certainly needs to be solved quickly and the perpetrators executed!" The General Manager continued to affirm that he fully supported the current government and Prime Minister Cagacikova and that he too, like many of his fellow Slovaks, was deeply concerned by what they saw as the EU's growing overreach.

At 11 am, the police were just finishing their interviews, having failed to obtain any useful information helpful for the investigation, when an officer from Interpol, Marek Farkas, arrived with his deputy. The name 'Farkas,' means 'The Wolf.' Marek was a shrewd, highly professional man, in his late thirties, and already well-experienced, who in his relatively brief career, had participated in a number of successful high-profile investigations across the continent.

Why he selected the Marrol as the hotel to visit that morning is unknown. Possibly, it was mere chance, pure instinct, or possibly, something in his keen insight told him that this was the place to be. However it happened, he was there now to supervise the local police as they concluded their interviews of the hotel staff.

Marek addressed the Detective Inspector. "What have you learned here thus far?"

"Nothing of value sir, I'm afraid," he responded.

"No, nothing at all," they responded almost in unison, shaking their heads solemnly.

"Nothing at all?" Marek repeated.

"No, sir," they responded again, with even more enthusiastic animation.

"Who has checked out of the hotel this morning?" Marek asked the manager.

"A family with two small children," the manager replied.

"How long had they been guests here?"

"More than a week," said the manager. "They were from Italy, traveling through Europe on a holiday sightseeing tour."

"Anyone else?" Marek pressed.

"An elderly couple from the U.S. celebrating their anniversary. No one else."

Marek walked outside and then back in again. "How long has that black Mercedes been parked out front?"

One of the bellmen answered him, "That belongs to the society couple, very special people. They ordered it to be out in front and ready for them at 10 am sharp."

"It's now 11:10 am, why haven't they come for it yet?"

The bellmen looked at each other and grinned, "If you saw her, the redheaded wife, you'd know why they are still in their room."

Marek ignored their enthusiasm. "How long are they staying?"

"Oh yes, I forgot to mention, they are leaving today also," responded the manager.

"Isn't it already past your checkout time?" asked Marek.

"Yes, but they have already checked out. I mean, Mr. Pearce went jogging early this morning and paid the bill when he returned, before going up to his suite."

"Did he also pick up their passports?" Marek asked.

"He did indeed."

"And neither of them has come down since?" Marek continued.

"No," they all responded, shaking their heads in unison yet again.

Marek turned to his deputy, "Go outside and run the license plate on the Mercedes. And do it quickly!" The deputy disappeared through the hotel's front entrance. Marek focused his attention back to the local police and asked more questions of them. Then turning to the front desk manager, he inquired, "You say the couple checked out and collected their passports earlier this morning?"

"Yes," the manager responded. "I believe it was about 8 am before I took my morning espresso."

"You didn't by chance take a copy of their passports, did you?" Marek inquired.

"Of course. Indeed, we do so with all of our international guests," the manager stated, his face brightening slightly. Turning to the woman from the back office, he asked her to retrieve the photocopies.

"How long did they stay? Marek asked.

"Only two nights," the manager answered, "but we all hope they will return often."

Just then, Marek's deputy reappeared and walking over to Marek whispered to him, "The Mercedes plates are not in the database, and there is a report of two black Mercedes 450s having been stolen from a Mercedes dealership across the border four days ago."

Marek turned back to the front desk just as the woman appeared with the two passport copies. Taking the copies, he told the manager to come with him and bring the room key. He directed his deputy and the three local policemen to follow. With his puzzled entourage in tow, Marek went up the elevator and down the corridor to the couple's luxury suite.

The manager knocked lightly on the room door. After a few moments, he knocked again, this time calling out, "Mr. Pearce, are you there?"

After a moment, Marek pushed him aside and pounded loudly on the door. No response. Marek took the key from the manager and opened the door.

The room was empty. No luggage. Nothing.

Marek hurriedly conducted the group back downstairs. He turned again to the Marrol's lobby employees and said, "Now think! Think very hard! Who else did you see leaving the hotel this morning?"

After a moment, the manager said he had caught a brief glimpse across the lobby of a young woman in jogging attire, who left through the exit on the far side of the hotel. "What did she look like? demanded Marek.

"She was slim, wearing athletic clothing, a baseball cap, and sunglasses."

"What color was her hair? asked Marek.

"I'm not sure, sir," said the manager. "She had on a hat, as I said, with a backpack on her back. She was all the way on the far side of the lobby, near the elevator, and I only had a fleeting glimpse of her … but maybe … red … yes, I believe her hair may have been red."

Trying to conceal his growing impatience, Marek, turned to the bellmen. "Did you see anyone else leave?"

"No, they both replied. No one other than regular guests who are still staying here."

Then one of the local police officers said, "I did see someone else when we first began interviewing hotel employees here in the lobby." Looking at the other two policemen, he said, "Don't you remember? There was that airplane pilot in uniform who came into the lobby pulling two flight bags. He was quite tall. He stopped at the front desk, didn't he?"

Marek turned once again to the front desk manager. "Did a uniformed pilot come to the front desk?"

One of the bellmen answered, "Yes, he inquired whether an Uber driver had arrived for him. I told him 'yes,' and he gave me a €5 note. But it wasn't the husband of the couple. The airplane pilot was clean shaven and had sandy colored hair."

"What color were his eyes," asked Marek.

"I'm not certain," replied the bellman, "He was wearing those aviator mirror sunglasses …."

"And pulling two flight bags? asked Marek.

"Yes," said the bellman as the other bellman nodded in agreement.

"Tell me, now, how often have you seen an airline pilot with two flight bags? Don't they normally have one piece of luggage and a pilot's flight case?" That seemed right to them all, and they nodded in agreement. Turning once again to the manager, Marek asked, "Do airline crews normally even stay in this hotel?"

He thought a moment and then answered, "No, they don't. This is a boutique hotel, for high-end guests."

Did you have any flight crews staying here last evening?

The manager thought again, then replied "No," and he couldn't remember the last time an airline crew had been booked to stay there. Once again, the others agreed.

Marek turned to his deputy, who shrugged his shoulders and shook his head. "What about the passport copies, do you think they'll be of any use?" he asked Marek.

Marek looked down at the two sheets of paper he was still clutching tightly in his left hand. "Their passports are undoubtedly forgeries, just as surely as the Mercedes is stolen."

Chapter 3:
The Meet Up

March 14*th*, Warsaw, Poland

In keeping with his surname, Franz Jäger was a hunter. A hunter of unique prey, or so he fancied himself. Human beings. To look at it another way, as a more rational person might, he was a *for hire hit man*, a contract assassin. And of the most deviant sort, in that he relished it. Not that he had always been this way, but Franz's perspective had been altered by a tragic turn of events years earlier. Now, he loved the hunt, but even more so, the kill. The challenge. The experience. Assassination had become more than a mere profession. Franz had, in fact, become his profession.

In contrast, it was not that Bruce and Sarah were any less assassins, but rather that they viewed their career choice purely as a profession, no different from a doctor, lawyer, business executive or any other professional occupation. After all, business is business. They did take pride in their work, given the skill, efficiency, and professionalism with which each assignment was performed, leaving no 'trail' or 'loose ends.' However, the Pierce's also sought, where possible, to minimize collateral damage. Just as much 'professionals' as was Franz, but with a profound difference: They took no joy in the hunt or act of killing and had no desire to inflict unnecessary pain on their victims.

Bruce and Sarah were consummate pragmatists, accustomed to a jet-setter lifestyle. They had expensive tastes. *The business,* as they referred to their profession, afforded them a highly lucrative vocation with travel benefits and a very enviable and flexible work schedule. For them, it was merely a financially rewarding business.

Sarah was whip-smart, an Oxford University graduate with double Bachelor's degrees in Mathematics and Philosophy, followed by a Masters in Advanced Computer Science from Cambridge.

Her father, a career British civil servant, had served at a variety of embassies during her formative years, with the result being that Sarah spoke fluent French, Italian and Russian as well as a smattering of Arabic, in addition to her native British English and its American derivative. She was the archetypal product of class and privilege, her education having been conducted exclusively in private schools and with tutors.

At the time her parents met, Sarah's mother was an American stage actress, whose flamboyance and self-assurance were traits readily passed on to her daughter. Somewhat spoiled by her indulgent father, Sarah, an only child, had grown up headstrong, opinionated and fearless—in a world predominantly populated by adults. Living abroad in diverse cultures, Sarah's privileged early life experience further elevated her sense of self and boundless personal confidence, though she could be quite petty and even childish at times.

Her father's title during the expat embassy postings had been Economic Attache, although this reflected only the public-facing aspect of his work. His involvement with the British Intelligence Service, more commonly known as MI6, in reality, constituted the core of his responsibilities.

Bruce had been educated in both the U.K., and the U.S., his parents, an Irish mother and American father had divorced when he was seven, and after that, his life alternated between London and Boston. Also the product of wealth and society, he earned an undergraduate Interdisciplinary Degree in Humanities and Engineering with a minor in Applied International Studies from Massachusetts Institute of Technology (MIT).

As a youth, his father had instilled in him a strong sense of individualism. A regimen of rigorous physical conditioning and survival skills training were honed by summer wilderness camping and rafting trips, winter skiing and years of decidedly disciplined martial arts instruction. Bruce's father regularly traveled internationally on business, taking his son with him whenever possible. In college, Bruce's avocation was crew. He loved water and any pastime that centered on it. Crew combined this passion for water with his belief in athleticism, leadership, and teamwork as crucial factors for success.

Growing up on both sides of the Atlantic, Bruce learned to readily adapt to the alternating worlds of his youth. Following college, he had planned on joining either the American or British military, with the goal of serving in a Special Forces unit. However, in his senior year, he was introduced to an elite, off-shore private security firm, owned by a business associate of his father. He quickly decided the contractor opportunity presented a more intriguing and lucrative future than military service. This pleased his father and placated his mother, who equated the words 'private security consultant' with being far 'safer' than a career in the military, particularly 'special ops.'

As contract assassins, Bruce and Sarah saw themselves as being in the business of 'eliminating obstacles.' Nothing more, nothing less. No different than if they had been arborists, eliminating trees which blocked the light due more desirable species or a company that tows away vehicles that have been in a roadway accident and are impeding traffic flow. What they did was more complex and intricate, but they merely engaged in the performance of a high-end service that needed doing, as is the case with any other profession. And it wasn't as if this rationale had been conjured up in their minds as a justification for a guilty conscience run amuck. No, they actually believed this to be the fact of the matter.

On the other hand, Franz hated most everyone. The vast majority of his professional contract assignments had been based in the Middle East and involved the elimination of high profile political or business figures, although the latter had often been individuals with dubious connections to criminal syndicates, drug trade or the illegal weapons market. He had made a 'game' out of these, in two instances, actually threatening the target for sport before closing in for the kill. It was for indiscretions of this nature that his professional 'reputation' had begun to suffer.

He was extremely intelligent and could be deceptively charming, if and when he so desired. However, beneath the convincing facade of amiability, with which he could mask himself, Franz often seethed with hostility. He despised his native German people for their weakness in not rising once again following WWII to rule over the entirety of Europe and whatever lands beyond which they might have encroached. He was not a Nazi; this must be understood. Nazi's were members of the National Socialist German Workers' Party. Franz spurned any political affiliations. In fact, he regarded himself as completely apolitical. He believed that all of Germany's Dukes, Kaisers and political parties, past and present, had let the nation and her people down over and over again. He had, some years earlier, resigned himself to the fact that Germany would never again rise to become a true world superpower, an empire. In fact, perhaps the age of great empires had passed completely. Today, it was all about globalism and the United Nations, the EU and ….

Of this, Franz wanted no part. No, Franz was solely for Franz. He would sell his services to the highest bidder, whoever that might be, in any given instance, but sell his allegiance to no one: no creed, country or political movement. He would not be like those 'corrupt, dirty politicians' who were always on television, pandering to whichever group they could promise some new free benefit in return for a vote at election time. They disgusted him, but he decided that as much as he hated them, they had created a system which worked for them; he had resolved to do the same for himself.

Naturally, Franz was a loner. He worked alone, lived alone, and in fact, spent nearly all of his time alone. And if on occasion he wanted the company of a woman, he would 'rent one.' He felt no need to complicate his life with a 'relationship,' as others termed it. His only relationship need was business related. He needed clients to keep him employed. Although of late, business had been more than a little slow. He had wondered why? Had the assassination business been slow for everyone or was it something about him?

This questioning had led him to ask one of the middlemen 'arrangers' if the market was soft. He was told that it was not the market, it was him. Some of the 'better clients' apparently no longer wanted to do business with him. They felt he was 'emotionally conflicted,' whatever the hell that meant. What it meant to Franz was less business, since they apparently feared he might let emotions get in the way of job performance. This was B.S. He had never failed to complete an assignment on time and without leaving any loose ends remaining. Still, as the arranger had insisted, 'perception is reality to the client,' warning him that he had better watch his step or his name would soon become *persona non grata*.

The good news was that this assignment was an excellent one, and it pleased him immensely that he had been selected to perform it. It was an important assignment. A very high profile target. This was the type of work that could rehabilitate his flagging reputation. He just needed to be extra careful to get it right in every respect. And he would. He was certain of that.

The assignment was also special, in addition to being high profile, it was also unlike any other he had ever been contracted to perform. Clients specify the target and typically the general conditions of the assignment, such as when and if they have a preference for whether or not the assassination is public (usually not). In fact, most want the hit to be as low profile as possible, depending on the circumstances. The details—the how, where and when—are as a rule the prerogative of the professional performing the service.

However, this client was unusual, in the level of specificity and detailed instructions with which Franz had been provided. His means of arrival, where he was to stay, his preparations for the kill shot, what to do with the weapon afterward and his escape had been carefully orchestrated for him. It was clear to Franz; this had been planned by someone who knew the business, not some wannabe amateur. But why such detailed planning and preparations? That question concerned Franz. Who was this client? And how were they involved? Answers to these questions had not been provided.

Despite his concerns and misgivings, Franz had accepted the assignment. How could he not? The fee offered was more than he had expected, and successful completion of the contract would undoubtedly position him at the pinnacle of his professional specialty—top choice for new and old clients alike.

The fact that the assignment was so entirely different did have Franz a little spooked. Everything down to the last detail had been specified. Moreover, the client had even provided the means, which was most unusual in this craft. Franz thought it was rather like a fine dining restaurant requiring a master chef to use a knife set provided by the restaurant instead of the chef's own set of knives. Strange indeed!

He was to use a unique weapon provided by the client. Additionally, the kill was to be accomplished with a single shot. A head shot at a target in a crowd, although the distance was not significant, only 700 meters.

Franz had honed his skills in Iraq and Afghanistan serving with the Kommando Spezialkräfte (KSK), the German Special Forces during the multinational Operation Enduring Freedom and after that, as part of NATO's International Security Assistance Force (ISAF). He was undisputedly one of the best high-powered rifle snipers on the continent, capable of complex shots at extreme distances. That was undoubtedly why he had been selected, Franz told himself.

He was especially proud of his Kommando Spezialkräfte's selection early in his military career. The process for combat positions was highly competitive and intensely rigorous, with only the very best of the best succeeding. Franz reminded himself often that he was the best!

The qualification process was divided into two phases: First, there was a three-week physical and psychological training regimen with a sixty percent washout rate. Then followed a three-month-long physical endurance phase, which had a ninety plus percent failure rate. The majority of this second phase was conducted in the Black Forest and included a grueling ninety-hour cross-country run plus a three-week international combat survival course. The very few who were able to endure these rigors then entered a multi-year intensive training program, which included jungle, desert, urban, and counter-terrorism training at a series of German and international locations around the globe.

Franz had arrived in Warsaw two days earlier to fully prepare for the assignment. He had carefully walked the site several times and meticulously studied the photographs provided by the client. He was comfortable with his route in and exit out. There would be no mistakes, he assured himself.

The first morning in Warsaw, he went over the timeline and details once again. On the second day, he carefully 'dry test fired' and checked the weapon one last time before it was pre-positioned for him later that afternoon. It would be too difficult to do so on the day, given the intensified security following the incident in Slovakia. He was not unreservedly comfortable with the arrangement regarding the weapon being out of his custody. However, the client had assured him that it was secure, and there could be no possible access to it by any unauthorized personnel.

A week earlier, he had carefully sighted-in the weapon. The Bavarian forest provided the perfect place to do so, and he knew the landscape well from his Kommando Spezialkräfte training days.

Franz's detailed instructions included him joining Bruce and Sarah at the Hotel Rialto's Salto Restaurant for breakfast that morning. Why, he had no idea, as they had no role to play in his contract. He had heard of this couple, but knew little as far as specifics about them and had even less interest. They were apparently 'posh' types. Not his kind of people.

As far as a hotel, the Rialto seemed adequate, but he would have been just as happy at a lesser place. The art déco interior did not impress him. Ostensibly it was the first boutique luxury hotel to open in Poland following the demise of the Soviet Union. In its advertising, the hotel boasted a long list of amenities: fixtures and fittings of the highest quality, an intimate atmosphere, and superb cuisine, as well as personalized and attentive service. He guessed that it had been chosen for or requested by the couple since he'd heard that they had a penchant for living a glamorous lifestyle. For his part, a quiet room where he would not be bothered, a comfortable bed, a TV with multiple sports channels and a restaurant that knew how to serve an exceptional steak and stout beer were all he required. The rest was just fluff paid for by silly people. However, as he wasn't paying for it, he decided that he would indulge himself and enjoy it to the hilt.

Bruce and Sarah arrived in Warsaw on the night of the twelfth after slipping out of Slovakia unnoticed. The first night in Warsaw, they stayed at a private residence, as arranged by the client. There, Bruce could remain unseen until again applying the temporary color to turn his sandy hair back to jet black. Stepping out of the bathroom that morning, Sarah walked up and hugged him, "I have my Celtic hero back! I think I could almost get used to you looking this way."

Bruce responded, "Don't get too used to it, I prefer the sandy-colored hair my parents passed onto me." Sarah laughed.

They laid low that day, resting and relaxing in their host's garden and once again enjoying the unusually mild weather. Late in the day, Bruce had arranged for an Uber to take them to the Rialto Hotel. Before departing, Sarah had again donned her wide-brimmed black hat and the Hollywood style dark glasses, and Bruce, the same outfit and the glasses he had worn in Bratislava, not the mirror sunglasses and uniform of an airline pilot.

The next morning, as they were preparing to meet Franz for breakfast, Sarah began to question, yet again, why they were doing this. What purpose could it possibly serve? After all, they were to have no operative part to play today. Bruce responded that they had been over this ground before. It was a fruitless exercise. The client had set the schedule, in exacting detail, and this is the way it was to be. End of story!

Sarah replied, "I've heard of this Franz guy, and I don't like him."

"How can you not like him when you haven't even met and know almost nothing about him," Bruce responded.

"That's inconsequential; women have a sense about these things, and I just don't like him. I see no point in our meeting with him, and I don't understand why we have to follow through with these crazy shenanigans. We've done our job; why can't we collect the balance of our fee and be on our way?"

Bruce gave her a long, hard look. There was no sense arguing the point. No matter what he said, it certainly wasn't going to change her mind. Sarah returned his stare until Bruce shook his head, turned away and continued dressing.

The restaurant was bathed in bright morning light by a wall of tall, leaded-glass windows. Its hardwood floor comprised a combination of blonde parquets outlined by dark cherry squares. Their reservation had been made under an assumed name, which both the Pearce's and Franz would recognize, so they could easily find one other. However, in reality, each party could have almost instantly identified the other, even in a room full of strangers, though they had never met before. Upon entering any room, they each knew how to recognize other 'professionals' amidst the remaining population, who were perceptibly unaware. They had been instructed to have breakfast together at a highly visible table.

Franz wore his usual disguise: a long-sleeve black tee, black Levi's, black combat boots, a black baseball hat emblazoned with the logo of an obscure German rugby team and mirror sunglasses. Fortunately, whether by forethought or chance, a table against the window wall had been reserved for them. This helped, at least a little, to justify the fact that the three were hiding behind sunglasses inside the restaurant. Although the bright light streaming in through the windows outlined them starkly, the glare also helped to conceal their features from those facing their direction.

For anyone observant enough to notice, they must have seemed an oddly matched trio. One might have thought they were three movie stars, making a half-hearted attempt to convince surrounding restaurant patrons they were incognito.

As soon as the obligatory hour had passed, they promptly left the restaurant and walked together through the main lobby and out the front doors, stopping just momentarily to chat. Then Bruce, acting as though there was something they had forgotten to do, turned around and the trio walked back into the Rialto and through the lobby a second time, affording copious front and rears views of the troika for CCTV cameras mounted on the lobby ceiling. Walking together from the lobby to the elevators, supplied one final parting CCTV shot before they ascended to their rooms.

Now back in their hotel room, Sarah demanded, "What the hell was that preposterous charade about? I have never been so humiliated in my entire life. And breakfast with that Neanderthal! I'm surprised that he knew how to use a knife and fork. And the so-called 'stimulating' conversation, limited to a singular topic, sports … and if that wasn't bad enough … soccer—on and on. Tennis, polo … these things I could at least tolerate, but soccer?

"Rugby," interrupted Bruce, "not soccer."

"Soccer, rugby, who gives a damn! Do you realize that he did ninety percent of the talking for well over an hour, you did ten percent, and I barely spoke!"

"It was only an hour, almost to the minute, so don't exaggerate, and you could have contributed if you had so desired," Bruce responded.

"Contribute to what? That moron's dronings on and on about some stupid team? I'd rather die!" Sarah moaned.

Bruce began to laugh. "You can calm down now. It's over."

"Oh no, it isn't! We'll be taking the train to Germany with him later today and then on from there! If I have to sit in a train compartment with that *IDIOT* for five minutes, I'm ... I'm likely to kill him!"

"We aren't being paid to do that termination," Bruce replied.

"Oh just watch me. I'll be more than happy to do him in for free!"

"Relax, Sarah!" Bruce now spoke to her in a low, soothing voice. "We won't be riding in the same compartment with him. In fact, our instructions are not to do so. We simply have to meet at the station, walk to the train, board together and then choose separate compartments in —Ready for this?—Separate cars! And here I was beginning to worry that you might be warming up to him ... and maybe I should be concerned about you two getting ... " his voice trailed off as he ducked to escape the shoe that she whipped at him. It struck the wall with a loud clap.

They spent the day out of sight in their hotel room as the client had instructed. Bruce read, and Sarah surfed television channels, something she rarely did, as she thought television programs were mostly an inane waste of time. Finding nothing that interested her after a few minutes, she moved from the broadcast programs to the pay-per-view movies. Over the next six hours, she started and stopped seventeen different movies, so many that the front desk called to see if there was a problem. She did so just to get under Bruce's skin, but he ignored her, ordering up lunch for two from room service without asking her what she would like. They ate lunch in their room sans conversation.

Chapter 4:

A Matter of Extreme Precision

March 15th, Sapiezynska 10, Warsaw, Poland

The Falck, a white building, four stories tall, with the exception of a small fifth story outcropping, houses a collection of business offices and shops, the primary tenant being the Warsaw branch of Falck, Centrum Medycyny Pracy—a medical center housing 25 consulting rooms, two treatment rooms, an outpatient rehabilitation facility, and a separate occupational medicine division comprised of six physicians' offices. There is also an occupational medicine unit with six physicians' offices.

The Centrum Medycyny Pracy is located just one block south of the General Kazimierz Sosnkowski Stadium, a large multi-use sports complex dominated by a soccer field. The medical center and sports complex are located near the Gdansk metro station, which provides convenient bus and tram connections to the city center.

Falck is the largest provider of emergency medical services in Poland, with twenty-five medical centers operating one-hundred-fifty EMT ambulances from sixty-six locations. Falck is also the country's largest private healthcare company working in concert with the State System of Emergency Medicine.

From the air, the building at Sapiezynska 10 forms a giant capital 'J,' with its long side lying to the south and the hook of the 'J' to the east. To the north are three other buildings, one immediately adjacent to the top of the 'J's' long leg and two directly in front of it. A parking lot forms a small asphalt island behind the two buildings and there is a 40' wide green space with trees sandwiched in between. This presents an open view, over the trees, of a section of the stadium's center-north stands from the east end of Sapiezynska 10's fifth-floor roof. Designed in an open style, without roof or overhangs, the stadium is oval with the long sides facing east and west and the short sides north and south.

Franz was an excellent marksman. In the Kommando Spezialkräfte, he rose to become a top sniper, both in number of kills and distance. But to hear it from Franz, he was their "best" marksman and sniper ever. Franz did not suffer from excessive humility.

Notwithstanding success at great distances, with some kill shots achieved at more than 1,800 meters, it was not for this proficiency that the client had selected Franz from a short-list of qualified candidates for this assignment. Rather, it was a combination of two traits. First, Franz possessed an uncanny ability to tightly cluster shots in extremely close proximity, causing him to stand out from other candidates. Not that being able to place multiple shots in a tight pattern would matter in this instance, as the client had been very explicit that Franz must only fire once and with that sole shot accomplish his goal ... without fail. However, his extreme accuracy with each shot greatly increased the probability of success with his first, and in this instance, only shot. The second requirement which had cinched the contract for Franz was that he had not operated before in eastern Europe.

It was around noon when he made his way to Sapiezynska 10, carrying only a small, black leather bag with him. The balance of his luggage, his roller-bag suitcase and a laptop case, he had taken to the Warszawa Centralna train station that morning and placed in an electronic locker.

Arriving at Sapiezynska 10, Franz entered the building through a service entrance which had been left unlocked a quarter of an hour earlier. Using the stairwell, as he had two days before, he quickly ascended the stairs to the fifth-floor. He proceeded down the corridor to another unlocked door, this one leading to a maintenance stairway and the fifth-floor rooftop. Once on the roof, he moved quickly to the ladder of the elevated HVAC (Heating, Ventilating, and Air Conditioning) mechanical platform and ascended. On top, he reached under the skid of the second cooling tower, his hand grasping a package wrapped in black plastic. He lifted its thirty-plus pound heft forward and clear of the skid and then upward. Unwrapping the protective plastic, he opened the case. Inside the case lay the weapon: a Barrett, Heavy Caliber M107/A1 .50 caliber U.S. LRSR (Long Range Sniper Rifle). The normal Leupold 4.5X15 Vari-X Scope had been replaced with an advanced design scope and targeting laser.

The M107/A1 is an improved variant of the original M107, a full five pounds lighter, but also stronger. The weapon alone, without a scope, weighs 28 lbs. and is 57" in overall length.

Guns of all kinds come in various calibers. The .50 caliber is a NATO machine gun cartridge, originally used in the Browning Machine Gun (BMG)—a large caliber heavy machine gun. With a cartridge diameter of half an inch and an overall length of nearly six inches, it was not originally designed to be a rifle bullet. It is available in various configurations, including an armor-piercing variety, which can penetrate light armored vehicles. The standard issue M1022 Long Range Sniper .50 Caliber cartridge has an olive green bullet coating. Designed for the long-range sniper, it exhibits superior accuracy and trajectory, with the bullet remaining supersonic to 1,600 meters. However, this was not the cartridge Franz would use today.

With an hour to go, he could hear the pre-game cheers coming from the General Kazimierz Sosnkowski Stadium. He stepped back under cover of a corrugated sheet-metal canopy to assemble the weapon. Helicopters were buzzing overhead, as part of the expanded security which was especially high at the stadium today, following the recent incident in Bratislava, Slovakia. Miroslav Cagacikov, the Slovakian Premier, had been scheduled to fly to Poland the evening he had been assassinated. His arrival would have been a prelude to traveling to Brussels with the Polish Prime Minister for the upcoming EU meeting.

The target, located at the north end of the stadium seating, was 640 meters from Franz's position. Such a shot was not at all extraordinary for an experienced military sniper like Franz. In fact, it was a fraction of the range of some of the shots he had successfully made in Afghanistan and Iraq. Nevertheless, it would be a difficult shot.

A warm wind was blowing moderately from the south across Franz's field of fire. Normally, this would not be a problem; however, the two large buildings directly ahead of him would serve to block the wind. Franz could and would compensate for the wind, as he did in every shot, but here the bullet would be subject to the wind as it left the barrel, then in still air during its flight between the buildings and, then again, the wind's influence would be exerted for the balance of the distance to the target, which comprised the majority of its journey. This added to the complexity of his task, but it was certainly well within his competency to overcome.

Nevertheless, Franz faced a far greater difficulty with this shot. He would be firing into the crowded stands. Despite being such a high profile figure and over the vociferous objections of his security team, the target always insisted on sitting in the crowd. Protecting someone seated in a crowded stadium is always difficult, even when this individual is seated in a protected VIP box. Sitting amidst the crowd makes it nearly impossible. Furthermore, the target and those around him would not be stationary—frequently and without warning, fans would jump to their feet, usually whenever an opportunity for a goal appeared imminent. Franz was accustomed to targets presenting a stationary or slow-moving profile, at least for a few seconds. Also, targets were not typically so closely surrounded by throngs of people. Today, it would be as though the target was employing six or eight human shields to protect himself.

In Franz's knowledge, no one had ever attempted a professional assassination under such circumstances. Regardless of the relatively short distance, the chance of missing the target altogether, or merely wounding him, was high—and the chance of hitting someone else in the row above or below instead was even greater. And the client had been explicit on two requirements: "You must eliminate the target with only a single shot, as there may be no chance for a second shot, and you will not miss the target or hit someone else." The client had allowed for the possibility, the likelihood in fact, that the bullet, even in a perfect shot, would also strike others, either directly, after passing through the target, or after ricocheting following the initial strike. Despite these complications, Franz knew he could do this … and do it right.

Military snipers typically work in two-man teams, with one being the shooter and the other the spotter. The spotter also protects the shooter. However, since leaving the military, Franz had always worked alone. That was how he wanted it—no responsibility for others; no one else to foul things up for him.

Wind, mirage, light, temperature and humidity, in addition to distance and bullet velocity, all affect the shot. There are various methods for estimating wind speed and direction to ascertain wind drift of the bullet. The 'clock system' is the method most widely used by snipers, but not by Franz. A tech zealot, he carefully monitored technological advances in his profession. Therefore, for today's kill, he would utilize the most up-to-date tools and techniques. His preferred choice was a Kestrel 5700 Elite Meter with Applied Ballistics, which not only measured but also compensated for sixteen discrete but interrelated variables, including:

- Gyroscopic spin drift and Coriolis effect
- Adjustment for angle
- Wind speed / Air velocity
- Temperature
- Wind chill
- Relative humidity
- Heat stress index
- Dew Point temperature
- Wet bulb temperature

- Barometric pressure
- Altitude
- Density altitude
- Wind direction
- Crosswind
- Headwind/Tailwind
- Pressure trend

He drew the Kestrel 5700 out of his black leather bag. Using the Bluetooth connection to his laptop, he had set up the Kestrel for this location on his first visit to Sapiezynska 10. He attached the portable wind vane mount and turned it on. The screen came to life, and the device began feeding data to the display. He had, on his previous visit, used his Mil Dot equipped scope to verify the distance to the reserved seat the target would occupy.

Franz left nothing to chance, especially given the importance of this target, and the fact that a failure on his part would undoubtedly damage, if not likely end, his career … an unbearable thought. This was why he had worked so hard to ensure success earlier in his career at the Kommando Spezialkräfte training school. It was all he knew, all he had as a profession, what he had become.

While he passed the time waiting for the soccer match to begin, he thought about the irony of this particular location. Here he was, standing atop the headquarters of the largest Polish emergency EMT and medical clinic service in the entire country. Undoubtedly, this company was providing the ambulances and EMT's for the stadium today. Yet, it would be from this very spot that he would fire the lethal shot. *Indeed*, he mused, *sometimes reality truly is stranger than fiction.*

Now he could hear that the soccer match was about to start. The periodic roar rising from the stadium as the teams were introduced was unmistakable. It was time. The weapon was assembled and ready. He reached into his bag and removed a plastic container that cradled a single .50 cal round. It was not the standard M1022 Long Range Sniper round. This single round, worth far more than its weight in gold, offered him the ultimate guarantee of success.

When he had first received the client provided weapon, in the Black Forest several weeks earlier, he had fired a few hundred standard issue NATO sniper rounds to acquaint himself with this individual weapon's performance, as each has its own unique feel and idiosyncrasies. Then, when he was ready, he had been given just three of these special rounds for practice, and one more for the assignment.

Developed by DARPA, the Defense Advanced Research Projects Agency within the United States Department of Defense, the priceless cartridge he now held in his hand was the fourth EXACTO cartridge (the Extreme Accuracy Tasked Ordinance System). He could not begin to imagine what it must have cost, even in production, or how it could have been obtained. He only knew that the round he now held originated from a limited production run in the United States and was still in the final T&E (Testing & Evaluation) phase, prior to combat fielding.

When he had fired the first cartridge, that day in the forest, he could not believe his eyes, even though he had previously been shown a YouTube video of the EXACTO's early testing program. The bullet came out of the barrel in normal enough fashion, but he could direct it inflight, so that even if the target moved in that instant between firing and striking, a certain kill was assured. It was like firing a miniaturized version of a laser-guided missile from a fighter aircraft.

EXACTO, he had learned that day, is a combination of a maneuverable bullet and a weapon-mounted, real-time laser guidance mechanism with the capacity to guide the projectile to the target, enabling the bullet to change its path up to 180 degrees while traveling. It contains miniaturized aero-actuation controls, a power source, an optical guidance system, and sensors which infuse maneuverability into the supersonic bullet. When the bullet is fired, miniature internal actuators receive data from the optical sensor in the tip to guide it to the target location. Tiny fins are used to change the bullet's trajectory so that it can correct the bullet's flight 30 times a second in response to any movement of the weapon mounted laser, which the sniper uses to continually track and light up the target.

When Franz had first fired it, he had asked his host where it came from. How was it obtained? The answer was a stony silence, followed by the admonition that it was better to just do his job without asking unnecessary questions. Still, he wondered ... even now. He had done some research since then and learned more about the development history of the DARPA program. Franz had also performed Google searches trying to learn more, but without much success. He continued to seek avenues for acquiring EXACTO, but even his 'special' sources, who generally could obtain 'anything' for the right price, had not even heard of it.

That was when he began to realize that this contract was for an assassination far beyond any ordinary kill, even a very high-profile kill. Whoever was behind all of this had to be extremely powerful and well-connected to have gained access to the EXACTO rounds, at any price. It was fortunate that the client had such unique connections to have obtained four, as Franz had wasted the first practice round, not even striking the target. He had been so busy trying to control the bullet after pulling the trigger that he had missed. An embarrassment he would not repeat. The bullet's supersonic flight time for 640 meters was akin to the blink of an eye. With the second and third rounds, he hit precisely where he aimed, even though as he fired the weapon, the target was mechanically moved to simulate the stadium crowd. Now, he held the fourth and final round in his hand, ready to chamber it.

Scouting the sky for helicopters, Franz darted quickly into position and chambered the round. From his earlier visit to Sapiezynska 10, he knew precisely where to place the weapon. Franz peered through the scope, a bit nervous at first, which caused him to look into the wrong section of the stands, but then he soon found his mark. There before him, clear as day, was his target: seated, but then suddenly jumping to his feet with the surrounding crowd, as their team nearly scored. The target moved to sit back down, only to quickly rise again.

Franz had practiced this at home. Going to soccer games and using his Bushnell Legend Ultra HD Monocular 10x42mm sighting scope, he had learned to anticipate the movements of individuals in a soccer crowd, suddenly rising and then sitting over and over again, like waves of the sea. There was a rhythmic flow to the crowd. He just had to pick up the subtle cues evidenced by spectators as they responded to the play on the field. He must anticipate as he would when firing at any moving target. Anticipate, lead the target and then ….

He was ready, but he waited for several more minutes as he followed the repeated rising and sitting of the crowd in the stands at

General Kazimierz Sosnkowski Stadium. Again and again, he watched until he felt their rhythm. Now, he could anticipate it.

He released the manual thumb lever safety, then placed his finger on the trigger. He paused, steadied his breathing, began to slowly squeeze the trigger, then held … waited. He measured his breathing. As the crowd rose to their feet, he waited once more for the natural pause between inhaling and exhaling, when his chest and diaphragm muscles relaxed … and then Franz fired. He followed the target, moving the weapon imperceptibly … the range so close that the bullet struck before he had even fully eased the trigger back to its rest position.

He was still waiting to inhale again when he saw the target's forehead explode rearward. A trifle higher than he had wanted, but without a doubt, a clean kill.

The Polish Prime Minister was dead.

Chapter 5:

The Escape

The assignment having been successfully completed, it was time for Franz to execute his escape. First, he retrieved the spent cartridge casing and placed it in his pocket. He then picked up the Kestrel 5700 and turning the unit off, removed the portable wind vane, placed it back in its protective case and into the black leather bag. Lifting the weapon, Franz headed for the mechanical platform ladder.

At the top of the ladder, he paused and swung the weapon over the edge, aligning it horizontally with a large steel weldment below which supported the HVAC piping. Steadying his aim, he dropped the weapon directly onto the weldment ten feet below. It hit with a loud crash, bounced once into the air, causing the bipod to break free and shattering the scope, scattering bits and pieces of glass and metal onto the roof below. The weapon itself, though bruised and battered, remained intact, due to its rugged construction, having been designed to survive maximum combat abuse.

Descending the ladder, Franz stopped at its base to survey the debris field. Using his right foot, he swept some of the debris to one side, clearing a small area directly in front of the ladder. Then, he unzipped the black leather bag, removing a squeeze bottle and a rolled-up half meter square piece of thin toweling with plastic backing on one side. Choosing the cleared area, he removed the leak-proof cover from the bottle. Squatting, he inverted the plastic bottle and squeezed until a small pool of human blood appeared on the tarred roof surface. Taking the toweling, he laid it over the blood, plastic side up, and then quickly dropped to his knees, onto the towel. He shimmied slightly from side to side smearing the blood, then stood up and lifted the towel. The blood was O-negative, not his O-positive.

He carefully rerolled the towel with the plastic side facing out and taking a plastic pouch from his bag, stuffed in the towel. Sealing the ziplock closure, he returned it to his bag. Franz scanned the path to the roof exit door, and began to walk slowly, squirting blood onto the roof, first a steady thin stream, then less, and finally only dribbles, until reaching the door, the flow had stopped altogether, but not before he stepped in the blood, at one point, smearing the roof again with one boot. Reaching into his bag, he retrieved another pouch, this one much smaller. Replacing the leak-proof cap on the bottle, he placed it into the pouch, zip-locked it shut and placed it into his bag.

Franz went through the door and down the service stairwell to the fifth-floor door. Opening the door slightly, he placed his foot in the opening and removed the surgical gloves he had worn since arriving at Sapiezynska 10, also placing them into his bag. He removed the Kestrel 5700 case from the bag and shoved it into the large front utility pocket of his windbreaker. Next, he removed a black plastic bag, and, closing his leather bag, placed it inside the black plastic bag and tied it shut. Using his elbow, he pushed the door further open and stepped through.

Now, he thought, *the assignment is complete—all but my rendezvous.* Entering the corridor, he strode toward the elevators. No one else was waiting. The elevator doors opened, and he entered an empty elevator. Franz pressed the ground floor button. Baseball cap and mirror sunglasses in place, he glanced up as the doors opened for the third floor. Two people entered, an attractive couple in their mid thirties. The man had jet-black hair, and the woman wore a wide-brimmed hat. Taking no notice of Franz, the woman's conversation did not skip a beat, as she nagged her husband about obviously trivial matters.

The doors opened to the second floor. There stood a smiling elderly woman with a cane in her left hand. She hesitated, and then slowly, unsteadily ambled into the elevator. The couple stepped to their left to make more room and Franz moved to the back right corner.

At the first floor, the others waited as the elderly woman slowly made her way out of the elevator and into the building lobby while the other man held the door *OPEN* button. Next, he gestured with his free hand for Franz to step out. Franz did, and the Asian couple followed, the wife continuing to fuss.

Franz made his way out of the building and turned toward the Gdansk station. He could hear the wailing of sirens, first one, two and then a chorus, as the alarm went out across all Warsaw. At the station, he purchased a one-way ticket in cash to Warszawa Centralna, a coffee, and a newspaper before heading to the platform. Waiting on the train platform, Franz opened the paper and removed the sports section. Walking over to a nearby trash receptacle, he tossed in the black plastic bag and the rest of the newspaper on top of it.

Warszawa Centralna, an unsightly vestige of the old Soviet era, is Bratislava's primary railway station. It was designed by architect

Arseniusz Romanowicz and constructed between 1972 and 1975. Located on the Warsaw Cross-City Line, it features four platforms with eight tracks underground and serves both domestic and trans-Europe trains. Built by the former communist People's Republic of Poland era (1952-1989), the project suffered major problems from the start. The modern functionalist structure, while in keeping with the minimalist communist vision of architecture, was plagued by design issues requiring repeated redesigns and alterations, as well as by sub-standard construction practices, as were common in the Soviet era. The railway station had been rushed into service to coincide with the then Soviet Premier, Leonid Brezhnev's, 1975 state visit.

✳ ✳ ✳

Warszawa Centralna

It was 3:30 pm when Bruce and Sarah arrived at Warszawa Centralna, after a delicious late lunch of Zupy Di Mare, Bistecca di manzo, an Altro Salad, and Tiramisu at Bella Italia Ristorante, located near the station. Sarah once again donned her wide-brimmed hat and dark, Hollywood-style glasses and Bruce his sunglasses with a baseball cap crowning his jet black hair. Both wore long-sleeved running clothes and windbreaker jackets, as the weather had suddenly turned chilly, back to a cool March afternoon in Warsaw. They stood in the station's main lobby, near the shops, so that as soon as Franz came into sight, Sarah would be able to meander away, browsing in one of the higher-end retail establishments she had found interesting.

It was nearly 4 pm when Franz ascended from the platforms below, his bandaged head showing beneath the baseball cap. He walked with a slight limp. Seeing Bruce and Sarah, he headed in their direction. At that instant, something in the nearby shop suddenly struck Sarah's fancy, and she pivoted and headed towards it. Bruce greeted Franz, who remarked sarcastically, "Sarah saw me coming and took off like a scared rabbit!"

Bruce, perturbed by Sarah's obviously impolite exit, responded unconvincingly, "You know women, always some shiny new object for sale to attract their attention."

"Everything go all right? As planned?" Bruce questioned.

"Of course! Like clockwork. Why wouldn't it?" Franz retorted coldly. Just then, on the giant TV screen to their left, a message flashed, "Breaking News Bulletin: There has been an incident at General Kazimierz Sosnkowski Stadium."

The woman who appeared on-screen was attractive and perfectly coiffured, the typical psychagogic news anchor, utterly devoid of emotion. She reported on the stadium story with the same superior aloofness as if she were announcing major street closings for roadway maintenance.

"This news just in from General Kazimierz Sosnkowski Stadium," she began, "where an incident is unfolding, the nature of which is at this time still unclear. We understand from eye-witness reports at the scene that there have been multiple injuries and possibly fatalities among spectators in the stands. There appear to be at least five ambulances and scores of emergency workers on site attending to the injured. We will be back to report more as additional information becomes available."

"Sounds like our cue to exit," said Bruce. The two started walking toward Sarah, who was just completing a purchase. As she turned toward them, Bruce said tersely, "We should go. Now!"

He turned and handed Franz a rail ticket. "What's this for?" asked Franz.

"I bought ours earlier and thought I might as well as purchase yours at the same time ... save you the effort," Bruce answered in a conciliatory tone. Franz stared at him. "It's fine, just take it and let's go," Bruce added. Together, the three proceeded past a set of CCTV surveillance cameras to the lockers, from which Franz retrieved his roller bag and computer case. With Franz limping perceptibly, they slowly walked toward the escalators, which would take them to the underground tracks and platforms.

The train had just pulled into the station as they made their way onto the platform. It had come from the cleaning shop and thus, had no passengers onboard. The doors opened, and they were able to board the empty train immediately. Sarah, guided from behind by Bruce, went first, turning right into the railcar's corridor. Bruce followed her with Franz behind him. As Bruce turned right, he looked back to Franz, who was about to head left. "All right, we'll see you later," Bruce offered.

Franz replied, "Yes ... and Bruce ... thanks for the ticket."

"Don't mention it," replied Bruce, as they both turned to find their first-class compartments.

Upstairs, sirens shrieked throughout Warsaw's city center, as the authorities learned, at least in part, the awful truth of what had occurred barely an hour earlier at the stadium—that the Prime Minister was dead. Police cars began arriving at the airport in force, and minutes later, at the Warszawa Centralna. As the police started fanning out across the first floor of the railway station, a train bearing the three assassins eased out of the terminal into the waning late afternoon light.

Chapter 6:
Marek on the Move

Marek was still in Slovakia investigating the assassination of the Slovak Prime Minister when the call came in from Interpol Headquarters in Lyon, France. Moving swiftly, Marek left his deputy to finish up the initial stage of the investigation, while he rushed to the airport to catch the first flight to Warsaw early that evening. Arriving after dark at General Kazimierz Sosnkowski Stadium, he was escorted by uniformed officers to the crime scene, where an investigation was already well underway by the *Policja*, Poland's National Police.

However, by this time the Agencja Bezpieczeństwa Wewnętrznego, Poland's domestic intelligence and internal security agency, along with the Government Protection Bureau, (tasked with protecting the Prime Minister, President and other high ranking state officials) had jointly taken control of the crime scene investigation. Having previously collaborated with individuals from both of these agencies, Marek held an overall high opinion of these organizations' professional competence and efficacy. In particular, he admired the thoroughness and tenacity of Domiik Figurski of internal security, and Jedrzej Lorbiecki, from the Government Protection Bureau, both of whom were on the scene. They had demonstrated themselves to be intelligent and were long-standing veterans of their respective organizations. Although vastly different in personality, physical appearance, and investigative approaches, they reminded him of a pair of Rottweilers in their relentless determination.

Although the soccer match had taken place in daylight, all of the stadium lights were now on. Portable lights had been brought in to further illuminate the section of the stands where the Prime Minister had been seated at the time of the assassination. This area was cordoned off with yellow police tape, and a group of more than one hundred officials was milling about just beyond the taped area. Marek immediately moved to greet Domiik and Jedrzej. Both appeared a bit startled by his sudden appearance. "You certainly don't let any grass grow under your feet, Marek," said Jedrzej.

"Nor do you let the corpse grow cold. You're worse than an undertaker!" smirked Domiik.

"My business is just as competitive," parried Marek wryly. The other two laughed.

"We need a little humor in the wake of this horribly tragic … " Domiik's voice trailed off.

Marek's tone grew somber, "May I offer both of you, and your country, my sincerest and deepest condolences. Prime Minister Binkowski was a fine man—a man of high character, dignity, integrity, and courage as well as a true patriot." The other men nodded sadly. Marek continued, "I hope that you will not consider my presence an imposition?"

"Old friend, your presence could never be considered an imposition. I more than welcome your involvement," Jedrzej responded with genuine sincerity.

Domiik nodded his assent, adding, "We will need all the help we can possibly get in solving this one. It was clearly a professional job, and definitely not some crazed lunatic or individual crusader. No, this bears the earmarks of an expert assassin. By the way, Marek, you weren't by any chance in Bratislava over the past few days, were you?"

"Yes," replied Marek, "I've been there investigating since the morning after the attack."

"When I first heard about Bratislava, I thought it might have involved a local or national issue," Jedrzej said. "Then, with this, I began wondering if they were related ... connected in some way?"

Marek nodded, "At this point, I know almost nothing of what happened here earlier today, but when I received the second call from Interpol Headquarters indicating that it may have been a high-powered rifle shot, coming so closely on the heels of the Slovakia assassination, I knew immediately that this would be a very unlikely coincidence."

Jedrzej responded, "The assassin did use a high-powered rifle, or something firing one massive projectile!"

"What do you mean, a projectile? It was a bullet ... wasn't it? You're aren't proposing that the Prime Minister was assassinated with a giant slingshot launching a rock, are you?" Marek inquired.

"To tell the truth, at this point we are at a loss as to exactly what it was that hit him. But I can tell you this: it was no bullet that I'm familiar with—no bullet I've ever seen before." Jedrzej told him.

Domiik shook his head, adding, "Have you ever seen a bullet with internal electro-mechanical parts?"

Marek asked, "What do you mean internal parts? Bullets are made of brass and lead."

Domiik answered, "Well, yes, the bullets we know are. But not this one. We've never seen a bullet like this before. Come, let me show you something." They walked over to where the internal security forensic evidence team had set up a table. "As best we can tell at this point, the bullet apparently passed through the Prime Minister's head, completely exploding above his nose, and I do mean completely—there was nothing left above the bridge of his nose ... absolutely nothing! The bullet then hit one of his security team's men in the row behind, tearing a hole through his chest big enough to put your fist through. After that, it penetrated the seat back, hitting the leg of the wife of an official two rows above the Prime Minister. Finally, it tore into the concrete step under her seat. At the time of the shot, our soccer team was just about to score a goal, so everyone had just risen from their seats. The bullet is here, in this bag ... what remains of it anyhow. Take a look and tell me what you think."

"Not much left of it, is there?" said Marek. "Of course, having gone through three people and a chair back before striking the concrete step, I guess we can't expect much to be left."

"Take a closer look. Here, use this magnifying glass from the forensics team. They're the ones who first detected it."

"Detected what?" Marek picked up the magnifying glass and plastic bag containing the bullet.

He tipped the bag back and forth in the glare of the portable lights. "I'll be ... could it be ... ?" asked Marek, his words fading as he stared through the magnifying glass at the battered remains of the bullet.

"That's what I mean," Domiik said. "We don't know exactly what it is, but it certainly isn't a normal bullet. It has some type of internal mechanism and almost looks like it may have contained miniaturized electronics. We'll know for certain tomorrow morning ... I hope."

"Can I take a closer look at the actual crime scene?" Marek asked as he set down the magnifying glass and plastic bag containing the bullet fragments. His asking was merely a polite formality, as he knew his colleagues would be more than happy to show him anything he wanted to see.

Walking over to where the yellow tape had been used to cordon off a section of seats, Jedrzej lifted the tape for Marek, Domiik and himself to duck under. Then he pointed and said, "It's the eighth seat over from the end of that row. That's where the Prime Minister was seated. He always sat there. Every game he came to, the same seat, same row. In fact, they kept it reserved for him. Whether he attended or not, it was always reserved for the Prime Minister and the seats, five abreast, two rows up and two rows down from his row were kept for his guests and security. We have never liked this arrangement, but he insisted on sitting among his people, not separated from them in a box seat enclosed by bullet-proof glass. You know how he was, as stubborn as he was courageous!"

"I know," said Marek, which is precisely why he was so well loved. How many people were injured?"

"A total of seven.

"*Seven?*"

In addition to the Prime Minister, one fatally, two critically, and three with minor injuries," Jedrzej answered.

"How on earth can one bullet kill two people and critically injure two more? And I thought you said the bullet hit three people, not seven."

"Yes, three were hit by the bullet. A fourth, another member of the security detail wasn't even hit by the bullet," Jedrzej said. "But it appears that he was struck in the face by a bone fragment from the Prime Minister's skull which was blown away with such force, that it went through his eye and lodged in his brain. The woman struck in the leg by the bullet is highly diabetic, she is the wife of one of our senior government officials and her doctors are doubtful about her ability to heal and recover. Her prospects are not good, as her overall health is fragile. Those two are in critical condition. The other injuries are relatively minor, people having been hit mostly in the face, one by splinters from the chair and two others, also by parts of our Prime Minister. The effect was more like an exploding mini-grenade than a bullet."

"How much longer will the forensics team be?" asked Marek.

"They're nearly finished, but we won't have any results back until later tomorrow morning. Although, they'll be working through the night," Domiik said. "Marek, have you had dinner?"

"No, but I'm not very hungry," Marek responded, turning away from the seats covered with spattered blood, human flesh, and brain."

"Come, Marek. I know a great little place where we can have a light meal and an excellent choice of beers. It's quiet there, and we can talk. Even if you don't need to get out of here and away from this horror, Jedrzej and I certainly do. You look exhausted—no, you look like hell! Come on, let's go!"

Retracing their steps away from the area, the three men headed out of the stadium to a waiting official car, which drove into the darkness, away from the intense glare of the stadium lights.

✳ ✳ ✳

Dom Polski Restaurant

It required several beers before the three had the fortitude to return to their earlier discussion regarding the events of the day. Domiik began, "Marek, what happened in Bratislava that makes you think—I mean, other than the timing of the two events—what makes you think that these assassinations are linked?

I don't have any solid evidence to base it upon, but first, it is certainly the timing: two political assassinations in two closely aligned countries within a few days, countries sharing a common border, countries in which the Prime Ministers were planning to meet later on the day of the first assassination to discuss their common concern regarding the EU. Far too much for a coincidence, don't you think?"

"Yes, I would agree with you, but you know that in police work strange coincidences often do occur, which could lead us to totally wrong conclusions if we are not very careful," Domiik countered.

"Agreed," said Marek, "but there is more. I can't quite put my finger on it, yet my whole being tells me that these two crimes are not only connected but that they may also play a part in something much larger … something more sinister and diabolical. I have no evidence for it yet, but I'm quite certain. I can just feel it … smell it. Call it intuition … whatever you want. I've been at this long enough, maybe too long, that I have developed a sense about these things. Maybe it's just the fatigue and the beer talking, but … no … I'm certain that these two assassinations are linked and that there is something dark and terrible behind them, the magnitude of which we have still have no concept."

Jedrzej nodded, "I understand completely, my friend, and I believe that you're right. Domiik and I are just trying to be careful not to jump to any conclusions which we might later regret."

"Professionalism!" Marek reiterated again. "It's all about professionalism. Our Bratislava investigation is obviously still in the very preliminary stages, but our initial findings thus far point to it having been perpetrated by a highly professional assassin … a very highly skilled killer. Actually, more than one, we believe that it was done by a couple, a husband and wife team."

Chapter 7:
Looking East

March 16th

It was 11 am, the following morning, before the law enforcement trio reassembled at the Warsaw Headquarters of the Agencja Bezpieczeństwa Wewnętrznego, having finally called it a night sometime after 2 am. They probably would have been in earlier, were it not for the multiple rounds of beer with which they had sought refuge to drown their sorrows. It didn't matter anyway, as the first real forensic evidence would not appear until just before noon.

The three, with much-needed coffees in hand, reconvened in a conference room to begin piecing together the scenario of what had transpired in Warsaw and Bratislava. Marek began, "As we believe that these two incidents are linked, we should look not only at the individual events but also at what common purposes may lie behind them."

"And who is behind them," added Domiik. "And by who, I am not just referring to the 'assassins' identities, as crucial as they are, but—more critically—who it was that hired and paid them to perform these acts, and, of utmost importance, why?"

Leaning back in his chair, Marek mused, "I can see only one plausible source for political intrigue of this nature and scale—and it lies to the east."

"East?" questioned Jedrzej.

Marek rose from the chair, walked over to the wall, and pointed to a world map, dropping his finger on Moscow. "From where else would such a treacherous plot emerge? This is not the work of Islamic extremists. It is far too sophisticated for that, and the crowing over who's taking responsibility would have begun long before now. No!" He shook his head. "This is not that crude, banal sort of terrorism. This is state-sponsored terrorism, and the only player I can see as a likely candidate is right there." His finger hovered over the Russian capital. "Think of it: Eastern Europe, two assassinations, merely days apart. And who stands to gain by it?"

"But the means of assassination isn't in keeping with the Russians, Domiik countered. Think of their attacks in Britain, Alexander Litvinenko, poisoned with lethal polonium-210 and then Sergei Skripal and his daughter, where a non-persistent nerve agent was used which nearly killed them both."

"Yes, Marek responded, "But possibly here they want it to be more public ... maybe they are purposely making a statement. We've all seen how Russia has been emboldened by the West's failure to respond to their increasingly overt aggression.

Jedrzej and Domiik had to concur. It was unquestionably the most plausible explanation. After all, the Kremlin had never fully accepted the loss of the former Soviet satellite states, as their aggression in forcibly annexing Crimea and threatening the Ukraine had all too recently demonstrated. The Great Russian Bear was still looking to retrieve her cubs. And of late, mother Russia had once again been ominously flexing her muscles in other parts of the world. It was for this very reason that the United States had recently reestablished its Navy's second fleet, responsible for protecting America's East Coast and the North Atlantic.

As the three discussed the likelihood of this scenario, Adrianna Bartoszek knocked and entered the room. Adrianna was striking in both appearance and personality. Five foot seven, with dark wavy hair, and translucent green eyes, she brought an air of feminine self-assurance into the male-dominated room, though she was barely twenty-seven. Rising from his chair, Domiik greeted her and, with a sweeping gesture of his hand, ushered her to the conference room table. "Gentlemen, allow me to introduce the newest member of our team, weapons forensics expert Adrianna Bartoszek."

"Your new expert?" Jedrzej said with more than a twinge of incredulity and maybe a hint of jealousy. "I see that I am working in the wrong part of the government," he continued as he rose to greet her.

"Don't let her youth deceive you," continued Domiik, "Adrianna earned her PhD. from Cambridge University at twenty-six years old. She is likely smarter than all of us put together. Adrianna, please take this seat," he said, pulling out a conference room chair next to his own.

"Not quite that smart," Adrianna quipped, flashing a disarming smile.

"What mysteries have you uncovered thus far?" asked Domiik.

Adrianna began, "Three. We have the bullet; we have, just a few minutes ago, identified the location from which the assassin fired, and we have recovered the weapon. The shot was fired from the rooftop of

Sapiezynska 10, a large, multi-tenant commercial building that houses a medical complex with a direct rooftop line of sight between two buildings which stand between it and the stadium."

"Excellent work," said Domiik.

Adrianna continued, "On the other hand, the bullet remains a mystery." The others looked and nodded at each other in acknowledgment that their on-site analysis the previous evening had been correct. There was something altogether unique about the bullet. She continued, "It was a .50 caliber round, which you had already surmised, although certainly not a standard NATO round, which I believe you had also suspected. The round contained a miniaturized actuation system, and we believe the bullet's nose contained a laser targeting receptor. Obviously, this disintegrated upon impact. However, the autopsy of the Prime Minister has revealed fragments of it, as well as those of a minute microprocessor."

The three looked perplexed. "Are you saying that this was some form of 'smart' round in an ultra-miniature form?" asked Domiik.

"That's exactly what I'm saying. And not just a smart round, but a laser-guided one, enabling the shooter to aim a laser targeting spot on the victim, fire and then guide the round in the event the target moved, which is what we believe happened here. The crowd, including the Prime Minister and the other victims behind him, were rising to their feet in unison like a great wave when the assassin fired. As best as we can ascertain from what is left of the bullet remnants, it also incorporated microscopic vanes and tiny actuators to control its inflight trajectory."

"So, that's how he was able to so accurately shoot into a crowded stadium filled with people moving up and down, and with a single shot hit his intended target with such precision. It wasn't merely a lucky shot," Marek concluded.

"Correct," affirmed Adrianna. "In fact, I would say there was no luck involved. This was not a random attempt on the Prime Minister's life. This was done with a level of calculated certainty that is quite extraordinary, and with a level of technology that is hitherto unseen."

"But where would an assassin get such technology … I mean this 'smart' bullet that you describe? It's not something you can buy off the street, or even on the black market … is it?" questioned Domiik, rubbing his forehead.

Jedrzej half shouted, "The Russians! It's the damn Russians again. Marek, you were right! Come to finish the job; take back Eastern Europe!" His fist hit the table with force, creating a loud bang, which reverberated across the room like a gunshot.

Adrianna intervened, "Before you draw any more conclusions, I think that you had better come with me. As I said, we have found the location from which the assassin fired and the weapon, but you need to see it for yourselves."

"Where is the weapon now?" asked Marek.

"At the spot where the assassin fired the shot. Well, not the exact spot, but only a few feet away."

"No professional assassin leaves his weapon at the scene of the crime," Marek responded. "Only a rank amateur like Lee Harvey Oswald would ever do so."

"Come, with me. Then you can see for yourself and draw your own conclusions," responded Adrianna as she rose from the table. Turning to Marek as they left the conference room, she stated, "And by the way, I never referred to the assassin as 'he.'" She proceeded through the door with the three in tow.

Chapter 8:

An American Connection

Sapiezynska 10, Warsaw, Poland

It was another sunny spring day, though not as warm as it had been. A cool breeze from the north added a chill to the otherwise temperate early afternoon.

They were driven to Sapiezynska 10, where the weapon had been found. Taking the elevator to the fifth-floor, they walked down the corridor to the maintenance stairwell and ascended the steps.

Emerging from the rooftop stairwell, they were greeted by a policewoman who instructed them to be careful where they stepped, as a blood trail on the roof led from the access door where they stood to the HVAC platform base. Seeing the blood immediately sent their minds racing. Had the shooter encountered someone else while on the roof and attacked them?

Without a word, they followed the trail of spattered blood, observing it carefully, like big cats stealthily tracking game through the tall grass. At the base of the ladder leading up to the HVAC equipment platform approximately ten feet above their heads, stood a gathering of

police. As they approached, the group of officers parted, to make way
for them, exposing the scene to their full view for the first time. "What
the hell happened here?" bellowed Jedrzej. There, on the roof before
him, was a smeared patch of blood, nearly a foot long. As they looked,
their well-trained powers of observation revealed that, although the
stain appeared quite large, in reality, it constituted less than a cup of
blood.

In response to their gaze, one of the policemen offered, "In his
hurry to escape, the assassin must have slipped and fallen from the
HVAC platform ladder while descending. The weapon landed over
there when he fell. He apparently dropped it when he slipped."

Jedrzej asked the police officer, "Was the blood stain just like this
when you arrived or was it smeared afterward?" The officer responded
that he had not been the first one to arrive on the scene and called over
two other officers. Jedrzej repeated the question to them.

"No, nothing has been disturbed. It is exactly as it was when we
arrived." They went on to explain that upon arrival they had exited the
stairwell and, as they made their way around the open door,
immediately observed the blood trail and had taken care not to step in it
or disturb anything. No one had even touched the weapon. And for the
same reason, they had not ascended the metal ladder to the platform
above, as there could be fingerprints or other minute forensic evidence
remaining on the ladder itself.

"Very good," said Jedrzej. "Excellent police work in fact. I
commend each of you for your presence of mind in what you did." The
two officers, both in their mid-twenties, smiled broadly at his
compliment.

The forensics team had arrived just minutes earlier and was still busy setting up shop on the rooftop a few feet away. Domiik approached them to ask how soon they would be ready, as he was eager to get a closer look at the weapon. They told him they needed just a few more minutes before they could begin. The four moved out of the way and waited. "Well, it's clear something happened up here in addition to the shot that struck the Prime Minister. What do you make of it, Marek?" asked Domiik.

"I'm somewhat mystified at the moment," was his the answer. Turning to Adrianna, Marek asked, "What made you say that you hadn't indicated the assassin was male?"

Wearing her best poker face, Adrianna quipped, "Nothing in particular. It's just that you assumed that the shooter was 'he,' a male, but we have no evidence of that. Why not a female? Couldn't the 'he' just as well be a 'she?'" And she smiled the wide grin of a Cheshire cat. Marek stared blankly at her.

"You see," Domiik added chuckling, "I warned you not to underestimate her. She'll keep you on your toes!"

The forensics team was moving into position. They began by taking a blood sample and photographing the entire rooftop crime scene. As they did this, Domiik asked his colleagues, "What do you make of the blood trail?"

"It would appear, Jedrzej responded, that he—or shall we say 'he' or 'she'—was coming down the ladder, weapon in hand, and lost his or her balance or slipped on the ladder and fell to the roof as the officer stated, causing an injury which at first bled profusely, but must have been quickly staunched to a trickle."

"All right you three, you can knock off the 'he'/'she' business. My point has been made, and you're now perfectly free to return to your habitual male thought patterns," Adrianna countered.

"*Touché*," applauded Domiik!

Marek smiled and nodded, "You won … that round, but I offer no quarter going forward."

"And I ask none," Adrianna volleyed back.

"Now, children," chided Domiik, "can we return to the matter at hand?"

By this time, the forensics team had lifted the weapon from its resting place to the right of the ladder and were zipping it into a large clear plastic bag. "Okay," said Adrianna, "We are now free to inspect the weapon." She took the nearly thirty-pound weapon in hand and, turning it over, gasped, 'It's American … 'Property of U.S. Marine Corps!' And the serial number has been expunged."

"American? exclaimed Jedrzej. 'It should be Ruskie! The Americans do have a wonderful .50 cal. sniper rifle, but so do the Russians. Why would a Russian sniper prefer an American weapon?"

Adrianna spoke next, "Then it is also possibly an American bullet? … I don't know, but who else would have the technology to create a laser-guided projectile that small? It is quite a techno-engineering feat. The Americans most likely … the Russians, possibly … not many countries could have done it. Is the ladder clear? Can we climb it now?"

"Yes," came the reply from the forensics team. "You may proceed."

Jedrzej went first, then Domiik. Pretending to 'hold the ladder' which was firmly anchored to the HVAC platform above and the roof at its base, Marek motioned for Adrianna to go next. "Ladies first," he quipped. She smirked and hurried up the ladder. Marek followed. Atop the platform, they walked towards the north edge where they found a sandbag on which the bipod supporting the weapon's barrel had been placed. They could still see the impression and small holes made by the spiked bipod feet. They searched the area thoroughly for the empty cartridge but found nothing. The assassin had taken the spent cartridge. Returning to the top of the ladder, they halted.

Marek spoke, "So our assassin picked up the empty cartridge and took it with … him … ?" he looked at Adrianna. She smiled knowingly and nodded her head in approval. Marek continued, "But then, he slipped and fell while descending the ladder, dropping the weapon there onto that large steel weldment," he pointed, "but the assassin landed on the roof, precipitating a sudden blood flow. And because of this fall, he left the weapon and hobbled off?"

"Too injured to carry it?" added Domiik.

"Or too worried that his escape would be impeded by his injuries?" Jedrzej conjectured.

"The weapon is large and quite cumbersome, heavy to carry. If he was trying to stop the blood flow, it might be more reasonable to leave it behind," Adrianna added.

Marek was thinking aloud, "But what if he didn't slip on the ladder and accidentally drop the weapon? What if he purposely dropped the weapon to damage it … and then leave it behind … knowing that in the course of searching all of the buildings in the line of fire, we would certainly find it?"

"And what if he purposely cracked his head against one of the steel HVAC pipes so that he could bleed profusely onto the ground for us to find the pool of blood as well?" Jedrzej shook his head doubtfully.

"You're probably right. But it all seems a little too convenient —the weapon lying here like this. What sniper leaves his weapon behind?"

"A dazed and injured one," suggested Adrianna.

"Yes, I suppose an injured one," Marek conceded. "But something doesn't feel right."

Descending the ladder, Adrianna headed over to the table that the forensic team had set up. The others followed. Once there, she lifted the weapon again and began examining it. "You're thinking it may be damaged, which would explain why the assassin left it behind?" Domiik questioned.

"It's a possibility. Obviously, the scope has broken off, but I wonder ... yes, the bolt carrier is pretty badly indented. The trigger mechanism is a bit twisted, and it would appear that the barrel itself may have been bent ever so slightly," she responded, sighting down the scope-less weapon's barrel. "Hard to tell for certain without the proper instruments back at the lab to check it. I'd say this weapon has likely seen the end of its service life." She placed it on the table and turned back towards the others.

"Too bad," added Jedrzej, "it's a really beautiful weapon." Adrianna looked at him in disbelief.

"Seriously?" she responded incredulously.

"Well, it is. I'm not referring to the purpose for which it was used here, certainly, but I'm a hunter, and I appreciate a really good rifle. Can you imagine how effective it would be up in the mountains for large game hunting? Even without the aid of a laser guided bullet?

"Don't look at me that way. I enjoy hunting in the Świętokrzyskie Mountains, and this—with the scope in tact, naturally —would make it so much easier. You wouldn't have to worry about chasing the game down after making less than a kill shot. It would be one shot, one kill. Very nice when hunting in steep mountainous terrain. Furthermore," a wry smile now appearing on his face, "it would be much more humane for the animal, as it wouldn't suffer. 'BANG' and down it would go. DEAD!"

"Ugh!" fumed Adrianna. "Authentic 21st-century cavemen!"

"Just because we like our red meat, you have a problem?" countered Jedrzej.

"Well, no, not at all," shot back Adrianna. "I'm as much of a carnivore as you are, but I like my meat to come from the butcher. It's more civilized!"

"Butcher? … civilized? … now that's an interesting juxtaposition," teased Marek.

"Alright, enough already" pleaded Domiik. smiling "I'm running the most crucial investigation of my career, of any of our careers, and I'm saddled with a team of wisecracking adolescents."

❋ ❋ ❋

On the way back to headquarters, the team stopped for a late lunch at a little French restaurant. While the others pondered the menu, Marek walked outside to call a friend at the U.S. European Command (USEUCOM), Patch Barracks, Stuttgart, Germany. The Lt. Colonel he contacted had spent most of his career in the U.S

Special Forces (SOF) and had been a sniper earlier in his career. Marek's question was simple: Had the U.S. developed a .50 cal. laser-guided round that could be fired and remotely guided to target by the sniper? Before answering, Lt. Colonel Mitchell inquired as to why Marek was asking. Marek continued, "If the answer is 'yes,' then the Lt. Colonel might be interested in acquiring some very sensitive information which would undoubtedly become public in Europe very shortly."

Lt. Colonel Mitchell hesitated a moment and then answered, "Yes, the EXACTO."

"What the hell is the EXACTO?" Marek asked. "Isn't that a commercial brand of knife with numerous interchangeable blades, popular with hobbyists for performing intricate detail cutting or carving?"

"That's correct," Lt. Colonel Mitchell replied, "I own a set or two myself." After a pause he continued, "But it's also the acronym for the Extreme Accuracy Tasked Ordinance System, a .50 caliber round that comes in various configurations, such as anti-armor and anti-personnel. The latter is designated for use by snipers. It's a relatively new creation of DARPA" (the Defense Advanced Research Projects Agency).

Marek fell silent. It was the type of silence that speaks volumes. Finally, Lt. Colonel Mitchell spoke, "I assume from your silence that I have something to worry about."

Marek said, "I can't talk now. I'll get back to you later, but before I go, can you answer two more questions? First, what other countries' militaries have developed such a round?"

"None," responded Lt. Colonel Mitchell.

"And secondly, how difficult would it be for someone outside the U.S. Military to obtain a few of these rounds?"

Now, it was Lt. Colonel Mitchell's turn for a long and uneasy silence. Finally, following a pregnant pause, he spoke again. "Next to impossible. And I mean that for someone within the U.S. Military, without very specific authorization. Outside of this ... utterly impossible!"

Marek thanked his friend, promised to call him back as soon as he knew more and hung up the phone. Returning to the table, he mentioned nothing about this latest revelation. When lunch was over, the group headed back to headquarters. Once they had all settled around the conference table again, Marek dropped the bomb.

"I need to tell you something," he began. "Before lunch, I called a longtime friend in the U.S. military whose career has been SOF, and who is also is well acquainted with snipers, their training, tactics, and equipment. The guided round is without question of U.S. Department of Defense origin, as is the weapon."

The others sat motionless, their faces transfixed in stunned disbelief. After the message had sunk in a little, Jedrzej spoke, "So now, in addition to a national crisis—make that two European crises—we now also have a diplomatic crisis on our hands."

"Indeed. My source informed me that the U.S. military does possess such a round, that they are the only military who has it and that it would be next to impossible to obtain it without top-level authorization, even within the U.S. Military, and utterly impossible outside of it."

After a prolonged silence, Adrianna reasoned, "Well, clearly someone did. Who? We don't know. How? We don't know. And most importantly, what is the motive for these assassinations? This also, we don't know."

Marek added, "This is true, but I am convinced that these two assassinations are the work of one mastermind with a singular purpose. The same entity is responsible for the work of the assassin couple in Bratislava and yesterday's hit here in Warsaw. But who? Why? And what is their end game?"

Chapter 9:
East West Dilemma

The others sat spellbound. What did this new information imply? Was it possible that the Americans were actually behind the brutal murder of the Polish Prime Minister? Could this, in fact, be an official, U.S. Government-sanctioned plot to assassinate him? And what about the Slovakian Prime Minister? Him too? Inconceivable!

Marek asked. "How far is the General Kazimierza Stadium from the American Embassy?"

"Only six or seven kilometers. A fifteen-minute drive at most. Why?" Domiik asked.

"I was just wondering, as the U.S. Embassy in Bratislava is just a few doors down from the restaurant from which the assassins triggered the bomb that killed the Slovakian Prime Minister."

Domiik responded, "Still, I cannot believe that the United States was behind the killing of Prime Minister Binkowski. Such a thing would have to be authorized by the President of the United States himself. Can you imagine President Michaels deciding to do such a thing? Why it was only six ... seven, months ago that Binkowski was in Washington meeting with Michaels. Together, they announced a new trade pact and additional defense cooperation ties in response to the escalating Russian threat. It makes no sense whatsoever."

"And what about Miroslav Cagacikova, the Slovakian Prime Minister?" pondered Jedrzej. "Even if the American president had received a perceived slight of some nature from Cagacikova, would Michaels have had him assassinated? Preposterous! And there could be no 'national interest' of the United States that could possibly form the basis of such reprehensible deeds."

Adrianna countered, "What if it was the Americans, but not authorized, at least not officially authorized?"

"What do you mean?" Domiik asked.

"What if it was a rogue CIA operation?"

"You've been watching too many action spy movies … entirely too much Jason Bourne," Domiik responded.

"That is undeserved!" shot back Adrianna. "Look, maybe I do have a vibrant imagination, but given these bizarre circumstances, anything is possible. It is certainly no more ridiculous than the American President having heads of two NATO states assassinated over 'perceived' personal insults."

"Yes, you have a valid point, Adrianna," interjected Marek, "But Domiik is also correct. It is highly unlikely that some miscreant CIA assassin or rogue, clandestine operation has run off the rails, resulting in not one, but two heads of state of neighboring countries being assassinated. No, such things only happen in Hollywood, not in reality."

Obviously miffed, Adrianna said nothing more.

"Alright," Domiik said. "So this is a conspiracy and some person, group or nation is behind the plot. It certainly wasn't orchestrated by a ghost. Let's consider the options. There aren't very many. As I see it, we have three. First, one or more Americans, or even the president of the United States himself, authorized the killing of two European heads of state for no conceivable reason."

"Utterly ridiculous!" spouted Jedrzej.

"I agree," added Domiik, "but for now, let's withhold all critique. Let's simply make a list which includes all possibilities, no matter how outlandish or implausible. We can eliminate both the unrealistic and the impossible later."

Marek rose and walked to the whiteboard. "Okay, number one, we have the U.S. President. Number two, we have a rogue American CIA operation—unauthorized, at least by the president—which has gone off the rails. What other possibilities do we have involving our American friends? Anything? Speak up if you have something … an idea … any ideas at all. Nothing? There must be other possibilities."

"Jedrzej's Russians," Domiik suggested. "Such a plot would have to have come from the very top of the Kremlin—agreed? No one in the KGB would dare run an unauthorized operation of this magnitude. I mean, such things just don't happen in Russia … do they? No! Russia runs strictly according to the book, the manual, the Kremlin rules … "

Jedrzej suddenly leaned forward, as if he were about to speak. Marek nodded at him, "Do you have something?"

"It just occurred to me that maybe we are missing someone."

"Who?" asked Marek.

"Organized crime! The Russian mafia … the Eastern European mafia … or perhaps some other organized crime syndicate."

"Killing heads of state?" responded Marek. "Isn't that a bit over the top, even for them?"

"I know it seems so at first, but since ISIS and linked terrorist groups began recruiting hardened criminals, the types of crime—the level of criminality—has been rising steadily across Europe, especially in Eastern Europe. What if their goal is to create a much greater level of political instability in one country after another, like dominoes, thereby fostering a climate for growing their criminal organizations? The thought crossed my mind just now as we were speaking."

"If your epiphany is correct ... or even a viable possibility," inserted Domiik, "then we have a new and far greater police problem than anything we have ever witnessed before."

"So, we have four options thus far, two American, one Russian, and, lastly, an unknown Middle Eastern, criminal terrorist organization, or group of related terror organizations, in league with hardened local criminals. Have we missed anyone else?"

Adrianna grinned, "Yes, the Martians! And these events are only the precursor of an impending alien invasion of earth!"

"From that 'insightful' observation I think we can conclude that no one has anything to add to our list," Domiik responded dryly. "Correct?"

They all nodded in agreement.

"All right, let's begin scoring them," and Marek hastily drew a crude matrix on the whiteboard. "On the left side, we have our four potential villains. Across the top, will be our categories, and in the boxes, we'll score each 1-5, with 5 being the highest potential and 1 the lowest."

Adrianna interrupted, "That should be 0-5, as some categories may have no possibility of being correct."

"1-5 or 0-5, what difference does it make?"

"From a mathematical probability standpoint it does make a difference that could significantly affect the outcome," she responded.

Marek looked at the other two, who seemed to be lost somewhere between bewilderment and amusement. "Alright 0-5, now what about categories?"

"Access to the weapon and a laser-guided round," Domiik began, "and to the explosives used in Bratislava."

"Which reminds me," Marek spoke thoughtfully, "I'm still waiting to hear back from my assistant as to whether they have determined the explosive type and origin. Let's take a few minutes' break while I call him."

"Good!" replied Jedrzej, "I've had too much coffee—I need a break."

The three drifted out of the conference room while Marek dialed his assistant's mobile number to inquire what overall progress had been made in his absence, specifically regarding the explosive used in the car bomb. At the response, his face turned ashen. He hung up the phone.

A few minutes later the group reassembled and collectively looked to him expectantly. "From your face," Domiik said, "the news does not appear to be good. Are they unable to type classify the explosive accurately enough to pinpoint the source?"

"Just the opposite," replied Marek, "they have done so with total certainty."

"And it's Russian?" asked Jedrzej confidently.

"I wish," Marek responded. "I can hardly believe this, but … its origin is, without any doubt, American!"

Chapter 10:
An Unexpected Visitor

Late that afternoon, as they contemplated this latest revelation, there was a sharp knock at the conference room door. Domiik rose and opened it. A member of his staff leaned in and murmured something in a low voice. "Who is he?" Domiik responded.

"I think that you need to see him," the man replied.

"Very well, show him in."

Domiik turned to the other three, "Apparently we have an important visitor who refuses to provide his name, but says that it is vital to our investigation that he speaks with us."

Marek looked up, "Well, this should be interesting!"

"This case seems to provide no end of surprises," Jedrzej quipped.

Domiik quickly flipped over the whiteboard so that its contents would not be visible to their mysterious visitor. Momentarily, the door opened again and in walked a tall, thin man, about forty years of age, dressed in a dark blue, American-style cut suit. His bright red tie made him appear presidential. He had sandy colored hair, actually more of a dirty blonde, and was clean shaven with a palpable air of self-assuredness. Entering the room, he looked at the four seated around the table, as if performing a mental analysis of each of them and storing it in his cerebral database.

Domiik motioned towards an empty chair, and the man seated himself. For a few uncomfortable seconds, no one said a word. Then Domiik began, "You wanted to see us regarding the assassination of our Prime Minister?"

"Yes," the man nodded as he spoke.

"May I ask who you are and the nature of your relevance to this matter?" Domiik continued, his voice evidencing a veiled, but still discernible level of annoyance at this unidentified stranger's brazen attempt to insert himself into their investigation.

The man leaned forward slightly and began to speak. "My name is Robert Murray, and, as you have probably surmised, I am an American." He paused.

"And so … ?" prompted Domiik impatiently.

"I have come to help you. To offer my country's assistance in your investigation." He leaned back in his chair.

Domiik was becoming increasingly annoyed with the man's obliqueness. "So, you are an American who has come to help us, sent by your government, I presume. Is that what you're saying … ?"

"Yes," the American answered.

"And, precisely who in your government do you represent? What department? Do you represent the President of the United States … President Michaels himself?" Domiik said turning to look at the others, who all seemed mystified by the course this strained conversation was taking.

"Yes, but not directly. I do represent the President of the United States but through one of his executive agencies."

"Which executive agency?" Domiik shot back.

"The Central Intelligence Agency," Robert Murray replied. He read the incredulous expressions on the faces of the four investigators, a stunned combination of surprise and disbelief. As his words began to sink in, he also noted, from decades of experience reading people, something else. What exactly, he wasn't immediately certain, but his skills as an interrogator told him that there was more than mere shock in their expressions, particularly Adrianna's.

Looking straight at him, Jedrzej was first to speak, "You are from the Central Intelligence Agency, the American CIA, and you are here to help us ... " his voice trailed off.

"How," Adrianna blurted out, "by assassinating us, too?" The import of her statement hung like a sudden storm cloud over the room.

Domiik jumped in, "You must excuse our young colleague. All we ever hear of the CIA is from movies, you know, Jason Bourne, and the like—spies and convoluted plots with the CIA somehow always surreptitiously at the nefarious center. The evil presence hidden behind the curtain and all that ... "

Murray smiled, "Yes, unfortunately, that perception has become almost universal thanks to Hollywood. It does make for exciting movie plots ... if not an accurate depiction of reality."

Adrianna's eyes continued to blaze as she stared at him.

Domiik began again, "I suppose that you do have some form of identification. I mean, anyone could walk in off the street and claim to be from the CIA. There are a lot of crackpots and overly zealous members of the media who might try anything to scoop a story regarding the assassination."

"Not that we're saying you are a crackpot," added Jedrzej.

"I fully understand," said Murray, removing his CIA identification credentials from the inside breast pocket of his suit coat and passing them to Domiik. Then he opened the slim black leather attaché case he had carried into the conference room and removed a letter which he slid across the table to Domiik. Taking the letter, Domiik scanned it quickly, passing it to Jedrzej, who did likewise before handing it on.

"Your credentials appear to be in order," responded Domiik. "You must excuse us; we have been terribly impolite. Please allow me to make introductions."

Murray interrupted him, "I appreciate the gesture, but I must confess that I already know all of your names. Domiik Figurski, of the Agencja Bezpieczeństwa Wewnętrznego, Internal Security; Jedrzej Lorbiecki from the Government Protection Bureau; Marek Farkas of Interpol, Lyon; and last, but certainly not least, the rising star of Polish Weapon Forensics, Adrianna Bartoszek, who is apparently current on all the latest Hollywood CIA plots." He smiled at her. Adrianna did not return the favor.

"That was impressive," Marek noted entering the conversation. "So, you know all about us, but we know nothing at all about you, other than that you are from the CIA and you are here to help us. How?" He paused and waited, watching Murray's emotionless face until he was just about to speak. Then Marek added, "And why?"

"Why? Are our countries not NATO allies, partners in keeping this world safe and ... on friendly terms?" Murray asked rhetorically. "It is natural that we would want to help you, our close ally in this troubled world. What has occurred here—both here and in

Slovakia—is a terrible thing. Of course, we wish to offer assistance. I understand that you are already collaborating with the FBI's Forensics lab located at the Quantico, Virginia, Marine Corps Base which has identified the Bratislava explosive as of American manufacture and that, at this moment, FBI agents are en-route to assist in your investigations."

"You are very well informed," Adrianna responded.

"The United States government will do everything possible to assist you, the Polish and the Slovak governments, in finding the perpetrators of these heinous crimes and bringing them to justice as quickly and efficiently as possible. President Michaels is very concerned and has offered all the available support we can provide from every U.S. diplomatic, law enforcement, and intelligence agency."

"That is very gracious," replied Domiik. "I'm certain that we are most appreciative of any help you can provide. And please excuse us. We have had little sleep these last … what has it been?" He turned to Marek, "about twenty-four or so hours—although it seems an eternity already."

"Not a problem," Murray spoke, now softening his voice. "I can appreciate your frustration and the distress that you are experiencing. I felt the same when our president was assassinated sixteen months ago. It is devastating. And all the more so as your Prime Minister was so highly regarded by the Polish people."

"Not highly regarded, Mr. Murray. Highly loved," replied Adrianna emphatically.

"Yes, excuse me. Your Prime Minister was much loved," deferred Murray.

"We are all tense, tired and angry, as you have pointed out, Mr. Murray," Domiik responded.

"Please, just 'Robert.'"

Sensing the heat from her superior, Domiik, and the rest of the team, Adrianna turned to Murray and said, "I apologize for what I said earlier. I guess it was, after all, the result of one too many action thriller spy movies together with the stress, grief, and exhaustion."

"Think no more of it," Murray responded in his most fatherly voice. "I am glad to see your passion. It is commendable, and it does you great credit."

Adrianna knew that she should make a show of contrition and appreciation for his fatherly demeanor toward her, even though inwardly she was seething from what she interpreted as a condescending manner toward her relative youth and the fact that she was female.

"How may I—that is—my government, and the Central Intelligence Agency, in particular, be of assistance to you in these two closely-related investigations?" Murray continued.

Seeing his opening, Marek spoke, "So I take it that your agency sees these two assassinations as linked?"

"Inextricably, yes, without a doubt. I suppose that one could argue the theory that it is sheer coincidence, the two attacks coming together like this, but reasonably … no. I believe that we must accept that these two assassinations are the work of the same people—not necessarily the same assassin, but certainly, they have been designed and coordinated from the same source. Do you agree, Marek?"

"Yes, and I am not alone … Robert," Marek responded. "We are all working from that assumption."

After running through the paucity of discoveries uncovered up to that point in the investigation, excluding the fact that the weapon and bullet had been recovered and identified, Domiik told Robert that they would stay in touch with him as more information became known. Robert provided them with his international mobile number along with the number of the hotel where he was staying, the Warsaw Marriott.

As he prepared to leave, Murray stood and shook hands with each of the four team members in turn. He came to Adrianna last.

As he took her hand in his, he looked directly into her eyes and asked, "Out of curiosity, why did you say 'too?'"

Adrianna, hesitated, then responded evasively, "too?"

"Yes," Robert stated, holding his gaze steady, "you said, 'By assassinating us, too?' What did you mean by 'too?'"

Adrianna averted her eyes momentarily as she sought how to formulate an answer that would sound plausible without giving away her true meaning. "You know, in the Hollywood movies, they are always shooting someone new ... to keep the action going. They are after all ... 'action movies.'" She tried to make her response sound as convincing as possible, but she could tell from his eyes that she had not succeeded.

He smiled, "You are by far the most charming forensic weapons expert I have ever met. I'll keep you in mind if there's an opening at Quantico. You would go far there, or even in our organization at Langley. Domiik, you'd better be careful, or I will steal her away to work on our side of the Atlantic."

He smiled again, picked up his slim black leather attaché case and walked to the door. Stopping just before opening the door, he turned back to them, "Anytime, night or day, call me if I can be of assistance."

"We certainly will," replied Domiik. "We'll stay in close contact. And, once again, thank you for your government's willingness to assist us!"

Chapter 11:

A Little Contrition is Good for the Soul

After the door closed behind Robert, they were all still standing near the conference table, a stony silence prevailing. Who would break the silence first? Finally, it was Adrianna who spoke. "I feel like a silly schoolgirl! I apologize for making such a mess of that. I spoke rashly without thinking ... my Polish temper."

Marek stepped closer to her, "Adrianna, it has happened to all of us at one time or another. It's part of the learning curve, and there is no way to avoid it. You can be told and warned a thousand times ... it doesn't matter. Until you've done it yourself ... believe me, you'll never make that mistake again."

"Thanks for the vote of confidence ... but how could I have been so foolish with that idiotic performance? I gave it away, didn't I? He knew exactly what I was thinking—that the Americans were behind the assassinations and probably the CIA! Urrgh! I feel so stupid. I let you all down ... miserably." She dropped back into her chair at the conference table and covered her face with her hands.

"No, you didn't Adrianna," Domiik placed his hand on her shoulder. You saw how he played us from the very beginning. He wasn't here to help us, at least not this afternoon. He was here for only one reason, to find out what we knew ... what we knew and weren't prepared to tell him. He probably knows all about the .50 cal. weapon stamped 'U.S. Marine Corps - Property of the U.S. Government.' Robert Murray is undoubtedly also aware that we know about the EXACTO bullet. Face it, either the Americans, the CIA at least, are in on these plots —even behind them, I should say—or, if not, they have heard by now what we know of the American connection. It wouldn't have mattered what we said or, for that matter, what you said or didn't say. It was a fishing trip, and he already knew far more than he let on.

"Chalk it up to a learning experience. As Marek said, we've all done worse than that … and most of us, far worse! In fact, if this turns out to be the biggest blunder of your career, you will truly be a James Bond 007!" Domiik added, smiling kindly at her, then sat back down.

Still somewhat deflated, a somewhat humbled Adrianna responded, "Thank you! I think I'll go outside for some fresh air."

"Good idea," said Domiik. "Let's all get out of here and have some dinner!"

Chapter 12:

A Picture Materializes

Returning from dinner, they reconvened. The four lead investigators were briefed on the current case status. While they had been away, the conference room had been transformed into the nerve center of the inquiry, and a full investigative team, which had by now grown to several dozen, was assembled and working just outside their door.

Shortly after midnight, an investigator carrying four portfolios entered the conference room. Laying one of the portfolios on the table in front of Marek, and three before Domiik, the investigator walked to the front of the room. The room grew quiet as she began speaking.

"Senior Detective Superintendent Marek Farkas, I will begin with the photos before you, forwarded to us by the Slovak government investigation team an hour ago. They were retrieved from exterior building cameras on Hviezdoslavovo na´mestie, near the Sky Bar & Restaurant. The top photo, the one that first triggered our attention, is actually the last in the series."

The others had gathered behind Marek and were also viewing the photograph. The investigator continued, "The photo you are looking at depicts a black Mercedes 450 parked around the corner from Hviezdoslavovo na´mestie on a side street approximately 100 meters northeast of the bar restaurant. The vehicle's license plate number matches one of two cars stolen about a week ago; the other was used to house the Bratislava car bomb. You will see a woman getting into the front passenger seat of the car, which then drives away. The time sequence on these photos occurred just minutes after the explosion of the car bomb.

"The next series of photos, clipped together, as you will see … yes … there … beneath the first—were taken earlier that same afternoon. These photos show the same woman, this time arriving on Hviezdoslavovo na´mestie driving the same Black Mercedes 450. Parking along the street, she then walked southwest to the restaurant. The license plate number is difficult to make out, but we have enhanced it and verified that it is the same Mercedes in the picture you just viewed, the one that drove away following the explosion. And it is the same vehicle that was left parked outside of the Marrol Hotel the following morning when the suspect couple vanished.

"If you will turn to the next photo, yes, that one, you can see in the distance a man approaching from the opposite direction, and, in the next photo, the man and woman meet in front of the restaurant and proceed together into the building. If you turn to the next photo, you will see an enlargement of the woman's right hand … and in it what appears to be the key fob of that Mercedes. In the next picture, you will notice that the man takes her right hand in his left. We believe that at that time he also took the key fob from her.

"The final clipped series of photos show the man emerging from the restaurant seventeen minutes before the Slovak Prime Minister leaves. He walks down the street northeast to the Mercedes, gets in and drives to the corner, turns right and parks the car just beyond the corner building. He remains in the car until, as shown in the later photos you viewed a moment ago, the woman rounds the corner and enters the car following the bomb blast.

"The photos of this man and woman were shown to the front desk personnel of the Marrol Hotel, as well as to many of the other employees. Eleven to be exact, have identified them as the couple who had been guests at the hotel. We also have photos available documenting the Prime Minister's times of arrival and departure, as well as the full videotape of that afternoon from the street side CCTV cameras, if you wish to see them."

"Definitely," replied Marek.

"Yes, sir, but before we do so, would you mind if we went through the other photos, the ones in front of Senior Detective Inspector Domiik Figurski?"

"Of course," answered Marek. "Please proceed."

"SDI Figurski, before you are three additional series of photographs."

Marek stood and, along with the others, moved around the table to behind Domiik, who at this point had returned to his seat. The three portfolios lay stacked before him on the conference table. He opened the top portfolio. The first group of photos was from the lobby camera of the Hotel Rialto in Warsaw.

The investigator continued, "The first set of photos, from the morning of March 14, show the couple dressed much the same as they were in the Bratislava CCTV footage. Please note the woman's hat and dark glasses, and the man's sunglasses and baseball cap. However, you will also notice here they are joined in these photos by a third man. They walked through the lobby coming from the Salto Restaurant in the hotel, where, according to the waitstaff, they ate breakfast together, and then proceeded outside to the curb.

"From outdoor CCTV, we know that a brief discussion ensued between the two men, following which all three walked back into the hotel. Although we do not have camera footage beyond the lobby, we believe that, once they entered the elevators, they likely proceeded to their rooms. We do have footage of the third man leaving in the later morning, shortly before 11:00 am. At that time we see him again in the lobby checking out and then leaving the hotel carrying a small black leather bag. There is no sign of a suitcase or computer bag as he leaves.

"We also have CCTV footage of the couple leaving the hotel just after 1:00 pm. They have two roller flight bags, the type that fit in airplane overhead compartments.

"Now, if you will open the second portfolio before you, you will see that same man, the third person of the group, coming up the escalator from the below ground arrival platform of the central train station late that afternoon. His head is wrapped in a white gauze bandage, which shows under the black baseball cap, and in the next photo—which has been enlarged—you can see that there appears to be a spot of blood on it. You will also note—sorry, back to the prior photo, yes that one—that there is what appears to be a large bruise on the of right side of his face. In the CCTV footage, which is also available for you to view, you will notice a pronounced limp in his right leg. He is initially carrying no luggage.

IMBROGLIO TRILOGY

"Now to the final portfolio of photos. Here that same man has met the couple, and they are standing in the main terminal lobby."

"Where is the woman?" Domiik asked.

"Yes, … the woman stands over there in the background. She was apparently looking at something in one of the railway terminal vendor shops and afterward, came away with a small paper bag, probably containing a purchase, which she then placed in her purse. We have checked, and it must have been paid for in cash, as there is no credit card record matching that time stamp …

"The second man then retrieves a single roller-bag and what we believe to be a computer case from the public storage lockers before the three descend the escalator to the lower level. The next picture shows the second man removing a rectangular black object from the front pouch pocket of his windbreaker. The object appears to have a brand name on it in white lettering. We cannot definitively identify it. However, we believe the first three letters are 'Kes' and that the last two letters may be 'el.' There is also what appears to be the image of a bird in flight preceding the letters. We believe that the object is the carrying case for a Kestrel meter. Kestrel's logo is a bird in flight. Kestrel is a manufacturer of a wide range of handheld meters for various applications, i.e., weather, fire, heat stress, and ballistics—the latter used for long range rifle shooting. Kestrel is a brand manufactured by NK (Nielsen-Kellerman) an American owned company. Before departing for the escalator and the lower level train departures, the second man places the object in his roller-bag."

"More American fingerprints?" observed Jedrzej.

The final photo shows the three suspects about to step onto the escalator, heading down to the below-ground train platforms. Please note that each of them is pulling one roller-bag suitcase."

"Any idea where they were headed?" asked Domiik.

"Yes, we have that information. Using the CCTV, we were able to determine the precise time when the first man, the one standing with the woman, arrived—twenty-seven minutes prior to the second man, the injured one. He bought three tickets. We know from the station's computer sales log, by the matching timestamp, that three first-class tickets were purchased, with cash, one-way tickets to Berlin on the 6 pm train."

"What time does that train arrive in Berlin?" asked Domiik who rose to his feet suddenly looking at the wall clock.

"It arrived on-time at 11:21 pm. We checked with Berlin as soon as we received this information, which was just before midnight, but by then the platform was deserted. The Berlin station master confirmed that the passengers had already departed the platform. We immediately contacted the Berlin authorities, but unfortunately, the police there were already too preoccupied with locking down the station in search of some other criminals or terrorists, to be of any assistance to us. We did request that they review the CCTV footage from all station cameras overnight, and we should receive the results by morning."

"Excellent work," said Marek.

"Indeed, yes," added Domiik. "You have done very well. Would you please cue up the CCTV of these in sequence, so that we may watch them at will."

"Yes, sir," replied the smiling investigator. She cued up the CCTV segments for them and then left the room, very pleased with herself.

"Well Marek," began Domiik, "you have your married couple from the Marrol Hotel in Bratislava, complete with the big black hat, and our shooter from Warsaw—all together. What do you think of that for police work?"

"Very good," Marek said turning toward him, with a smile. "I now know what my mystery couple looks like, as well as having a visual of your injured shooter. And there can now be no doubt whatsoever that the three assassins and the two assassinations are integrally linked."

"Berlin, ... ah. Berlin!" Marek repeated. "Why Berlin?" he asked rhetorically.

Adrianna questioned, "Why not Berlin?"

"I think you missed his point," Domiik responded. "What Marek meant was what could be in Berlin which would cause them to go there? This trio is very professional, focused and determined. I am certain that there is nothing they do without it being carefully preplanned ahead of time. The question is: What drew them to Berlin?"

"A place to hide ... a *Safe House* possibly," Jedrzej suggested.

"Possibly," Marek said as he stood up to wander the room.

"The source," Adrianna began, then paused.

"More ... keep going ... " Marek encouraged.

Still thinking as she spoke, Adrianna continued, "What if the organization ... or whoever is behind this international plot ... is centered in Berlin?"

"Could be," Marek mused, adding thoughtfully, "Yes, it could be. It's possible ... But would the masterminds want to draw the assassins, and our attention, to themselves?"

"Maybe, depending upon their ultimate purpose" interjected Jedrzej, "or what if Berlin wasn't their destination at all. What if it's somewhere else and Berlin was merely a stopping off point … in transit to some other location."

Now looking at Jedrzej, Marek asked, rhetorically, "Where would you go from Berlin, that you wouldn't want or couldn't go to directly from Warsaw?"

Domiik got up and walked to the door. Opening it, he called out to the room full of investigators working on the case, "Do we have any information on our three conspirators once they reached Berlin? Any CCTV hits at the Berlin Hauptbahnhof? Or the airport? Or anywhere?"

After a few moments, he closed the door and returned to his seat. "Nothing so far. By morning, probably, once the Germans finish chasing their other miscreants."

"What a strange, unfortunate coincidence that at the very moment our three conspirators arrive at the Berlin station, the police there happen to be busy looking for a different set of criminals and can't be bothered with ours," Adrianna reflected.

"No stranger than the rest of this case," Jedrzej added.

"That's the truth," Domiik rejoined.

"They could have gotten off the train before reaching Berlin," Adrianna posited.

"Yes," Marek reflected thoughtfully, "but it would have had to have been at Poznan, here in Poland. I've taken that train recently, the 6 pm train, the one they took, and Poznan is the only stop between Warsaw and Berlin."

Domiik rose again and headed for the door. Opening it, he yelled across the room for all to hear, "Check Poznan ... the station CCTV. And check Berlin again. That is the largest station in Europe, and —since the recent upsurge in terrorism—I think it must have half of all the video surveillance cameras in Europe."

He closed the door and looked at his watch. It was now nearly 1:00 am. "Colleagues, it is already tomorrow. Last night was a short one, and tomorrow is likely to be a very long day again. I suggest that we call it a night and get some sleep. Quarters have been set up here in the building, or you can go home, or Marek, to your hotel, if you prefer. Let's start again in the morning with fresh eyes and brains."

Rising to leave, Marek placed his hand on Domiik's shoulder. "I'll go to my hotel. I'll walk; I need the exercise and to take some air ... to think ... or at least to clear my mind. Rest well, my friend. We will find them."

Chapter 13:

To Berlin

March 15th — A Day Earlier

Given the total success thus far of their assignment, the conspirators were able to relax and enjoy their rail journey onboard the Berlin-Warszawa Express. It is one of the finer trains in Europe, particularly in first class, where they sat, the Pierces in one car and Franz in another. This arrangement suited Sarah, although she would have been happier if Franz were not on the train at all. Better yet, if she had never set eyes on him.

Departing Warsaw at 6:00 pm sharp, the Warszawa Express arrived in Berlin at 11:21 pm, with only a brief stop in Poznan, Poland, completing the 570km (356 mile) trip in five hours and twenty-one minutes, certainly longer than the ninety minutes of flying time, but it afforded travel in a far more civilized manner. Despite the additional time involved, the elegance of rail travel more than made up for the speed of flying, with its crowded airports teeming with security. A further benefit, especially for these three travelers, was the absence of any mandatory check-in or security screening checkpoints before boarding the train.

First class cars, configured into compartments, each seating six passengers on plush magenta seats offered spacious and relaxed accommodations. Franz settled into an empty compartment, which suited him just fine. If no one else entered it, that would please him. However, just before 6:00 pm, two Romain Catholic nuns entered the car breathlessly, inquiring whether the seats opposite from him were unclaimed. Franz answered, "Yes," coldly.

They proceeded to try lifting their heavy bags onto the rack above their heads. Franz, watching their futile efforts, stood-up, and taking the bags from them, placed them securely onto the rack. As they thanked him, he asked, "What do you have in them? Gold bullion?"

"Oh no," the younger nun blushed, "books, books for children."

Silence settled over the compartment as the train pulled away from the station. "Such confusion outside! Police swarming into the station," the younger sister remarked to no one in particular.

Franz decided that under that ridiculous habit she might be quite pretty after all. She had delicate features, warm hazel eyes, a beautifully sculpted nose, and full, well-formed lips. Even without a stitch of make-up, she was attractive. Deciding to engage her in conversation he asked, "What confusion?"

"Why the trouble at the stadium. Police racing around the city and just now, upstairs in the station." the other sister answered. "Apparently, there has been a terrorist attack."

"Probably Islamist Jihadists," Franz responded.

"Perhaps," the older nun answered, shaking her head in dismay. "So much terrible violence in the world today, wouldn't you agree?"

"Sometimes the only answer to violence is violence. That's all some people understand."

The older nun stiffened and responded sharply. "No monsieur! You are wrong! Violence is never the answer."

Franz looked straight at her,

"'A time to kill, and a time to heal;

A time to love, and a time to hate;

A time of war, and a time of peace.'

"You haven't served as a soldier as I have in Iraq and Afghanistan. The Taliban, ISIS, they are no longer even human. The things I've seen, the things they've done. The only solution is to utterly obliterate them from the face of the earth. Don't you agree?" He directed his question to the pretty young nun.

"I'm sure I know nothing of the terrible things you have witnessed in war," and she looked down. The older nun frowned with disapproval at her young companion's ambivalent answer.

Franz decided that he would say no more, as any further conversation would likely be between himself and the older nun, a prospect in which he saw no advantage. From the side compartment of his computer bag, he withdrew two American magazines, the latest issues of *Tactical Gun Magazine* and *Guns and Ammo*. Franz tossed *Guns and Ammo* conspicuously onto the seat next to him, turned so that it faced the nuns. Then he opened *Tactical Gun Magazine*, and, holding it high so that they would be sure to see it, he began to read silently.

At this, the older nun turned to her younger colleague saying, "Let us go to the dining car for dinner." They got up and, with the older nun in the lead, departed the compartment, but as they did, the younger nun turned back, looked at Franz and smiled, then crossed herself.

After they were gone, Franz dropped *Tactical Gun Magazine* on the seat on top of *Guns and Ammo* and, reaching back into his computer bag, pulled out *Art Culinaire* and *Gourmet*, with which he whiled away the time until he fell asleep. The nuns did not return to the compartment to retrieve their luggage until the train arrived in Berlin and Franz had departed.

As Bruce and Sarah entered their railcar, Bruce directed her to a window seat in the first compartment, knowing that other passengers, seeing a couple there, would be more likely to continue down the railcar looking for an unoccupied compartment. Sarah, still peeved by the overall state of affairs, began complaining again as soon as the two had taken their seats in the empty compartment. "I wish there were single compartments for only two instead of six. No doubt we'll have four more people come squeezing into our compartment before the train pulls out. I hate being among all ... "

"Stop! You've been whinging ever since we met Franz for breakfast yesterday morning. Get over it," Bruce chided, with a degree of annoyance audible in his voice.

"It's not that ... it's him ... that Neanderthal! We did our part, so why the need to partake in this silly charade yet a second time? All I want to do is to get away for our vacation ... with you ... just the two of us." Bruce didn't even look up from the newspaper he had purchased before boarding the train. "And another thing, why wasn't there a first-class waiting room in the Warsaw station? At least Berlin provides the

DB Lounge for first class passengers. You'd think Poland could do as well. Instead, we were forced to wait in the main lobby with everyone else!" her voice trailed off.

Bruce knew the wisest course was to ignore her childish pouting, the carryover of an over-indulgent upbringing. Although smart and highly sophisticated, there remained another side to Sarah's persona, that of a spoiled little 'daddy's girl.' Peeved by Bruce's icy silence, she now sought to console herself, opening her purse and taking out the jewelry trinket she had acquired at the station.

It wasn't long before the last boarding call for the train sounded from the platform. Sarah felt relieved that no other passengers had entered their compartment, although a number of people had passed its sliding glass door and looked in at them. She knew Bruce's choice of the first compartment had been strategic. It was so typical of him, always pre-planning their every move, great or small, leaving nothing to chance. That was one of the characteristics that had initially drawn her to him, when they had first been introduced. He was always thinking, anticipating, planning his next move. Taking off her hat, she stood momentarily to place it on the rack above the seat across from them.

Sitting down again, she tucked her dark glasses and new jewelry into her purse. As the train eased out of the station, she sighed with relief. Bruce looked over at her sitting in the seat next to his. Pulling up the armrest between them to its stowed position, he placed his arm around her and pulled her close, her head resting on his chest. "For such a brilliant woman, you can be so childish at times."

"Would you have me be otherwise?" Sarah asked looking up at him as she slid down in her seat and turned her face toward his.

Bruce laughed softly, "No, I guess I'll keep you just the way you are." He pulled her close, and it seemed to her that every muscle in her body relaxed.

The sudden slowing of the train awakened Bruce but startled Sarah. "Now there," Bruce said as he stroked her hair softly.

"Why are we stopping?" she asked drowsily.

"It's the normal stop for the city of Poznan, Poland, nothing unusual ... nothing to worry about."

"Who says I was worried?" she said, snuggling back against his chest.

Sarah had almost fallen back asleep when the compartment door rolled open, and, just as the train lurched forward, two middle-aged businessmen stumbled into the compartment, the first nearly falling onto Sarah. "Pardon me," he said, looking at Sarah's face as she turned to him in surprise. His gaze did not leave her as he straightened up and stepped backward, collapsing into the seat across from her.

The other man sat across from Bruce. "Sorry, I wasn't expecting the train to move just then," the first man offered.

Bruce responded, "That's alright," although he fully realized the maneuver had been contrived. Sarah avoided eye contact with the man and sat straight up in her seat. Then, turning to Bruce, she requested the newspaper that was now lying on the seat nearest the compartment door. He passed it to her, and she began reading intently, holding it high to hide her from the two strangers.

Bruce's face revealed a slight smirk as he removed his arm from around Sarah's shoulders. He was going to enjoy this—even though he knew she'd be annoyed.

The man across from Sarah attempted to strike up a conversation with Bruce. "Did you board in Warsaw?" Bruce responded that they had. "Then possibly you haven't heard the news?"

"What news?" Bruce replied blankly, as he listened to the man recount the news of a shooting at the Warsaw stadium, right near where the Prime Minister was sitting for the soccer game. "No, I hadn't heard. Was anyone injured?"

"No one seems certain," the man replied. "It was reported that a number of ambulances were dispatched to the stadium, according to the television reports we watched while waiting for the train at Poznan station. The situation seems to be very uncertain."

The other man nodded, adding, "At least it appears that the Prime Minister is all right."

At this Sarah slowly lowered the newspaper to her lap and looked up.

The first man continued: "After that business the other day in Bratislava, it almost makes one wonder if today's incident wasn't an attempt on the Polish Prime Minister's life." Looking at Sarah, he continued, "Is there anything in the paper about the Bratislava investigation?"

Sarah looked at him, the folded paper in plain view on her lap with a portion of the headline 'Slovak Prime Minister's Assassination Investigation Continues' showing and said, "No, nothing at all about it in the paper."

The compartment lapsed into silence. Then the man across from Sarah, looking intently at her (in fact, he had not once taken his eyes off of Sarah) asked, "Are you traveling beyond Berlin?"

Sarah looked up at him again, taking her eyes off the folded newspaper, and turned to Bruce. "I'm hungry," she whispered, loudly enough for the others to hear.

Bruce rising to his feet and, taking Sarah's hand to lead her from the compartment, said, "Excuse us."

"That was pretty cold," the second man said to the other after Bruce and Sarah had left the compartment. "Obviously, nearly falling into her lap didn't win you any points."

"I didn't do it on purpose!"

"Well, if you say so, but I don't think she bought it, and I'm certain her husband didn't. Nice try, anyhow. She certainly is a looker. Better luck next time … provided you don't make a move on a married woman with her husband sitting right next to her."

Bruce and Sarah made their way through the train to the bistro-restaurant car. Finding a table for two, Bruce ordered sandwiches, along with a glass of merlot for Sarah and a dark German beer for himself. It was now completely dark outside, and the car was dimly lit. Music played in the background interrupted only by the softly clattering syncopation of the train car's wheels periodically striking track switch points or crossovers.

Beer in hand, Bruce chuckled, "Poor fellow stumbled when the train started."

"Poor fellow! That oaf pretty much landed right on top of me."

"Just a harmless accident," Bruce countered.

"Do you seriously think so? I don't for one minute. I think he did it on purpose!"

"And why ever would he do that?" Bruce questioned.

Sarah looked up from her sandwich. "I wasn't born yesterday. I've had plenty of guys flirt with me, but that was obnoxious." She studied his expression. "You know he did it on purpose. You could have said something, instead of just sitting there enjoying the whole farce."

"What was I supposed to say? 'Yes, my wife is gorgeous, but please don't fall for her—or worse yet, on her?'" Bruce smiled his obnoxiously all-knowing grin.

"So you knew it was a ruse intended to get my attention."

"Yes, I saw him staring at you through the compartment door before he opened it. He was no doubt smitten by your dazzling beauty."

"And you just let him fall into my lap?"

Still wearing his wide, boyish grin, Bruce added, "What could I do but enjoy the moment?"

"Hmmf! Men. You're all alike. Either you're making a pass at a woman, or you're enjoying watching someone else do so!"

The couple lingered long after dinner. Bruce ordered two coffees with Baileys and a dessert. Sarah said she didn't feel like a rich dessert. However, after watching him polish off more than half of a generous portion of luscious tiramisu, drizzled table-side with warm dark chocolate sauce, and then being tormented by his obvious delight in slowly licking the fork after each delectable bite, she snapped. Reaching out quickly, she snatched the plate from him and placed it directly in front of her. With one hand securely anchored to the plate, she devoured the rest of it.

"Still hungry?" he asked innocently in a playful tone.

"No ... I just don't want you getting fat!"

After she'd finished scraping the plate clean with the fork, Bruce said, "Let's go back to the compartment." But Sarah wasn't ready to do that, so he ordered a brandy old fashioned for her and a rum and coke with a twist of lime for himself. They sat quietly with their drinks, watching as the lights of Berlin's suburbs began flashing past. Then the conductor came through, announcing that the train would be arriving at the Berlin station in ten minutes. They could sense the train perceptibly slowing. Rising, they walked back to their compartment.

As they approached the first compartment, they could see the two men still seated inside. Both men looked up as Bruce opened the door and they stepped in. "Still here I see. No more problems losing your balance?" Sarah questioned sarcastically, looking directly at them.

"No," the first man responded. His companion held out his mobile phone, so they were both able to view the news headline.

"Now that we're in Berlin, we finally have internet," he remarked. "I don't understand why the train doesn't have it. Airplanes do, and so do some trains, why not this one? This is an interesting article. The Slovak police have a lead on the assassination of their Prime Minister." Thrusting his phone even closer for Bruce and Sarah to see, he continued, "They have a picture of the couple they are looking for … "

Bruce took the phone from him. "Could be anyone," Bruce said as he handed the phone back.

"Could even be you two," the second man said, then laughed.

"Could be," responded Bruce, "had we been in Slovakia instead of Poland the past week."

The brakes squealed as the train came to a stop at Berlin Hauptbahnhof. "After you," said the first man.

"No, go ahead," Bruce responded. "I'm afraid my wife had one too many drinks with dinner. Now that the train has stopped, she'll need a few moments to regain her balance before we can go."

The two men laughed again. "A pleasure sharing the compartment with you," said the first, as they got up to leave. Exiting the compartment following his colleague, he took one last longing look at Sarah, but she was staring out the window, the dark glasses, clutched in her hands. Closing the compartment door behind him, he suddenly froze, his eyes fixed on the black hat poised on the rack over where he had been sitting. Then he glanced at Bruce, who was looking directly at him, his expression darkened with a coldness devoid of any human feeling. The man's face became ghostlike as he quickly spun around and hurried to disembark the train.

Sarah turned to Bruce, "He noticed the hat, didn't he? I was watching his reflection in the window."

Bruce's expression returned to normal, "Yes, he did indeed. Time for us to go."

Chapter 14:

Warsaw

March 17

At 7:30 am, shortly after the four investigators arrived back at police headquarters to begin the new day, the conference room door opened. "Sir," an officer interrupted the four, "we have just received a call from Berlin. The couple from Bratislava that Interpol is seeking has been sighted. As we suspected, they were traveling on the evening train from Warsaw that arrived in Berlin minutes before midnight."

Marek jumped to his feet. "Are they certain?" he asked.

"It would appear so. We have a conference call for you coming through from Lyon shortly. They'll be providing a full briefing."

Minutes later, the conference room phone rang. Domiik answered and placed the call on speakerphone. A female agent was on the line from Interpol, Lyon. "Mr. Marek, we have reported sightings of the couple first identified in Bratislava. And they were accompanied by another man, the same one identified by Polish authorities as having been with them at the Hotel Rialto and again at the Warsaw train station."

"So they were traveling together on the train," Marek responded into the speaker.

"No ... well, not exactly. Allow me to explain. We have CCTV photos of the three walking together in the Berlin Hauptbahnhof and then exiting the station together. They subsequently got into a private car, a black Mercedes, which then drove off. Unfortunately, we were unable to obtain a clear photo of the license plate.

"However, for some reason, they did not travel in the same compartment on the train—we don't know if they were even in the same railcar. We are, at the moment, trying to track down the first class conductor for an interview.

"We know the couple traveled together in the first compartment of the lead first-class car. Two businessmen joined them in that car, getting on at Poznan, Poland—the only stop between Warsaw and Berlin. The men made several unsuccessful attempts at conversation with the couple, and in fact, soon after the men boarded the train, the couple left the compartment and went to the Bistro-Restaurant car for dinner, remaining there until just minutes before the train arrived in Berlin. They know this because one of the men also went briefly to the Bistro to buy sandwiches, which he brought back to the compartment. He noticed the couple seated in the Bistro car, presumably having dinner.

"It was only as the train approached the station in Berlin and one of the two witnesses was able to connect his phone to wi-fi service that he saw the news article and photo of the Bratislava couple. However, he didn't immediately associate the couple in their compartment with the one in the news photo. He told the Berlin police that he had even joked with them about it, suggesting that they might be the people in the news photo and showed them the image on his mobile phone. He said that they laughed and said something to the effect of, 'Yes, us and every other thirty-something couple.'

But as he was leaving the railcar, he caught sight of the woman's black hat on the rack above his seat, identical to the one in the police photo. And on her lap were the matching dark glasses as in the photo. At that point, it occurred to him that this was more than mere coincidence. Once inside the Berlin station, the two men conferred for several minutes, as the second man advised that they not get involved. Finally, they agreed, found a uniformed policeman, and related the entire story about the glamorous couple they had met on the train and their suspicions. However, by the time all of this had transpired, and the police took action, the couple was nowhere to be found—along with the other man in the Warsaw photos, as they had already departed the station, as we now know from the CCTV footage."

"Damn!" explicated Jedrzej slamming his fist on the table. "We could have had them if only the spotters had acted sooner in contacting the authorities."

Marek did his best to calm his colleague, "No, realistically it wouldn't have mattered how quickly the two men had alerted the Berlin police. It no doubt took the couple only two or three minutes to rendezvous with their companion—who was probably traveling in the next car of the train—exit the station and get into the waiting pick-up car. I am quite certain that the driver of that car knew exactly how to navigate his approach to the station, precisely where to park and the best escape route, ensuring that the station's outdoor CCTV cameras would not be able to record the license plate.

"This is all too carefully planned and far too professional an operation for them to have been apprehended at the Berlin train station. Nor did they wish the car's license plate to be seen and traced. They were not so concerned about being seen with their faces obscured from the cameras by disguises, but did not intend to give us a photo good enough to be utilized by facial pattern recognition software. Just be glad that the men traveling in their compartment had the presence of mind and courage to notify the authorities, even if they initially debated doing so. Many people wouldn't have bothered, or even wanted to involve themselves in such a high-profile criminal matter."

Turning back to the phone's speaker, Marek asked, "Did the Berlin authorities have them collaborate with a police sketch artist to create an accurate drawing from their descriptions?"

"No," the voice on the phone answered. "They provided only a general description of the couple, which both described as being very attractive and well dressed, but it was nearing 1:00 am, by the time the police had locked down and searched the entire station. It's the largest train station in Europe, and by that time the two men said they were exhausted and needed to get to their hotel, as they had early morning meetings. They told the Berlin police that they would be tied up in meetings all day today and then had an important client dinner engagement this evening, but that tomorrow morning, before leaving Berlin, they would be willing to meet with a sketch artist at police headquarters."

At this, the conference room erupted in angry shouts directed at the phone. "What! The hell they will!" barked Marek. "By the time those two idiots finally get around to finding a convenient time to meet with the police sketch artist, they won't even remember what the couple looked like! We'll end up with sketches that look like everyone ... and no one. You tell Berlin to go immediately to wherever they are now, their hotel or wherever their 'important' meetings are taking place and insist ... no, just escort them to police headquarters immediately for the sketches to be made now. And if they refuse or try to delay even one minute, direct the Berlin police to arrest them for withholding evidence! We need those sketches now! Not tomorrow."

The agent on the other end of the line affirmed that she would call Berlin to ensure this directive was carried out immediately. Marek added, "If Berlin gives you any trouble, call me right away, and I will kick their asses so hard they'll never forget it!"

"Yes, Sir!"

The call ended, and the conference room fell silent. "So now we know which dangerous criminals the Berlin police were pursuing last night with such verve that they had no time to respond to our people's request for assistance. Another sterling example of police coordination ... at its finest!" Domiik smirked.

"Just standard German efficiency," Jedrzej muttered. "Too busy to answer the call that would provide them with the information they needed for the search they were so very busy conducting!"

Adrianna asked, "Do you think they'll be able to provide us with drawings that are accurate enough to run facial recognition?" Marek just groaned loudly. "I take that as a no," Adrianna voiced, assessing from her colleague's distorted facial expression.

Domiik answered her, "As Marek said, I'm sure they will be good sketches. Sketches of every attractive man and women their age ... and of none. Unless these two men or at least one of them, has developed remarkable powers of observation and memory, don't expect to get anything definitive enough to be useful. The average untrained citizen has the recollection powers of a goldfish ... and you know what they say about the memory of goldfish."

By late morning, Berlin had transmitted the completed sketches of the couple. These were projected onto the conference room screen. After studying the artist's renderings, Adrianna was the first to speak. "Now I understand what you meant, Domiik. These renderings are quite detailed and artistically very good, but they could be just about any attractive Caucasian man and woman with the right hair and eye color."

"Yes," Domiik replied, "and heaven only knows what their real hair and eye colors are. Does the woman really have brilliant red hair and bright blue eyes, or are these the result of a bottle of hair coloring and blue contact lenses. She undoubtedly has fair skin, but that's all we can ascertain with any certainty from this sketch. She's just as elusive here as when she was wearing her black hat and dark glasses. And as for her husband—we don't even know if they are married, although in the CCTV photos she does sport a rather ostentatious rock on her left hand—either he's unusually good-looking or our two travelers have confused him with someone they've seen in the movies. I'd bet this rendering has more in common with a youthful, dark-haired version of Robert Redford then it does with Bruce ... what's his name ... "

"Bruce Pierce," Adrianna answered.

"Yes, Mr. Pierce, or whatever his real name is."

Jedrzej stood up suddenly. "I know her," he announced excitedly, in a loud voice, pointing to the image projected on the screen. "Domiik, you do too. Look at her face closely. Now, mentally change her hair color to dark and her eyes to green—we have her."

"What do you mean?" Domiik sputtered.

Meanwhile, Marek joined in, "Yes, I see it too. We need look no further."

Somewhat confused, Adrianna, queried, "So who, who is she?"

Domiik, not typically one to be slow on the uptake, now joined in with the other two. "You're right! I should have seen it before. It's plain as day. Am I ever getting slow! Time to retire."

"Yes," Marek added, "she certainly is a beauty. WOW!"

"Will someone please tell me what's going on?" Adrianna's voice was exasperated and demanding.

Marek turned to her, and leaning across the large conference room table and in his most serious deep voice, asked, "Tell us, Adrianna, why did you do it?"

"Do what?" she retorted.

"How did you get involved in all this? And why? Who is that man, your accomplice?"

At this, Adrianna turned on them. "You idiots! Men … you are all alike! Every time I begin to think that maybe … just maybe, you have begun to grow up, you start in again and prove me wrong. Ugh!"

"Oh well," Marek announced, now laughing heartily with the other two, "We can forget facial pattern recognition with this artist's renderings. The mystery woman could have easily been our Adrianna!"

Adrianna was not amused, and her face showed it. "Can we possibly get back to work? Now that you 'boys' have had your fun!"

"Ah, but, remember ..." Domiik, turned to Adrianna, "Marek did say that he thought you are 'very beautiful.'" Adrianna was caught off guard … speechless for a moment. She didn't know how to take it. Was this still part of the joke? Or was Domiik hinting that Marek meant what he said about the artist's rendition of the woman being beautiful? Surely, he was referring to the woman portrayed in the sketch … or did he mean her?

She was flustered and felt certain that her face must be turning beet red, which was the last thing she wanted them to see, especially Marek. Her mind was swimming; above all, she knew that she couldn't look at Marek. As Adrianna struggled for words that would turn the joke back on them, she felt the eyes of all three men fixed upon her. Looking up, she quipped, "Why, I thought Marek hadn't noticed."

"Woo, Marek, you'd better watch yourself. She's a cool one." Jedrzej warned.

"Alright. Let's begin again. What do we have?" Domiik's jovial voice sounded.

As she felt the attention shift away, Adrianna breathed a quiet sigh of relief. Was she just being silly and thin-skinned, or was there another not so subtle conspiracy developing in the room. A conspiracy on behalf of Marek—and she the unsuspecting target?

"So far we have our four possible perpetrators: the American President, the CIA—without their President's knowledge or sanction— a Russian conspiracy sanctioned by the Kremlin or lastly, criminal underworld elements in Eastern Europe," Jedrzej recapitulated. "Until yesterday, I would have completely discounted both of the American options. However, the very idea of a friendly visit from that singularly unhelpful CIA operative does make me wonder … although it still makes absolutely no sense at all to me."

Marek chimed in, "Premeditated crimes such as these, state-sponsored assassinations of friendly heads of state, would need to be sanctioned at the very highest levels, if ever. Whether or not it is the Lee Harvey Oswalds' of the world who actually pull the trigger, someone much more powerful is pulling the strings. What we have before us is nothing like that Hinckley maniac who shot Reagan! This is a full-fledged conspiracy emanating from a very high level … somewhere."

Having regained her composure, and wanting to feel that she was holding her own again, Adrianna added, "We have the weapon, and we know that both it and the round originated with the Americans. And the Kestrel ballistics meter as well. These may have been given to the shooter or stolen and sold to him by someone, but there is no question that the round originated from a highly placed source within the American Department of Defense."

"Adrianna's right," Marek cut in. "We need to find out how the assassin obtained that round. I, for one, think it's time we contact our American friend and ask some pointed questions. Agreed?" They all concurred. He picked up the phone and dialed Murray's mobile.

"Hello?" Murray's voice sounded friendly and cheerful on the other end of the line.

"This is Marek, and we need to see you immediately."

"No problem, I'm on my way over to see you now. In fact, my taxi is just down the block. Be there momentarily!"

Murray hung up, and Marek touched the 'Call End' button on the conference room phone. "Domiik, do you want to handle this?"

"Not particularly. Marek, why don't you do it? You undoubtedly have more experience dealing with these American 'spook' types."

Minutes later, a smiling Robert Murray strode confidently into the conference room, slim black attaché case in hand. He greeted each person by name and then seated himself at the table. "You would like my assistance?"

Marek opened the portfolio that was before him on the table and, removing four photographs, slid them across the table to Murray. "The first photo is of the gun recovered from the scene of the Warsaw shooting, the Barrett, Heavy Caliber M107 .50/A1 Caliber Sniper Rifle — LRSR, (Long Range Sniper Rifle)."

"One helluva gun!" Murray nodded, smiling as he picked up the photo and carefully examined it.

"Yes, and not the kind of weapon you see everyday. Not even among hired assassins. It's clearly of military origin," Marek continued.

"You're right," Murray agreed, still deep in thought.

"Robert," Marek used his first name as a sign of acceptance and to demonstrate a cooperative spirit with the CIA operative, "This isn't used by just any military, but one specific military! It is American design and issue, and, as you'll notice in the second picture, a magnification showing the words, 'U.S. Marine Corps - PROPERTY OF THE U.S. GOVERNMENT' indelibly stamped on its side."

At this, Murray straightened his back and tightened his grip on the second photo.

"And then there is the third photo before you. The bullet. A .50 cal round so badly mangled that at first, we thought nothing more of it. But then our forensics team, headed by Adrianna," Marek glanced towards her, "noticed something very peculiar about the bullet. It was not solid. Instead, it had a tiny microchip and battery fragments. As you will notice in the fourth photograph, it also has vanes and what were apparently miniature fins, before they were crushed by the impact."

As Marek spoke, Murray's brain rapidly processed this information, like a miniature supercomputer. He picked up the fourth photo, a further enlargement of the bullet. While it was impossible for him to distinguish the individual component parts Marek was describing—or rather, their remnants—he instinctively grasped what Marek was describing.

"As you can imagine, Robert," Marek continued, "you don't buy this type of hardware on every street corner ... not even in America, where you have more guns than you have people."

The room fell silent as Murray continued studying the photographs, going back through them several times. Finally, after a hiatus that seemed like an eternity, Murray spoke ... utterly shocking his hosts. "The weapon is clearly of American design and origin. I know it personally ... not this one specifically ... but this weapon type, the Barrett LRSR. I've fired it. In fact, I've used it myself, operationally. I am also familiar with what I believe this round to be—it's called the EXACTO, a recent creation of DARPA, the Defense Advanced Research Projects Agency, part of the U.S. DoD. And I know of no other round like it in the world ... not from any other country."

It was as though a diplomatic bombshell had just been detonated in the conference room. The same alarming thought raced through the minds of the four investigators: Why would Murray so openly and without further prompting or pressuring confirm this most incriminating and damning evidence—especially after being so deliberately evasive at their first encounter the previous day?

"I suppose you're all waiting for an explanation … as to how this is possible," continued Murray, after the mental dust had settled. "Unfortunately, I do not have one … not at present. I wish I did. What I can do is assure you that despite the fact that this weapon and its extremely unique bullet somehow found their way into the hands of Prime Minister Binkowski's assassin, this in no way, and I repeat, absolutely in no way represents an officially or unofficially sanctioned act of the United States government."

Turning now to Adrianna, Murray eyed her intently. "I now understand your comment yesterday, Adrianna. At the time, I was mystified by such a remark coming from you, a young woman who has so quickly risen to a high status of respect within this organization, undoubtedly for your talents and clear thinking. Adrianna, the simple truth is that neither the CIA nor DoD had anything to do with this assassination. Nor the one in Bratislava!" Even after he had finished speaking, he kept his gaze locked upon Adrianna.

Finally, she looked down, saying quietly, "I understand. Thank you."

Murray now turned and addressed the entire group. "I am as shocked by this information as you must have been when you first discovered it. I confess that when I came here yesterday, it was not merely as a simple courtesy visit or a token effort to offer you my … my government's assistance. I came to learn something … something I did not know, but now do. To speak plainly, a source we have in Brussels heard 'noise' of something, again, something nebulous that he could not pin down, emanating from Germany, from Berlin, something purportedly to do with us, the U.S., related to these two assassinations. We could not obtain any further information. I came to you, primarily,

I'll admit, on a fishing expedition on behalf of the U.S. Government, and not just the CIA, but also at the behest of the Department of State, to ascertain the answer.

"That, in all honesty, is all I can tell you at this time because it is all I—we—know—at this time. I only wish I could explain by what machinations this weapon and bullet were misappropriated and, as a result, are now here in your possession. But I cannot!"

Adrianna wrote something on her notepad and slid it over to Domiik. He read it and passed it to Marek and Jedrzej, who with barely perceptible nods agreed. Domiik pushed the notepad back towards Adrianna, saying, "Go ahead."

Adrianna turned to face Murray. "Mr. Murray…"

Murray interrupted her, "Please, Robert."

"Robert," she continued, "I want to show you a picture of the Prime Minister's head wound." Opening her portfolio, she removed a single photograph, handed it to him and waited.

Murray took the photograph and examining it intently, asked, "At what range was the shooter?"

"640 meters, about 700 yards by American measurement," Adrianna answered.

Murray began again, "I am familiar with the damage a .50 cal can do and at such a short range. It is massive. However, this … this appears to me to be more than what I would expect. Adrianna, I am not a forensic, or even a weapons expert like you. However, I have extensive personal experience with weapons of various types, including the .50 cal. No, this looks like too much damage for even such a large and powerful bullet as the .50 cal."

"That was my first impression also," Adrianna agreed. "The Taylor KO factor," she went on. Murray looked puzzled, " ... the Strike Energy," she said. Murray nodded his understanding of the second term. Adrianna continued, "for the .50 cal, although very high, a TKO of 147 for the Browning Machine Gun is likely insufficient to do this level of damage. At first, I thought that possibly the bullet was a hollow tip, but then we learned it was a military round which, as we all know, under the Geneva Convention must be FMJ (Full Metal Jacket). So, we did some further testing.

"As you can see from the photographs, the bullet is severely deformed. But the bullet's impact, together with the velocity with which the skull fragments and cerebral material of the Prime Minister were scattered, led me to believe that this could not be the result of a standard NATO round. Then, in the course of our laboratory analysis, initially, to determine the strange nature of the electromechanical bullet fragments which had been identified, we detected traces of mercury fulminate. Are you familiar with the substance?"

"Yes," Murray answered, "it's an impact-sensitive explosive which, when packed into the tip of a hollow point bullet, will explode upon impact, causing a significantly larger wound and much more damage than an ordinary FMJ, or even a hollow point bullet. But, the U.S. military does not use hollow point rounds of any type, nor does any other legitimate military, as this is also contravened by the Geneva Convention. We certainly do not use mercury fulminate exploding rounds for anti-personnel. Additionally, this round if indeed it is the EXACTO, has never been produced as a hollow point and could not be modified to a hollow point, as the laser guidance sensor is in the tip. I'm at a loss in regard to the presence of the mercury fulminate." The intensity in Murray's face and speech left little doubt in the minds of the others that he was speaking the truth.

Chapter 15:

The Perpetrators Found

Robert Murray had left with the promise that he would return with hard answers as to how the weapon and EXACTO cartridge had found its way into an assassin's hands. The investigators ordered in a late lunch. It was delivered, and the group was reassembling following the break when Adrianna returned to the conference room.

"Quick, turn on the TV," she said.

"What's happening?" Marek asked, as he picked up the remote and clicked it on. Scenes of angry street protests filled the screen.

"Is something going on?" Domiik inquired, walking back into the room. "We've been locked up in this room so long that I have no idea what's going on outside of these four walls."

"There's growing anger here in Poland—and in Slovakia, as well as in other eastern and southern European member countries, regarding the EU Brussels announcement which followed yesterday's meeting," Adrianna apprised them.

"What announcement?"

Adrianna responded, "Apparently, the EU called for increased centralized control of member countries' economies and banks, as well as stricter enforcement of trade agreements against the U.S. All this comes immediately on the heels of the assassinations of two of the eastern European Prime Ministers who vocally opposed such measures. I think there may be a high price to pay over this!"

"They're just peaceful protests, aren't they?" asked Jedrzej returning to the room.

"So far, but the question is whether they'll stay that way, given the rate at which they are growing."

Domiik picked up the conference room phone and spoke to someone. Hanging up, he said, "That was our internal security division head. It looks as though this could rapidly get out of hand. The protests in Slovakia already have escalated into confrontations between angry crowds throwing rocks and riot police firing tear gas. This isn't what we need right now."

The team ate their lunch in silence while continuing to watch the news of growing protests unfolding in Warsaw and around Poland. After lunch, they returned to the work at hand, reviewing the facts known thus far regarding the two assassinations.

Late in the afternoon, the phone rang. It was the Interpol agent again, calling from Lyon. "Marek, we've had a tip as to the whereabouts of our three suspects."

Marek switched the call to speakerphone. "Please repeat that again so that we can all hear."

"We've had a tip as to the possible whereabouts of our three suspects."

The team came to life as if struck by a high-voltage electric shock. "Where?"

"I'm conferencing the Berlin authorities into this call," she stated. "Berlin, are you there?"

"Yes, we're on."

"Go ahead; we have the investigative team in Warsaw on the call."

"Okay. Warsaw, we believe that we may have located the three suspects here, on the outskirts of Berlin. We have a response team headed there now, ETA twenty-two minutes."

"Can't they get there any faster?" Marek asked.

"Unfortunately, not, it's rush hour here, and the location is some distance outside of Berlin's city center. We have also dispatched a police helicopter which should be arriving momentarily. The location is a private residence … a house with a stand-alone garage. From the satellite map, which should be coming into view for you via a video link, it appears to be in a semi-rural area. The house, if we have the right one, is located on about 2.5 hectares—that's roughly six or so acres if you have any American friends there with you—and has a detached garage building. Hold on; we are getting an update from the helicopter now."

"What do you mean, 'if we have the right house?'" Marek barked.

"The tip we received wasn't precise … there was no actual address provided, just a description of a house and the general location. You must understand that in these more rural areas, small roads and addresses can at times be somewhat difficult to locate quickly from the air or satellite."

"I'm going to add in the live helicopter video feed now. There will be a moment of silence as I bring them online."

The Warsaw team sat in silence as they waited, wondering if this could actually be their opportunity to apprehend the suspects.

"Warsaw, this is Berlin, we have the helicopter on the call now, and the video link should be up for you."

The news images of the growing protests were still on the television screen, though the volume had been muted earlier, following lunch. Domiik walked to the door and spoke to someone. Moments later, a police technician came into the conference room and connected the widescreen TV to Berlin's video and audio feed. Now the screen came alive with an aerial image from the helicopter closing in on a modest country house on the outskirts of Berlin.

"Go ahead, eyes in the sky," Marek responded into the speakerphone.

"We've sighted what we believe to be the house. We're standing off about a kilometer, so as not to spook them. Zooming our video camera in now! There's a black Mercedes heading down the gravel driveway away from the house as we speak and another one parked outside of the house. Do you want us to follow the moving car?"

"Which way is the car traveling?" Marek asked.

"It's turning out of the driveway westbound, headed out toward the autobahn."

Following several seconds of silence, Berlin Police Headquarters responded, "No, let it go, stay with the house as long as the other car remains parked. We have a second helicopter arriving momentarily; they'll intercept and follow the moving car. And maintain your standoff. We don't want whoever is in the house to panic and flee before we have sufficient assets in place.

"Warsaw, the second helicopter has intercepted the Mercedes and will follow at a standoff distance."

The minutes ticked by as the first police helicopter hovered just outside of earshot of the house. Then the call came that the first response team had arrived and taken a position on a nearby hillside with some trees for cover and an unobstructed view of the house.

"Are you certain that you have the right location?" Jedrzej asked.

Berlin responded that they were, as long as their tip was accurate, and they had a high confidence level that it was.

"Warsaw," a voice from the second helicopter crew broke the silence, "We are likely to lose the second Mercedes. The light is fading quickly, and the car has turned onto the autobahn, this section of which is highly congested at this time of day. It's doubtful we'll be able to maintain tracking without getting too close or spotlighting the vehicle, either of which might cause the occupants to phone the house and warn them. Do you want us to move in closer or spotlight them?"

Marek looked at the others and then responded, "We can't take that chance before there are sufficient assets in place to prevent an escape from the house. Just maintain your present surveillance as long as possible. Maybe we'll get a break in the traffic. Under the circumstances, better a bird in the hand."

"Understood!" the helicopter crew replied. Moments later, "We have lost the Mercedes."

"This is Berlin, we've pulled back the first helicopter, as the response team has night vision and can maintain surveillance without the potential of alerting the people in the house of its presence. It is landing nearby and will be joined shortly by the second helicopter. They'll both keep their engines running and can be back in the air on a moment's notice and in place over the house in under two minutes if we need them. We have five more response units on the way and will have the full compliment of response personnel placed in position around the house, ready to move within the hour. We also have the local police ready to block the surrounding roads when we move in."

The hour passed slowly for the team in Warsaw. They requested more coffee, meanwhile cake fortuitously arrived from another department where a retirement party was just concluding.

"Retirement," said Jedrzej, "now that's an idea that has held growing appeal for me of late."

"Nonsense," replied Domiik. "You're far too young to even consider such a thing."

"My wife and I have been talking about it for a while now: Miedzyzdroje, on the Baltic. Magnificent white sand beaches with tree-covered hills behind. The Wolin National Park next door. Most beautiful spot in all of Poland! I'm tiring of this life. Too often not home at night, stress, politics … I'm ready for something slower. A more relaxed lifestyle. And quieter. With time to enjoy our grandchildren. We now have three, you know, and they're growing up before our eyes! I've been thinking that I could retire to Miedzyzdroje and write crime novels. I was a literature major in university before entering the Federal Police Academy in Szczytno and have always loved writing. Just sitting on the beach writing books … that's the way to go out."

"You could never afford to live on the beach in Miedzyzdroje anyway," Domiik interjected.

"Maybe not right on the beach, at least not until I've published my first best-selling novel. Maybe it will even become a movie … a great detective mystery interspersed with exciting action scenes. Then we'll move to a big house on the beach. I can't wait."

The phone line came back to life. "Warsaw, this is Berlin. All teams are in position and ready to move. Anything, in particular, you want to add to their final instructions before they move on the house?"

The Warsaw team looked at each other. Marek spoke, "These three are cold-blooded killers, so your people need to treat them as such. At the same time, we need them alive. Bodies won't tell us who is behind these assassinations or what is the ultimate objective, and these three are our only link to the source of this plot ... and whatever else may be planned. They must be taken alive at all costs, even to jeopardizing the lives of the response teams. But be careful!"

"We understand what's at stake here," was the answer from Berlin.

"Good luck!" No one added anything more. Marek had expressed their thoughts perfectly. Now, it was just a matter of waiting. Marek spoke again, "As soon as we know that you have them secured, we'll be in the air on our way to you."

"Understood!" came the voice on the phone. "We'll keep the video feed live as we move in on the house. We're going over to a matrix screen display where you'll see six boxes; each one will show you the view from one of the six response team lead's helmet cameras. The response teams are all night-vision camera equipped. We are now patching you into our feed from each team's leader's video, and audio feeds."

The screen went blank, then static, then blank again and then ... a matrix appeared, three boxes wide and two rows high. One by one, the matrix boxes filled with live, eerie green night vision feeds from the six teams on the ground positioned around the house.

"Both helicopters are in the air," Berlin reported. Both still in standoff mode and running dark. They'll light up the house when the response teams strike. The Warsaw investigators watched as the six response teams moved slowly into their final assault positions. Two spread out and surrounded the house at a twenty-five-meter distance, while two began to move in close, one toward the front and the other, the back doors. Two teams took up reserve positions front and back, very close to the house, while the door teams crept silently up to it. "We see lights on throughout the first floor and a light in one room of the second floor. This house design typically has five rooms on the first floor, and we anticipate two upstairs," the response teams' leader advised. "We're ready to go."

"Let the helicopters move in and then go on your mark," a Berlin voice said. Each of the six teams responded in turn with their ready status, and the teams switched their cameras from night vision to daylight. Two members of each door team held blast shields as the remaining members crouched behind them.

"We can hear the helicopters approaching, we have 'Go' in 30 seconds," the response teams' leader repeated, " … 15 … 10 … 5 … GO!"

The scene was instantly awash in brilliant white light, like noon on a sunny summer day, as the two police helicopters directed their searchlights onto the house and yard. Two nearly simultaneous blasts were heard, and small white flashes could be seen on the screen emanating from explosive charges that the teams had placed on the locks and hinges of the front and back doors of the house. Both doors blew inward, and the two teams rushed inside amid the smoke.

The front door team went in through the living room while the back door team entered through the kitchen. Through the still-swirling smoke, Warsaw watched as the five interconnected first floor rooms were cleared. As the last "clear" call was heard, one team headed upstairs. Two officers crashed through the door to the lighted room. Seconds later they cried out, "Clear!" Then two more officers did the same in the room without lights. There was a several second pause and then "clear" was heard once more as the second upstairs room's lights went on. A shout was heard from the stairway, "Cellar!"

The back door team was the first to locate the cellar door. Opening it, all they saw was blackness. A stun grenade was immediately thrown down the steep and narrow stairway. The grenade exploded, then the team members turned on their night-vision and began their descent down into the silent darkness. The stairs were so steep that the team had difficulty negotiating the steps wearing all of their protective gear and holding their assault rifles ready. At the last step, the leader halted … holding up one finger to signal he heard the sound of movement. He paused, then burst forward, his weapon aimed straight ahead. The two men behind him leapt down the last few steps, one landing to his right and the other his left, their weapons aimed outward. They did so snapping the flimsy railing with a loud crack.

That team leader's voice was heard faintly, "There are some rooms with closed doors." He signaled his men, and they advanced on the three doors, two forward of the staircase and one behind. Two men moved to each door. Their leader signaled the first two, and they crashed a door. A second passed, two, three … then "Clear!" As soon as their shout was heard the leader and his partner crashed the second door. Again, a "clear!" was signaled. Now, those four moved to support the last two who stood facing the door behind the stairway. The team leader held up three fingers … then two … one and the final team burst through the last door. There was a second of silence and then a sudden burst of fire from an assault rifle. Then total silence. The two emerged again from the room. "Rats … I hate rats!" one exclaimed.

"Nothing down here: the cellar's empty and all clear!" the cellar team leader shouted as they headed back up the stairs.

Domiik turned to Marek with a stunned look, "Where the hell are they?" Now one of the teams that had held back in reserve was moving in on the garage, as one of the helicopters trained its searchlight from above. Their night vision on, in moments the team was inside and had cleared it, then turned on the light switch. Night vision switched off once again, their leader's helmet camera panned an empty garage, except for an old lawnmower, a few rusty garden tools, and a decrepit lawn chair.

"Room to room again … and this time checking everything," came the command from the response teams' leader. As the two teams moved through the house, their helmet cameras gave Warsaw a full view. The house appeared neat and clean. There was food on the kitchen table in closed containers, a tea kettle on the stove, still warm, they were informed, and a few items of perishable food in the refrigerator, along with eight beers. "On the dining room table we have photographs of various government buildings in downtown Berlin," came a voice from inside. "There's a group here of maybe twenty photos of the Bundeskanzleramt Federal Chancellery Building, all clipped together, and another of what appears to be the rest of the Reichstag Parliament and adjacent buildings. The chancellery group has a large '#1' written on it, and the Reichstag a '#2' on it. Both appear to be in black marker pen. There's also a paper map of the area surrounding the Parliament.

"There are multiple handguns in the dining room, and in the corner, what looks like a rifle case." One of the response team members lifted the case and placed it on the table. He opened it. "Oh yes, what do we have here," he spoke as the group in Warsaw watched with rapt attention. "It is definitely a military-style sniper rifle. It's a SAVAGE 110 BA 338 LAPUA Sniper Rifle. I know the weapon ... I've used it. And there is a box of ammo for it. Soft point ... but they have been filled with some substance ... a greenish-brown in color .... wait ....

"Something else here ... " another response team member was just emerging from a closet off the dining room. "We have a large satchel bag" ... he placed it on the dining room table. Opening the bag, he continued, "Whoa ... it's full of C-4 ... has to be close to 10 kilograms of plastic explosives. Enough to blow ... "

"Hold it," another voice shouted over his. "There's an open laptop on the bookshelf ... there," as they all turned to look, Warsaw could see the open laptop, its blue power LED glowing even though its screen was dark. One response team member walked toward it. Suddenly stopping dead still, he said, "I think its camera is on. We're on camera!"

With that, the response teams' leader shouted in a loud voice, "Clear the house! ... Clear the house now!"

IMBROGLIO TRILOGY

Chapter 16:

Beholding Horror

The two matrix images on Warsaw's TV screen which were streaming images from inside the house suddenly lost picture as well as the video feed from one of the team's stationed immediately outside of the house. Static was all that remained. But the other three video signals were still live, leaving no doubt about what had happened. First, a bright yellow-white flash had appeared momentarily across all three remaining images, and then the roar of a mighty explosion. With it, the terror of the blast seized everyone in the Warsaw conference room.

The room reverberated with the appalling sounds of anguished screams and shouts coming from the audio link of the remaining three teams, as the wounded and those desperately trying to reach them reeled from the blast. The sound was so loud that the conference room door burst open and several investigators working in the outer office rushed in to see if everyone in the conference room was all right. By now, all standing, they watched in anguished disbelief; the images gyrating wildly, as the Response Team members struggled to pull those near the blast zone away from the inferno which only seconds earlier had been a bucolic rural setting.

As this unspeakable horror played out on the screen, all color drained from Adrianna's face. Trembling, she dropped back into her chair and began to retch. Marek told one of those who had just entered the room to escort her out of the conference room. Screams and cries for help assaulted their ears as the three remaining video frames continued streaming scenes of the Response Teams' futile attempts at beating back the flames engulfing their burning comrades on the ground.

"How many are down!" shouted Domiik, at the screen, the speakerphone and the scenes of horror playing out before them. Marek sat back down with the weight of a bag of cement dropping onto the chair. "Who can know … " he muttered, burying his face in his hands. The others likewise recoiled from the vivid nightmare in stunned silence.

Chapter 17:
Aftermath

It was late in the evening before any sense could be made of the situation on the ground. At 11:00 pm Warsaw time, the call came through connecting Berlin police authorities and the Berlin office of Interpol, together with Lyon, Bratislava, and Warsaw.

Berlin began, "We have an update on this evening's events. To begin with, we lost fifteen officers," then in an emotionally strained and tense voice, "Incinerated!"

"My God!" Domiik gasped.

Adrianna's eyes welled with tears.

Sitting next to her, Marek leaned over and, speaking softly, suggested, "You don't have to stay here through this. It's already been a long and very heart-rending day. You can get some rest and come back in the morning."

Adrianna, with tears streaming down her face, shook her head slowly, "I want ... No, I need to hear what happened," she said softly. Marek touched her arm as she struggled to maintain some semblance of composure.

Berlin continued, "There are also another six in the hospital, three in critical condition with blast wounds and severe burns ... two of them with missing limbs. Most have a very doubtful prognosis. The injuries are in keeping with a war zone, not a Berlin police action.

We lost everyone who was in the house at the time of the blast plus three outside. Most of what we know is from the video transmissions from inside the house prior to the explosion. Unfortunately, all the evidence from inside the house was destroyed in the inferno. There is literally *nothing* left of the structure and its contents, other than an empty, burnt-out cellar.

"Instead of apprehending the three suspects, we have suffered a terrible loss of life, as well as appalling injuries, and we are still left with far more questions than answers. Who was in the Mercedes that left the house just as the first helicopter was arriving? Was it the suspects and, if so, how many and which ones? Why did they leave the handguns, a sniper rifle, photographs, the map, etc.? Were they tipped off to our strike teams' imminent arrival and thus fled in haste, leaving these items behind, along with the photographs and map? And, finally, the satchel of C4: Was it intended as a booby trap or did our team accidentally trigger a detonator inside of it?

"Which also raises the issue of the laptop computer on the shelf. Was the camera on? And was that camera being monitored, enabling a remote detonation? Regarding the last question, our people are working with IPB, the sole internet provider for this locale. Although the computer may also have been using a cellular phone hotspot, and as any phone was destroyed in the explosion along with the laptop, that inquiry may be a dead end.

IMBROGLIO TRILOGY

"Now for what we do know: The Mercedes that was parked near the house was engulfed in the subsequent fire, but we retrieved the VIN. It's no surprise; the car was stolen … from the City of Cologne two days ago. We suspect the other Mercedes was also stolen, as that seems to be the pattern. However, we can't know this with certainty, as we have no a license plate number or VIN.

"We have all of the airports, train and bus stations on full alert and have distributed the CCTV pictures that you provided, as well as those from the Berlin Hauptbahnhof and the police artist's drawing, to all the taxi companies, Uber drivers, etc. For now, this is all we have to share with you. We'll reconvene by conference call in the morning as soon as we have new information."

"Thank you," Marek responded. "And again, please accept our most heartfelt condolences on the enormous losses you have sustained today. The thoughts and prayers of the entire team here in Warsaw are with you and the families who have been so devastated."

"On behalf of all of us here in Germany, thank you. Good night."

The call ended. Exhaustion and sorrow for their German colleagues clouded every face in the room. Domiik was first to speak, "My friends, let's call it a day. I think we all have experienced more than enough tragedy for one day, and we can't accomplish anything more here tonight. And take a little time in the morning to sort yourselves out … emotionally, I mean. I don't expect that we'll hear any more from Berlin until at least mid-morning, so don't feel the need to rush in here early.

They all departed in silence, each carrying a burden of grief and a profound sense of failure.

IMBROGLIO TRILOGY

Chapter 18:

An Unwelcome Surprise

March 18, Warsaw, Poland

A Dismal Morning

Marek took Domiik's advice to heart and slept in a little; then indulged himself in a leisurely breakfast at the hotel restaurant. Not that he had an appetite for a big breakfast, but he was in no hurry to return to police headquarters, with its memories of the previous evenings' nightmarish events. By the time he left the hotel, large groups of protesters were already forming. Apart from some scattered violence the night before, precipitating the police use of tear gas, most of the Warsaw protests had remained relatively peaceful. Still, as a seasoned law enforcement professional, he could already see indications that today's crowds would be larger and more likely to become violent as their tenor was turning dark. He supposed that news of the events in Berlin the previous evening was doubtlessly contributing to the growing unrest. *This is certainly not what we need,* he thought.

While getting dressed earlier that morning, he had turned on the television in his hotel room to images of widespread demonstrations the previous day, across eastern and southern Europe. In some places, violent confrontations with the police had occurred.

Arriving at headquarters midmorning, Adrianna found that the rest of the team was still drifting in. There were no smiles, personal greetings or small talk this morning. She sensed the deep despondency overshadowing the entire investigative team, which by now numbered more than seventy people. Even the copious provision of delectable pastries and coffee that Domiik had ordered did nothing to brighten the disconsolate atmosphere.

✳ ✳ ✳

Robert Murray's Announcement

Once the four were assembled in the conference room, Domiik opened, "I'm glad to see that you took my advice. I hope that a brief time of solace has helped to begin the healing … at least a little. Despite what has happened, we all need clear heads if we are going to find and capture these perpetrators. And this we must do." As he was still speaking, the conference room door opened and Robert Murray strode in.

Murray sat down without a greeting. Domiik addressed him, "I hope you bring us some definitive news this morning that will help to move our investigation forward."

Murray leaned back in his chair, straightened himself to his full seated stature, cleared his throat and began, "I believe that I can shed some light on the issues you raised yesterday, but before I do so, I need to inform you that we have a new—and at least from my government's standpoint, very serious—problem."

Everyone's gaze was fixed upon Murray. "What exactly do you mean?" asked Marek.

"I received a disturbing message early this morning from a very senior level at the Department of State, that someone from the EU, someone in Brussels, an unnamed official, was about to leak a story to the European press that the American CIA was behind the assassinations. I don't need to tell you what this would mean to relations between the United States and the various European countries involved in this situation. It would be nothing less than disastrous, especially at a time when violent public protests are escalating across Europe. None of us needs this kind of unwarranted trouble."

The shock with which this news was greeted by the others in the room was palpable. "This can't be possible!" stated Domiik in utter disbelief. "I don't believe it!"

"I was assured that our source for this information is highly reputable, and it is most certainly true. Although, like you, I find it impossible to comprehend why any responsible official within the EU would fabricate such a story and leak it to the press."

There was a knock, and the conference door opened. A young woman from the larger team of investigators stuck her head in, "Excuse me, but you had better turn on the TV and see what's happening."

Domiik asked, "Increased violence in the streets?"

"No, not yet, but I'm sure it won't be long. Just turn on the TV, and you'll see troubling news bulletins on every channel."

Domiik grabbed the remote off the table and clicked the TV on, but there was only static. Perplexed, he sat for a moment wondering why they had no reception.

Then Adrianna intervened, "I think it's still set to live streaming from last night. Switch it over to broadcast." Domiik glanced down at the control in his hand with a blank expression. Then he clicked the controller to the broadcast setting. On the screen before them appeared one of the European news talking heads. And below him scrolled the words: *Breaking News: Assassinations of Slovak and Polish Prime Ministers linked to American CIA.*

"This is unbelievable." Marek fumed.

The news anchor went on to report that a confidential, high-level source within the EU, Brussels, had purportedly told a reporter, on condition of anonymity, that Interpol had determined that the explosive used in the Bratislava, Slovakia, bombing death of Prime Minister Miroslav Cagacikova was of U.S. origin. Furthermore, the sniper rifle used in the Warsaw assassination of Polish Prime Minister Binkowski had been identified as belonging to the U.S. Marine Corps, and the bullet it had fired was a new 'secret' design of the United States Department of Defense. "From this and other information which has not yet been publicly released," the anchor stated, "Interpol has concluded that there is compelling evidence of the United States' Central Intelligence Agency's direct involvement in these assassinations."

Domiik muted the television, "I can't listen to anymore of this nonsense. Murray, I hope that you have brought us facts that will refute every word they are spewing."

Murray cleared his throat again and began, "To begin with, I trust that it is still Robert and not 'Murray' in this room."

"Yes, yes," Domiik replied.

"I can't tell you anything more than you already know about this 'supposedly' confidential high-level, unnamed EU source. But my government is furious over this utterly baseless allegation, and there will be hell to pay when we find out who this 'supposed' confidential source is—and why they're spreading these damnable lies."

Domiik stopped him there, "Unfortunately, Robert, they aren't all lies! We've already confirmed days ago that the C4 was American-made, and—as you know from the photographs we gave you—the weapon was of U.S. Marine Corps origin. You confirmed that the bullet was EXACTO. These are facts … truth!"

"Yes, you're right," replied Murray. "But that isn't what I was referring to as 'lies.' The lie is that the United States government, or for that matter the CIA, had anything to do with these assassinations".

"The problem, Robert," Marek interjected, "is that, although we in this room believe you, how do you expect the media and Europe's citizens to believe you with such a 'smoking gun' now publicly revealed?" After a short pause, he grinned and shook his head. "No pun intended."

Expressionless, Murray responded, 'I see I should have 'scoped out' this group better before engaging." That brought a tension-breaking chuckle from the others."

Murray opened his black attaché case. Removing several documents, he placed them on the table. "As to the weapon," he began. "Although the serial number was obliterated, we believe it was used in Afghanistan by a Marine Corps sniper team. They were killed, both the sniper and the spotter, during heavy fighting with the Taliban in and around Kandahar a little over a year ago. Their bodies were recovered, but not the sniper's weapon. The DoD listed it as taken by the Taliban fighters." He handed the document to Adrianna, who was seated closest to him. "The EXACTO round, or rather, a total of eleven EXACTO rounds," he continued, "disappeared … and were presumed stolen, from Picatinny Arsenal, ARDEC (Headquarters of the Army, Armament, Research, Development and Engineering Center), in Dover, NJ, two months ago. How they disappeared or were stolen, is still under investigation by the DoD. And, as you'll see from this set of documents, this investigation is being taken very seriously by my government, both from the standpoint of the loss of SECRET level technology, possibly to a foreign, hostile government, as well as the concern that the rounds may have fallen into the hands of an international assassin. Which is precisely what seems to have happened here." Murray passed the second set of documents to Adrianna.

"Taking you at your word, which I do," Marek noted, "it appears that this entire conspiracy has much broader and more significant implications than we realized up until now. For instance, the apparent theft of the EXACTO round from Picatinny Arsenal. I assume that one does not simply walk into an American SECRET level R&D command and walk out with their pockets bulging with stolen high-tech bullets. Which means that this conspiracy must involve multiple people in high places, in both Europe and the United States, either as willing accomplices, or individuals who have perhaps been coerced, or bought, for the right price."

"Your observation is correct," Murray acknowledged. "An immediate concern in Washington is that we know only that one EXACTO round has been fired. That leaves ten more rounds unaccounted for. The DoD presumes that the assassin would have fired several in practice while preparing for the assassination, but it is unlikely that as many as ten would have been used for practice."

"So, Washington fears that more assassinations are probable?" Jedrzej posited.

"That is an unknown, but certainly very real possibility and a grave concern of my government, especially as the entire world now knows that the bullet was unique and originated from the U.S.," Murray replied.

"We may not be any closer to knowing the truth about who is behind this plot or why, but we're beginning to perceive the menacing scope of it, which I believe will become more and more evident as we move forward in the investigation. I assured you yesterday that you had the full cooperation of the United States government. I will tell you now, without even speaking to my superiors first, that after this purportedly leaked news story there will be nothing, no resources, withheld in supporting your efforts to resolve this conspiracy."

Marek looked directly at Murray, "I believe I can speak for everyone around this table in saying that we welcome your country's fullest support and participation. Also, I must say, although I have not spoken to my superiors at Interpol headquarters in Lyon, there isn't the least possibility of any senior Interpol official having told the EU in Brussels or anyone else for that matter, of a purported conclusion that the CIA was in any way involved, either directly or indirectly.

"First of all, I can't believe that an Interpol official at any level would undertake such irresponsible action, and, furthermore, had Interpol come to such a conclusion, which they certainly have not, I would have been informed of it. I can also confidently say that no

Interpol official would have communicated the information we have about the weapon and the EXACTO bullet's origin to anyone at the EU Headquarters in Brussels. Which leads to the additional question: How did whoever leaked this report know about EXACTO?

"Lastly, as we in this room are all well aware, the United States is a full member of Interpol with an office in Washington, DC, the U. S. National Central Bureau. However, this is something that many in the media and public at large do not even realize, as they tend to think of Interpol as being a purely European organization.

"The open questions I currently have regarding this matter are, first, how quickly will Interpol and the EU officially denounce these news reports and, second, who is the purported unnamed, highly placed EU source for this ridiculous and highly inflammatory story?"

Marek and the others didn't have long to wait for Interpol's response. Within an hour of the story breaking, Interpol, Lyon released an official statement denying any knowledge of a CIA or other foreign government involvement in the two assassinations. However, it wasn't until just before 5:00 pm Brussels time that the EU finally issued a similar 'official' denial, albeit vaguely worded. To this Murray responded that he had once had a friend who was a Colonel in the U.S. Army who referred to such obscurely worded affirmative statements as being 'damned by faint praise!'"

In the streets of European cities, these denials did little to quell the fermenting anger of the growing crowds, who now had a more conspicuous target to vilify than the EU—the United States. Meanwhile, with the three suspects seemingly having vanished into thin air in Berlin, the Warsaw team struggled to make any real progress on the case, even with the help of Robert Murray and the CIA's global network of resources.

Given the team's unanimous agreement that neither the United States government nor the CIA was involved, they turned their attention to the other two remaining possibilities: Russia and Eastern European organized crime. The notion that these two entities could be linked to this conspiracy was also not lost on the investigators.

IMBROGLIO TRILOGY

Chapter 19:
Athens

The investigators finally had a breakthrough later that afternoon, when a call came in from Prague. A gate agent for Aegean Airlines became suspicious after watching the news during her lunch break and seeing a photo of the three suspects. She recalled three passengers who matched their descriptions in Prague, boarding a flight bound for Athens. Airlines throughout Europe had been alerted to watch for a couple and a man with a bandaged head. However, the three people who had boarded this flight were all traveling individually. Furthermore, one of the men—the one who seemed most like the man with the bandaged head in the photograph—was wearing a black stocking cap pulled over his ears, although a bit of the bandage was visible. It was only after watching the news program on TV that she connected the three individuals as possibly being the suspects.

Obtaining the flight information, Marek immediately contacted Athens airport and the Greek Interpol office in Athens. The ninety-five-minute flight had landed at 3:47 pm, twenty-five minutes prior to Marek's call, but not arrived at the gate until seven minutes later due to aircraft congestion on the ground. Athen's airport security sprang into action. Immediately contacting the gate personnel, they learned that the last passengers, a family with several small children and an elderly woman requiring wheelchair assistance, were just deplaning now. Not wasting any time with the flight arrival area, airport security notified Immigration and Customs, then focused on the terminal exits, knowing that by now the suspects would very likely have to be intercepted as they left the terminal building. Fortunately, a significant number of heavily armed security personnel patrolled the main terminal area at all times, enough to have at least one cover each exit as well as the bridge connecting the main terminal to the Suburban Rail/Tram building, until additional security personnel could arrive.

Meanwhile, Athens police were rapidly converging on the airport, which is located not far from the city center, in the hope of arriving in time to fully secure all of the entrances before the suspects left the terminal. Airport security alone was spread too thin to accomplish this adequately, especially if an armed incident ensued. The police had been instructed not to use their sirens and to turn off blue emergency lights before approaching the airport, so as not to alert the suspects to the closing net.

The Warsaw team waited anxiously, hoping almost against hope that this time they would not be too late. "Deplaning, Immigration —although they are undoubtedly traveling under forged EU Passports, Customs—they'll only have carry-on roller bags, nothing to declare, and will just head through the airport to the exits … if they're lucky, twenty-five minutes. If we're lucky … maybe a bit longer. Pray that many flights came in simultaneously or better yet, just before theirs," Marek voiced his thoughts audibly, more to himself than the others. The phone line to Interpol's Athens office and the airport security office was live on the conference room speakerphone. The minutes ticked by as they waited. They were told that an airport security office employee had been dispatched to the exits with a stack of photocopies of the Warsaw train station CCTV photo. She was tasked with distributing them to security officers at each door.

From the speakerphone, the team learned that the Athens police were now arriving in force and that, within the next two to three minutes, all exits would be blanketed. "Well," said Jedrzej, breathing a sigh of relief, "if they are still in the airport terminal, we should be able to capture them."

"Yes … but that's still a big if!" Domiik replied, looking first at the wall clock and then fixing his gaze intently on Marek, who seemed lost in thought.

The speakerphone came to life again. It was the Athens airport security. "We have all exits sealed; no one will be permitted to leave until they have been compared with the photograph you furnished. Furthermore, we now have enough police in place to begin sweeping the entire airport terminal building. If they are here, hiding anywhere, we will find them."

Domiik leaned toward the speakerphone, "Remember, they are extremely dangerous, and you are dealing with an airport full of civilian travelers … women and children."

"We recognize the risks. We're well aware of what happened in Berlin yesterday. We're also well prepared for whatever occurs, including a hostage situation, if that should arise. We regularly practice counter-terrorism drills, especially at the airport."

"That's a blessing, at least," Domiik declared to the others in a hopeful voice. Another few minutes passed, and Domiik looked at

Marek again. "I know you are worried that we may have already missed them, but they're doing everything possible in Athens."

"Yes," Marek responded, "I know." Another minute passed. "What is the photo they are distributing for identification?" Marek suddenly burst out, jumping to his feet.

"The one from the Berlin train station," Adrianna answered, "but we've told them that the second man is wearing a black stocking cap, not a head bandage."

"A photograph of the three of them, right?"

"Yes, it was as they were just getting on the escal … "

Interrupting Adrianna mid-sentence, Marek shouted into the speakerphone, "Don't look for a woman and two men traveling together. The Prague gate agent said they were traveling individually. If they have any hint that you are looking for them, they will most certainly split up and use different exits. And forget about looking for a man in a black stocking cap … he's probably already ditched that in a trash can … and the head bandage, for that matter."

The others looked stunned. "Don't tell me that Athens is looking for a trio … " Jedrzej thought out loud.

"Athens, did you hear me," Marek shouted again.

"Yes … yes, we are relaying that message to security personnel at all exits … don't look for the three together … look for each separately … and no hat … no black stocking cap or bandaged head."

Marek sat back down; slumping in his chair, he folded his hands and raised them to his face. Domiik looked at him, "It was just too fast … it happened so fast … I can understand the mistake. They had a picture of two men and woman traveling together, so as they raced to seal the exits, that was the thought in their minds … a woman and two men … together."

"I know," Marek responded in an exasperated tone, " … I know … I know … not their fault!"

Adrianna sat in silence, feeling disheartened, disappointed with herself. "I should have realized that sooner."

"We all should have, Adrianna," added Jedrzej, "We all should have."

"The problem is that it's always the very last moment with these three," Domiik reflected. "There is never a minute to plan … to even think. Don't blame yourselves, we have undoubtedly missed them again, but we will find them. It's only a matter of time."

"We've found them!" an excited voice proclaimed the triumphant message. An air of hope and disbelief simultaneously flooded the conference room. The air was electric with anticipation. "Yes, it appears we have them," the voice rang out again. Wait … we're getting more details from an exit door … no … from the Suburban Rail/ Tram bridge checkpoint. "Go ahead … you have them there?"

"No … no, only the woman in the photo, not the two men, she was alone, but I'm certain it was her … she passed through here a few minutes ago, but she was alone … no men with her."

"How do you know it was her?" Marek demanded into the speakerphone.

"She was ΄Ομορφο΄!"

Marek looked up from the speakerphone puzzled. "΄Ομορφο?΄"

"'Bella' … pretty … in English." Jedrzej smiled. "He's a Greek man, after all!"

Marek placed his hand over the speakerphone mic, "Oh, so now we let assassins run freely through the arms of our security lockdown if they happen to be a beautiful woman?"

Domiik exclaimed in disgust. "Greeks … and I thought we only had to deal with this kind of behavior from the Italians!"

"The French aren't any better," Jedrzej exclaimed snidely.

"She passed through the bridge to the trains a few minutes before I received the photo, but I certainly remember her," the voice on the phone continued.

"Is the train or tram or whatever it is gone—or could she still be waiting?" barked Marek. "That depends on which one it is and which direction she's traveling," another voice responded.

"Well, get your asses over there and find out .…. Find HER!"

"I can't believe this … " Marek groaned.

"Turning back to the speakerphone, "Athens, any information on the male suspects?"

"We have a possible sighting at Exit Door 4 where the taxi queue begins, but not certain as yet."

"Do they have the suspect there now?"

"No, apparently he passed through while they were still looking for three suspects together."

A few minutes passed and then, "This is security at the bridge. We have checked the boarding areas for trains and trams, and the female suspect is not there."

"Did you check the bathrooms in the area?" Domiik asked.

"Yes, we had a woman on the security detail do so, and she reports that the bathrooms are clear also."

"Thank you," Domiik responded half-heartedly.

"Again!" Marek grunted. "They have slipped through our fingers once again!"

"Shall we have the police check all of the train and tram stations on the airport routes?" Adrianna asked Marek.

"Yes, please do so ... but by the time they get there, she will no doubt have slipped away. I would bet money that by now she has already been on and off a train and has disappeared into the city. There is no question that we are dealing with experienced professional killers! If we are to capture this trio, we will need to get ahead of them—not keep chasing them around Europe, always one step behind."

IMBROGLIO TRILOGY

Chapter 20:

On to Prague

Earlier — Late Afternoon of March 17th

Twelve minutes after departing the country house on Berlin's outskirts, the trio's driver in the black Mercedes had exited the autobahn. The departure route and timing coincided with the "tip" phoned in to the police, as well as with Berlin's rush hour traffic. In Germany, daylight savings time had not yet begun, providing the additional benefit of darkness to conceal their escape.

Upon leaving the autobahn, they pulled into a car park building. On the second level, they advanced toward two cars parked facing outward with their headlights on and an empty parking space between them. As they approached, a man exited one of the cars and quickly removed the orange cone from the empty spot. The black Mercedes glided into it.

Franz, Bruce, and Sarah exited the Mercedes. Franz slid into the driver's seat of a waiting Lexus coupe, while Bruce and Sarah got into a Volvo Cross Country. They took nothing with them during the car exchange, which was accomplished with perfect German precision and efficiency. No words were spoken between the trio and the drivers of the other cars. In under sixty seconds, both the Lexus and the Volvo were on their way out of the building.

The cars contained medium sized duffle bags for Bruce and Sarah, a larger one for Franz and also a suit bag for Bruce, stowed in the trunk of their respective cars. The passenger compartments contained chilled water bottles and an assortment of snacks: healthy snacks for Bruce and Sarah and luscious ones for Franz.

After three hours, both cars stopped along the route at Lovosice, Czech Republic, for the night. Franz stayed at Penzion Dubina, and Bruce and Sarah had accommodation at Hotel LEV.

※ ※ ※

March 18th

In the morning, they were off again on the half hour journey to the Prague airport. Franz arrived thirty minutes before Bruce and Sarah, despite having stopped along the highway for a leisurely coffee and pastry. As prearranged, he parked the Lexus in a remote parking lot and took a shuttle bus to the terminal. Bruce dropped Sarah off at the Villa St. Topez Hotel, where she visited the gift shop, made a costly purchase, and then caught the hotel shuttle to the airport. Bruce then drove on to the Dolce Villa Hotel, where he parked the car and took a taxi to the airport terminal. Having previously checked in online, they had selected seats scattered from front to back in the airplane. They soon cleared security with their carry-on luggage in hand and individually boarded the plane for Athens, Greece.

In-flight, the three took turns visiting the lavatories at intervals. While there, they changed clothes before returning to their seat. In this way, the glamorous Sarah was transformed into a young woman on spring holiday in tight jeans and a casual sweater with a silk scarf tied around her neck, her brilliant red hair now tucked under a chic, floppy, Athleta straw hat with a ragged fringe, her eyes hidden by aviator mirror sunglasses. She pulled the front of the hat down so that the back could ride-up on the seat back, further concealing her features. Gone was the Hollywood look, with the mysterious black hat and dark glasses shielding her face.

Bruce was recast as a smart looking businessman, wearing a finely tailored beige Giorgi Armani summer suit, Fendi tie with matching pocket scarf, a classically understated black Bulgari Octo Velocissimo Ultranero wristwatch, Illesteva Sunglasses, and handmade Fratelli Borgioli shoes. Deplaning in Athens, he carried a slim brown Armani leather attaché case and a Wall Street Journal under his arm.

Franz, however, would have won the prize for best transformation. From the 'man in black' with a bandaged head and stocking cap, he was remade into a charming 'good ol' Texas cowboy, complete with authentically 'weathered and worn' Levi jeans—not the pretentious designer washed and ripped style—brandishing a huge, silver belt buckle, two pocket plaid shirt, crumpled and weather-beaten straw cowboy hat, which he placed on his lap after returning to his seat, sunglasses, and of course, to ensure complete authenticity, cowboy boots. Franz stuffed his pants legs into the cowboy boots so that they would be all the more obvious.

Leaving the Athens airport from the train/tram terminal, Koropi is the first stop on the Proastiakos Kiato-Airport line. Served by trains every quarter hour to and from the airport, the stop was a mere five-minute ride for Sarah. Exiting the train at the northern end of the Koropi station platform, she descended the stairs from the open platform and stepped into a waiting taxi. It was a warm, sunny afternoon in this Athens suburb and the glow of spring sunlight shone upon her.

Turning onto the Leoforos Possidonos, the main coastal highway leading into Glyfada along the scenic Aegean Sea sometimes referred to as the "Athenian Riviera," the taxi took her the short fifteen-minute drive to the Palmyra Beach Hotel. From a text message received on her mobile phone, she knew the room was 0307, and that Bruce was waiting for her. Sarah's face fell as she entered the room; it was typical by European standards for a so-called "Superior Room with Seaside View." But Sarah was not pleased. "Is this the best they can do?" she cringed.

"We'll be gone in the morning," Bruce responded, "and then you can finally relax and enjoy the beach vacation."

"I didn't say I wasn't relaxed; I just said the room is minuscule … cramped. You know I don't like claustrophobic spaces!"

"It's small by American standards, I will grant you that, but calling it claustrophobic is a little over-the-top. Anyhow, it's after five. Why don't you get dressed for dinner? We should meet Franz for a drink beforehand, and he's probably already waiting."

Sarah glowered, "We aren't having dinner with him, are we?"

"No, but it is only polite to meet him for a drink. Anyway, I don't think he wants to have dinner with us—with you, my dear—any more than you do with him. We'll have the obligatory drink, converse politely for 30 minutes and then go our separate ways for dinner … we'll dine at a restaurant other than the hotel's. And please … try to be 'sweet' … or at least civil."

Sarah just shrugged, "You mean, like I was on the train from Warsaw toward those two businessmen morons?" Bruce starred at her, his dismay evident.

Full sets of luggage had been delivered to the two hotel rooms earlier that day. Bruce and Sarah changed for dinner and headed down to the Waves Bar. Franz was waiting. "Well, hello to my favorite glamorous couple. And how was your trip from the airport down to the beach, Sarah?"

"Fine … uneventful. I don't think our friends had any idea."

They joined Franz at a table overlooking the turquoise sea and ordered drinks. "This is on me," Franz told the waiter. Then, turning to Bruce and Sarah, "In reality … on our employer," he chuckled.

"The airport went flawlessly for me. Just as I was headed for the exit, I saw the airport security scampering to block the doors," Franz chuckled. "A small queue was already beginning to back up at Door 4, where the taxis wait. So I just joined the queue, stayed cool and took my turn … waiting. No rush, just an American tourist on *vacay*."

"When I reached the queue, the police reinforcements were just arriving, doubtless adding to the confusion of who was in charge. I just stood there nonchalantly while the airport security officer and the police argued about jurisdiction and who had authority. When they had finished, and those in front of me had passed through the door, in my best southern drawl I loudly announced, 'Texan,' pointing first to my hat and then down to my cowboy boots. They looked down at a poor resolution photocopy of a CCTV image they had of some girl and a couple of guys, shook their heads and said 'πάει'—'go' in english—and waived me on. So I departed!" He grinned broadly and pointed to his boots, which were now comfortably occupying the empty chair next to Sarah.

"You can put those back on the floor now," Sarah responded, shaking her head. "A Deutsche Texas drawl? They must have been deaf to fall for that one."

Her sarcasm was not lost on Franz, and he was quick to counter, "You are in the habit of grossly underestimating me, but I am no fool. And I can do far more than shoot a man in the head at 1,400 meters," he said in a lower voice. Then raising his voice with a flourish, "I speak four languages fluently, three with or without an accent, as I choose."

"That's impressive," Bruce chimed in.

"How did you fare?" Franz asked Sarah.

"No problems. I was just about to enter the pedestrian bridge to the intermodal terminal when two airport security men closed ranks in front of me." Sarah paused, for dramatic impact. One would have thought she was on stage at London's West End.

"Then what," Franz asked. Silence. "What happened?"

"Oh that … well, I simply turned on my best British accent and asked them if there was a terrorist alert or something I needed to fear."

"Of course not," they responded, "No reason to worry."

"So I told them how relieved I was, as travel these days has become so very unsafe, what with dangerous assassins on the loose in Europe. Then I smiled and well … "

"Yes, and well what … ?" Franz urged her on.

"Oh, I just talked about how glad I was to have brave police there to protect the public. They assured me that I was absolutely safe and that they were there to protect innocent travelers. So, I smiled again, thanked them and slowly walked away, making sure to sway my hips just enough to keep their minds distracted until I passed from sight."

"I'd wager you've charmed your way out of every traffic ticket as well," Franz lamented.

"All but one ... of course, that was from a female officer. There should be a law against them."

"Damn! Women certainly do have an unfair advantage over men, don't they?" Franz protested.

"Can't help that. We just happen to be the fairer sex."

Franz just stared at her. "You are fair, that I will readily admit."

"Fair, as in complexion?" Sarah responded feigning innocence.

"Yes ... as in complexion, but ... also ... fair as in beauty."

"Now that is a compliment I never thought I'd hear out of you, Franz. Why thank you!"

"You're welcome—it's well deserved."

"Let's drink to that," Bruce raised his glass. "To Sarah ... a true beauty." Franz raised his glass and clinked both of theirs.

"What about you?" Franz asked Bruce. "Any problems?"

"None whatsoever. I didn't see any security, other than the usual rather bored police with sub-machine guns slung over their shoulders, prowling about the terminal building. I chose the right lines for Immigration and Customs and sailed through the airport and out Door 1 just as we'd planned. I passed through the airport so quickly that I missed all of the free entertainment.

"Once outside, I walked to the hotel shuttle pick-up stand and took the first shuttle that arrived. It was bound for the Sofitel. The driver asked if I had a reservation, and I told him that I was meeting some hotel guests for business. He dropped me off in front. I started for the entrance, and then, while he was busy helping other passengers with luggage, I turned back and got into a taxi which brought me to the town of Glyfada just down the road. I milled around for a few minutes and then took another taxi here. I even arrived before Sarah, possibly because I didn't do any shopping along the way," Bruce continued, now looking intently at Sarah, who coyly averted his gaze "As long as they don't have a clearer and more recognizable photo of us, eluding these amateurs will remain easy!"

An hour of amiable conversation passed as well as a second round of drinks before Franz said that he felt like dinner. Even Sarah had enjoyed herself, a fact that Bruce thought better not to mention to her. Franz paid the bill, and Bruce and Sarah headed off to a small, romantic restaurant nearby, overlooking the Aegean. A soft evening breeze was blowing off the sea.

In the morning, a silver 640i Beamer convertible arrived for Bruce and Sarah's departure. An hour earlier, Franz had driven off in a shiny red Jag F-Type convertible.

As they followed the coastal highway, Sarah turned to Bruce. "Next time, I would prefer a white Bentley!"

Chapter 21:

Berlin Calling Again

March 19th, Warsaw, Poland

The previous evening had ended in utter frustration and despair for the investigative teams in Warsaw, Bratislava, Berlin and, finally, Athens, where the police and airport security were still sorting out the blame for missing the trio. In reality, their efforts were essentially doomed from the start, given the few minutes they had to organize their disparate airport security and city police forces into one integrated corps to intercept the conspirators. The attempt was made especially difficult due to the absence of clearly recognizable photographs of the suspects' faces.

The Warsaw team knew all of this. Their frustration was not with Athens, per se, but with the fact that the trio had now twice slipped through their fingers. They determined that it must not happen a third time.

By mid-morning, the real break they had been waiting for was precipitated once again by a phone call from Berlin. This time Interpol was on the line. The caller directed Marek to travel to Wiesbaden,

Germany, the German Federal Criminal Police Headquarters, immediately for a meeting. A source, this one verified as legitimate, had come forward with information which appeared to present a possible breakthrough in the case. The confidential source was in Wiesbaden awaiting their arrival.

The Warsaw team lost no time in booking a flight to Frankfurt and preparing to leave. Marek immediately telephoned Robert Murray, briefed him on the information just received from Berlin and asked if he wanted to accompany them. Murray inquired as to the flight they were booked on and arranged to meet them at the gate. Arriving in Frankfurt, the five agents were greeted by Interpol representatives and driven the twenty-two kilometers to Wiesbaden.

Once there, they were immediately introduced to Herr Helmut Kohler, CEO of Euro Strategic Security Services, headquartered in Berlin. The German Interpol representative asked Kohler to relate his story.

Kohler began, "I have been reluctant to come forward with this information, not for fear of any involvement or illegal activity on my part, or for that matter of my company, but because I find it difficult to believe that the individuals I am about to name could possibly be involved in the villainy which has transpired in recent days in the cities of Bratislava, Warsaw, and Berlin.

"Please, allow me to begin by giving you an overview of my company, Euro Strategic Security Services, and its operations. We provide strategic security services across Europe, as well as in the UK. We have also performed client assignments in a number of Middle Eastern countries and elsewhere. Our typical clients consist of either corporations or very wealthy individuals. On the corporate side, we furnish advisory services, as well as protection for high-profile executives either in-country or when traveling globally. In terms of individual protection, we offer security for high net-worth individuals, and their families and properties, as well as celebrities—movie stars, singers and the like— whose fame can subject them to stalker fans or kidnappers hoping to collect a ransom.

"I founded the company in 1990, after the fall of the Berlin wall the previous November. With the subsequent reunification of Germany, I felt it was the perfect time to embark on a business of this nature.

"As I'm sure you understand, in our line of business both clients and contract staff require a high degree of anonymity. Most of our contract hires come to us through personal referrals, generally from either security and intelligence agencies around the world or the militaries of NATO countries. We screen and vet each new applicant very carefully. It is a lengthy process requiring sixty to ninety days— sometimes longer. This vetting includes comprehensive background checks, rigorous psychological testing, and multiple interviews, as well as lie detector tests. We ... I, take my business very seriously and actively strive to provide the very best and most effective security services for all of our clients. We have built an elite team of contractors on par with any in our field globally, and I am sufficiently familiar with each of them to be willing to place my own life, or the lives of my family, in their hands with total confidence.

"I tell you this to explain my initial hesitancy and delay in contacting the German Federal Criminal Police as well as in my subsequent conversations with them and Interpol because what I am about to tell you directly concerns several ... more specifically, three, of my contractors." Hearing these words, Robert Murray and the Warsaw team experienced a heightened sense of anticipation, focusing their full attention on Herr Kohler.

Perceiving their keen interest, he continued, "The three individuals of whom I speak are two men and a woman. Again, I must preface what I'm about to tell you, and what I've already shared with the Federal German Criminal Police and Interpol, by saying that it is simply impossible for me to imagine that these three individuals could in any way be involved with the recent nefarious doings. That absolute certainty is why I did not come forward sooner. However, after the horrific incident in Berlin, I felt I had no choice except to notify the authorities despite my confidence that what I'm about to share represents nothing more than a strange, random coincidence.

"The three contractors I am referring to are Tom Barrington, Ryan Flynn, and Rebecca Moore. All three are American citizens living and working for us here in Europe. Again, I must re-affirm that my confidence in each of them is absolute, as I have never had any reason to doubt their integrity.

"Tom Barrington was a US Marine Corps Raider, which—I assume you know—is one of the Marine's Special Operations Units. He is very familiar with Europe and quite European himself, as his father was a senior executive of a prominent German engineering firm and the family lived in Germany during much of Tom's childhood and teen years. His Marine Corps specialty was as a sniper. He served with distinction and was credited with numerous combat kills in Iraq and Afghanistan.

"He then moved to the CIA. What he did there, we have never discussed ... or, more accurately, he was not free to discuss. He came to us highly recommended, as did each of these three, nearly two years ago. Obviously, being a civilian security company, we do not utilize snipers. However, Tom's skills go far beyond that of being a crack shot with a high-powered rifle. In addition to his exceptional physical prowess, he is also extremely intelligent and possesses superior problem-solving capabilities.

"Ryan Flynn, came to us directly from the US military, specifically the Army, about two years ago as well, where he served, also with distinction, in explosives and demolition. I can honestly tell you that I don't think there exists anything in the field of military explosives and related devices in which Ryan is not an expert. Once again, as a civilian security provider, we don't have a need for defusing IED's (Improvised Explosive Devices)—or for building them. But, like Tom, Ryan possesses many other extraordinary skills and specialties gained during his army service, also in Iraq and Afghanistan. These competencies ideally suit him to our security requirements.

"Rebecca, who joined us only about eighteen months ago … well, she is unlike any young woman I have ever met. Her specialty is Cyber Security, but she is also one of the most socially perceptive people I have ever known. Her skills encompass virtually anything computer related. In addition to Cyber Security, she is excellent in remote and on-site access control, electronic surveillance and a host of related activities. She is a cyber wiz, who possesses an extraordinary ability to walk into a room and read those who are present, just as you or I would read a book. I admit that I am no amateur in this regard myself, nor are any of our contractors. However, Rebecca's perceptive cognitive abilities are quite unique.

"I don't know exactly what she did before joining us, except that her work at the American NSA (National Security Agency) was shrouded in secrecy. One final thing about Rebecca: although an American, she has the bearing of a fiery red-haired Irish beauty. When she walks into a room, heads immediately turn. Men, well, they naturally look—but women as well, and I suspect that for some it may cause a twinge of envy.

"Against my better judgment, I have come to you. When I first saw the picture of the three you seek from the Warsaw train station; I didn't pay much attention. The individuals in that photograph could be almost anyone. But as I learned more details of the events in Bratislava, Warsaw and finally, Berlin, from the news, I came to be at war within myself. On the one hand, I feel certain that my three contractors—Tom, Ryan, and Rebecca—could not possibly be involved in these awful events. At the same time, as I looked at the photograph again, and again, having downloaded it from the Internet, printed it and pinned it on a cork board next to my desk, I kept thinking about their uniquely specialized skills and wondering whether this is just a strange coincidence or something worse. It all seemed surreal, but the pieces do undeniably fall together … well, rather like a jigsaw puzzle.

"Still, I would have summarily dismissed it all from my mind, but for one more fact. In January, the three of them informed me that they had been contacted by a third-party on behalf of an extremely wealthy Greek family with deep ties in the international shipping business. It seems the three had been told, that this family would be holding a series of business/social meetings and events at their private estate compound located on the Greek coast. A third-party go-between had been tasked with hiring a top-notch security team of three for a six to eight-week timeframe, before and during these events, to provide security for the family and their international business guests, who would be coming and going during this period.

"They said that the offer was extremely generous, but that the third party would only contract with them directly, not through an agency, such as ours. You might think that this was an unusual request which would arouse suspicion. However, in our business, it isn't at all unusual. The business people we protect … or, I should say, provide security services for, often have a rather … shall we say exaggerated view of the potential threats they face. Such people often have not risen to the top without making enemies, some considerably more than others, and some of these enemies can be ruthless.

"My three contractors requested a leave of absence for a sixty-day period, beginning in early March, allowing them to accept this private engagement. At the time, I thought that it might not be just for the money. All three had been working very hard on demanding assignments. You must understand, some of our clients are a pleasure to work with, while others can be quite disagreeable, from the standpoint of believing too much in their own press, resulting in an overinflated view of their importance. The latter also has a tendency to flagrantly ignore the professional advice of the security professionals we provide. To put it more articulately, a significant portion of our clients can be exasperating to deal with. A real pain in the ass, to be blunt about it.

"The engagement offered by the Greek family was apparently pitched to them as being low-key and as much a spring vacation on the Greek coast as a work assignment. I felt at the time that it would be good for them, a welcome break from the intensity of their recent assignments. I anticipated that they would return refreshed and renewed. Ours is a demanding business, and as I said, all of my employees take what we do very seriously. That results in a great deal of stress at times which can lead to burn-out, and we all need a periodic break from it. I regard my contractors more as family members than employees, and I am concerned for their well-being. In this instance, I felt it was best for all of us to grant the leave of absence they had requested ... so I did.

"Their leave commenced on March 6th. I haven't heard from them since, nor did I expect or even want to, as I hoped it to be a real break in routine for them. I expected they would contact me toward the end of April, with news of their return by early May.

"I have struggled for two days now about what to do. Finally, I felt that the circumstances demanded that I come forward. So, here I am."

"This is incredible," said Marek, looking at the others. "I am astounded by what you've just told us. And, Herr Kohler, I know that I speak for all of us when I say that we certainly appreciate the dilemma in which you find yourself. Your business depends upon absolute faith and trust in those with whom one works. Without this faith and trust, it would be impossible to do anything effectively. That said, we thank you for coming forward and sincerely hope that, as much as this would be a tremendous break in the case for us, your friends do not turn out to be at the heart of this conspiracy."

Interpol had requested full facial photographs of the three suspects as well as their employment records, fingerprint cards and other identifying information, which Herr Kohler was told to bring with him to the Wiesbaden meeting. Upon seeing the faces of the three for the first time, the four agents and Murray simply stared at them. "Finally, we get to see them ... actually see what they look like, who they are, these Americans! It has almost felt like we were chasing phantoms around until now … but, finally, we see that they are not phantoms." Jedrzej smiled, the first time he had done so in days.

Looking at Rebecca's photo, Domiik remarked, "I see what you mean Herr Kohler. She is an outstanding beauty."

Adrianna leaned over to look at the photo Domiik was holding, "She's pretty all right. I'll give her that!"

The men all looked at Herr Kohler, who was intently watching Adrianna looking at the photo. He smiled, "See what I mean about her effect on other women?"

IMBROGLIO TRILOGY

Chapter 22:
The Hunt Begins

The investigative team promised Herr Kohler that they would do everything within their power to ensure that the three would be apprehended without violence, if at all possible. Although the four investigators and Murray did not share Herr Kohler's belief in their innocence, they understood and respected his deep sense of commitment and loyalty to his people.

They thanked Herr Kohler for coming forward with his information, and he departed with the reassurance that he would notify them immediately of any contact from the three. Following a brief break, the team reassembled.

"Well, what do you think Murray?" Domiik asked. "CIA and NSA! Part of your 'Brothers in Arms' from the past?"

"I don't believe it! Not for a minute," Murray replied. "I'll get to the bottom of this!"

"You do that, but in the interim, we need to move on this information post-haste," Domiik responded.

"Understood!"

"It would not be the first time agents have gone rogue on either side," Marek interjected. "I remember reading how, back in 1968, the Russian sub K-129 was commandeered by a group of eleven KGB fanatics who fired a ballistic missile with a nuclear warhead at the U.S. Navy fleet in Pearl Harbor, thinking they could fool the U.S. into believing it was China who had launched the attack. They were convinced that the U.S. and China would obliterate each other, leaving mother Russia to dominate the world ... what little would have been left of it after the radioactive fallout and nuclear winter.

"Fortunately for all, the missile Fail-Safe detected an unauthorized launch and self-destructed the missile upon ignition in its tube, sinking K-129, but preventing World War III. There are enough die-hard crazies and fringe lunatics in each of our countries' intelligence communities to destroy us all, given half a chance. Possibly some of yours are trying to do so now!"

"That may be, but it had better not be these three," Murray replied, already rising, cell phone in hand, to leave the room.

With photographs and personal identification information for the three suspects provided by Kohler, the full team of investigators quickly launched into action. The photos were scanned, and—together with the personal identification information—were flashed to Interpol, Lyon, and from there to Interpol offices and national federal police headquarters across Europe. Robert Murray simultaneously transmitted the files to CIA Headquarters in Langley, VA, with an urgent request for full background information on each of the suspects.

Meanwhile, Athens airport authorities were contacted and asked to transmit all digital CCTV files from the timeframe covering the suspects' arrival at Athens airport. The team also requested relevant

CCTV footage for all of the tram and train stations located along the airport route. Within hours, the data was flowing into Wiesbaden German Federal Criminal Police Headquarters. Soon video files were being scanned for facial recognition. It didn't take long before they had confirmed matches. The three suspects were picked up by cameras first in the main terminal arrival area and then departing through Door 1.

When the investigators regrouped in the large conference room to plan their next steps, Marek asked Domiik for the Athens file. Leafing through the file, Marek remarked, "This is a bit strange. The interviews and reports from Athens airport security personnel and police on the scene indicated that they had possibly sighted two of the conspirators. One, the woman, was at the entrance to the bridge to the city trains and the other, possibly the shooter, seems to have been sighted exiting Door 4. Both apparently identified after they had already departed the airport. Yet here, in these Athens airport CCTV camera photos matched by facial recognition to Herr Kohler's photographs, we see all three exiting Door 1 together. And neither of the suspects described in the two purported sightings by Athens airport security, are dressed anything like this video footage or as they were described by the gate agent when they checked in for the flight in Prague."

Jedrzej looked up, "I'm not at all surprised! You're talking about airport security and police attempting to recall who they remembered seeing among hundreds of faces. In the case of the shooter, their identification may have been made 20 minutes … 30 minutes … or maybe an hour after he had exited the airport terminal. And in the case of the woman, who knows what 'bella' woman the Greek security personnel were infatuated with.

"Given the low definition CCTV image they received and then printed, at what level of resolution we can only imagine—probably 72 dpi—they may well have identified my dog as one of the conspirators, had it been there. Remember Marek, at the time we agreed that it was extremely unlikely, under the circumstances, that a correct visual identification would be made in an after-the-fact situation like this, with people trying to recall who they saw, and where, amidst the confusion. It is unlikely that they could do so accurately and, unfortunately, far more likely that an incorrect identification would be made in their eagerness to be of assistance.

"As to their clothing, wouldn't you have expected them to change their disguises before departing the Athen's airport? What surprises me is that they exited the airport together. They're certainly brazen, I'll give them that much."

"Or maybe they think so little of police proficiency that they simply aren't worried about being apprehended," Domiik added. "And they may be right!"

"That was a little harsh, don't you think?" Adrianna shot back.

"Don't mind him, Adrianna," Jedrzej shrugged. "He's just frustrated!"

"I suppose you're right," mused Marek. "I just don't like discrepancies in an investigation. It always makes me wonder what I've missed."

"Don't worry, they won't slip through our grasp the next time —not now that we have recognizable photographs and their real identities," Jedrzej responded confidently. "The question we must focus on presently is: why Greece? Why are they there? Is it to carry out yet another assassination? Or to hide? Or for some other, still unknown reason? If we can discern why they're there, it will make finding them more likely."

"I think they are likely headed for a Safe House in Greece to wait until its time to unfold the next step of their plan," Domiik responded. "I find it difficult to believe that they would be planning on assassinating the Greek Prime Minister. That country has so many economic and social struggles ... what could possibly be the point."

"Fermenting more social unrest and instability," Jedrzej opined.

"More than already exits in Greece? Now that would be a feat!" Domiik countered.

Adrianna questioned, "What if Greece is merely another transit point for them, rather than a destination?"

"Adrianna makes a valid point," admitted Jedrzej, "We don't know with any certainty that Greece is their final destination."

"Or in fact that they are still there," Adrianna added.

Marek stood and walked over to the conference room wall, where a floor-to-ceiling map of the world was displayed. "If you are correct Adrianna, then they may have already left Greece, or are about to do so," Marek postulated, pointing to the map. "My guesses would be, first, Turkey, then Cyprus, and finally, North Africa—probably Tunisia or Egypt. That's where I would go if I wanted to vanish from 'sniffing range,' but still remain in the relative 'neighborhood' for whatever is to come next."

"And why stay close ... that is, in the neighborhood?" Adrianna asked. "You're assuming more activity ... ?"

"Yes, because their work is not yet finished," Marek answered. "Whoever is behind this plot ... whatever their purpose ... it is clearly not over. I don't believe for a moment that their end has as yet been fully accomplished. Nor that this trio has left Greece. I think they are still there and will remain until the next step in their plan has been executed."

"All the more reason for us to find them now. They are our only trail to the real perpetrators! And I agree with you," Domiik concurred. "We must end this conspiracy before it leads to more killings, which I am certain will come soon … if we fail."

The Greek authorities initiated facial searches of all government controlled CCTV in and around Athens but turned up nothing more. Likewise, the privately controlled CCTV cameras throughout the city provided by Athen's businesses also came up empty.

Athens police reviewed the CCTV footage from the train stations between the airport and downtown Athens However, only one passenger disembarked within the two or three minute timeframe in question: a casually dressed young woman with a hikers backpack. Obviously a student tourist, so they didn't bother to pass on that footage to the team in Wiesbaden.

Over the previous several days, Marek had been privately communicating with his friend Lt. Colonel Mitchell at U.S. European Command (USEUCOM), in Patch Barracks, at Stuttgart, Germany. Now he called upon Mitchell once again, updating him on the Wiesbaden developments. Mitchell related that he had encountered Ryan Flynn briefly in the context of his Afghanistan SOF involvement. Although he did not know him well, he was surprised to learn that he had become a primary suspect in the assassinations and Berlin booby trap bombing. Other than that, he could not shed much light on the events or the investigation, other than to say that a firestorm was in progress within the U.S. DoD, the intelligence community and the State Department over the 'facts' and public accusations emerging from the EU in Brussels.

As their conversation concluded, Mitchell painted a picture of the DoD's own high priority internal investigation into the weapon and EXACTO bullet, which he was certain would now expand to include any possible connection to the three named suspects.

Meanwhile, Murray had been busy pursuing information through his own unnamed sources. Uncharacteristically, for once the CIA appeared to be openly and fully cooperating, not only with the rest of the American intelligence community but also with European intelligence—and the civil police authorities. The picture Murray gained from his sources was that there appeared to be a concerted effort underway to foment violent clashes with police across Europe. But who was instigating this and why remained shrouded in mystery, even to Murray and the CIA. Or at least, that was what he claimed.

Marek gathered the lead investigators from the various organizations now represented in Wiesbaden, numbering over a dozen individuals. "As much as none of us wants to hear this, I believe that we need to wait … wait until we receive some sighting or other indication of the suspects' whereabouts. Herr Kohler could not tell us where in Greece this 'mystery assignment' was to take place—only that it was a spacious villa somewhere along the coast. But, as we all know, there are innumerable large villas along thousands of miles of Greek coastline, including the islands.

"While we do have mobile numbers for the suspects, which Herr Kohler provided, he told us that it was company policy—that is, Euro Strategic Security Services policy—to maintain the location services of all security personnel's mobile phones in the 'off' position while on assignment, in order to prevent them from being tracked by a foe.

"Although the suspects are not on Euro Strategic Security Services business, they are likely to follow that same protocol on this assignment. And no signal whatsoever from any of the three suspects' phones has been picked up since March 6th by any cell tower. That final phone access was in Berlin, which means that their phones, the ones we are aware of, have been switched off since then. Thus, calling or trying to track tower connections will not help us to locate them.

"Simply put, I believe that all we can do is to wait. We don't want to spook them since doing so will likely only drive them further underground. They have successfully eluded us thus far, and it would be best for them to think that they can continue doing so. There is no reason to believe that they know of Herr Kohler's visit and revelation, or that we now possess their real identities and photographs. We've distributed their information to every law enforcement agency across Europe. It cannot be long before they surface on the radar of law enforcement somewhere.

"My question to you is this: Do you agree that we wait and allow them to continue their assumed anonymity, or do we broadcast their photos and real names through the media across Europe, in an attempt to flush them out? There are risks to either course of action. We must determine which alternative creates the least degree of risk. As I have stated, I think we are better off waiting, at least for the moment."

A debate immediately ensued which was vociferous and at times heated, as there were no 'weak' personalities in the room. Understandably, due to the horrendous losses suffered only days earlier, the German Federal Police wanted the suspects flushed out immediately. The Germans were understandably out for blood and did not attempt to conceal their intense animosity, despite Herr Kohler's insistence on the suspects' innocence.

Murray and the Warsaw team thought it better to bide their time and hope for a lucky break in the case. One which would provide a vital clue to the suspects' whereabouts, without alerting them. The Germans, however, feared a repeat of the Athens debacle or, worse yet, another Berlin tragedy. Thus, the debate continued for over an hour, until Jedrzej and Murray, as unlikely a pair as any, proposed a compromise. By this time, it was late in the day, and they suggested that the group recess for the night and reconvene in the morning with the intention of waiting one more day for an opportune development before taking any further action.

Exhausted emotionally as well as physically, everyone agreed that this proposal was reasonable. However, the Germans were adamant that the delay be no longer than twenty-four hours. Murray, Marek, and the Warsaw team headed to their hotel for dinner and some well deserved sleep.

IMBROGLIO TRILOGY

Chapter 23:

The Long Wait

March 20th

Dawn broke cold, with a steel-gray sky. Earlier it seemed as
though winter had fled, vanquished, yielding to the welcome arrival of
an early spring. Now, its promise of warmth and rebirth had been
suddenly snuffed out, taking all hope with it.

Based upon their decision the previous evening, the group
gathered to wait for a break in the case. Murray spent most of the day on
the phone, working every official as well as off the record CIA asset he
had at his disposal. He also reached deep into his own not unsubstantial
cache of personal contacts accumulated over the course of his career, in
an effort to turn up any information about the three American suspects.
However, his efforts were to no avail. Normally, given his senior level
and the extensive internal contacts he had forged over time within the
CIA, he would have been able to find out the contents of Tom
Barrington's personnel file, if not obtain a full transcript. However, when
he requested access, the file had been inexplicably locked, blocking all
access.

As morning passed into mid-afternoon, the Germans began to grow ever more anxious. "What if … ?" they would venture. "What if they, the suspects, were about to execute another assassination or some other lethal plot? What if they had slipped out of Greece and were already at their next destination, preparing to commit some monstrous deed there? The 'what if's … ?" went on, envisioning ever more dire consequences as the day progressed.

And then, there were the 'CYA' issues. "What if the assassins had just vanished, never to reappear again?" Everyone involved had agreed that their pernicious plot was not yet complete. There certainly had to be more to it. But what if they were wrong—and there was no more? How would they explain to their respective agencies and superiors that they had just sat on their hands and done nothing for a full thirty-six hours while the assassins had bolted and escaped justice forever? And imagine the countless conspiracy theories which would proliferate wildly across the media, internet and elsewhere! Their reputations would be ruined, not to mention their respective careers

Notwithstanding the other investigators' concerns, Murray, Marek, and the Warsaw team held their ground, insisting that, as difficult as waiting was, it offered the best hope. The instant the suspects' identities were made public, they would certainly be on the move, and the chase would be on again. Once more, the 'good guys' would be in hot pursuit—likely a step behind the conspirators at every turn. There simply was no good option, but a 'chase' at this juncture, they argued, was far less likely to yield the outcome they needed.

No one wanted to leave the command center, so as the day wore on they sent out for dinner as they had for lunch. But dinner brought with it renewed contention, as they were now approaching the twenty-four-hour deadline to which they had all agreed. Adding to the mounting pressure to act, was the increasing frequency of calls emanating from each agency's senior leadership, demanding progress updates. The decision to wait for the suspects to make a move was hardly viewed in a positive light by their superiors.

Finally, as they concluded dinner, the issue provoked a more heated debate. The Germans received an unequivocal mandate from above to take immediate action. They were informed that if the group did not act in unison, they would be forced to act unilaterally, releasing the photos and other identifying information to the German media. As the release in one country would result in its viral spread across Europe within hours, the decision to move forward in unison was quickly, if reluctantly, agreed upon.

With this decision made, a news bulletin was hastily composed for release to the European media. Once finished with this task, the group of investigators decided that an early night would be their best course of action. They fully expected the following day to bring about some result, although of what nature and outcome remained to be seen.

IMBROGLIO TRILOGY

Chapter 24:
Vacationing
Mykonos, Greece

Rising early, Bruce, Sarah, and Franz drove their vehicles the eleven miles up the coast from the Palmyra Beach Hotel, outside of the seaside town of Glyfada, the short distance to the Port of Piraeus on the outskirts of Athens. Their cars were soon loaded onboard the 7:00 am *Sea Jets* high-speed ferry for the scenic two hour-forty-five minute voyage to Mykonos. The passage was smooth and the spring air balmy. In fact, while temperatures in the upper seventies (25° C) were typical for the time of year, since arriving in Athens, they had enjoyed days in the mid-eighties (30° C) and delightfully cool evenings in the upper-sixties (20° C).

Approximately one-hundred nautical miles southeast of Athens in the Aegean Sea lies a small cluster of islands known as the *Cyclades*. The smallest of these islands, Mykonos, encompasses an area of just one hundred square kilometers. Nicknamed the *Island of the Winds,* it has also been referred to as *Little Venice* having become a popular mecca for tourists from all over the world.

According to the Greek custom of *Chora,* meaning *The Town,* the ultra cosmopolitan main town of this small island also bears the island's name, *Mykonos.* During high season, July and August, it attracts the rich and famous, including movie stars and scores of paparazzi. However, spring (late March through early June) and fall (September through October), offer the best climate and tranquility, without the hordes of day-tripping summer tourists who disembark each morning from a steady stream of colossal cruise ships. Spring is, without a doubt, a perfect time to vacation on Mykonos.

From the harbor, Bruce and Sarah drove the silver Beamer convertible, and Franz the red Jaguar convertible to a picturesque villa overlooking the aqua-blue Aegean Sea on the west side of the island: a gleaming, white structure set among terraced gardens leading down to the sea. The couple moved into the main house, with its six spacious bedrooms, while Franz settled happily into the three-bedroom guesthouse, connected by an expansive cobblestone terrace and arbors overlooking the sea—fragrant with the sweet scent of jasmine emanating from the shaded alcoves beneath a riotous profusion of bougainvillea and mandevilla.

This arrangement afforded the couple privacy from Franz, although Sarah's warming to him had begun the previous evening over drinks and continued unabated during their ferry sailing. She had gone from detesting Franz to tolerating him, and when he was his most charming self, usually after several drinks, she found herself almost enjoying his company.

She had come to realize that he wasn't actually the cold-blooded neanderthal devoid of social graces that she had at first assumed. Maybe he had mellowed—or perhaps they all were being impacted by the breathtaking beauty and azure tranquility of the Greek

Isles. After all, these islands are legendary, storied for their mesmerizing effect on visitors. The famed home of Aphrodite.

Earlier, Sarah had insisted to Bruce that if they had to stay at the same villa complex as Franz, at least they would not share meals with him. On that account, she had been uncompromising. Sarah did not want anything more to do with him. But now all that was changing. In fact, that very afternoon, Franz had suggested that he should prepare dinner for them in the outdoor terrace kitchen overlooking the sea. Bruce was about to decline, explaining that he had already planned dinner for two at a local restaurant that he wanted to try. To Bruce's surprise, Sarah beat him to it by accepting Franz's offer.

"But can you cook?" she teased.

Franz grinned, "Ah, yet another baseless misconception! You continue to misjudge me. See for yourself by the dinner I prepare for the three of us at sunset on the villa's seaside terrace."

With that, he headed off to the market in search of the ingredients for dinner. He returned with multiple bags brimming over with vegetables, fruit, meat and fresh locally caught fish, along with several carefully chosen bottles of wine. "We are going to feast and be merry tonight!" he called out exuberantly, as he passed them lounging on the terrace near the pool on his way to the guesthouse kitchen.

Late that afternoon, as the sun began its descent toward the Aegean, there appeared on the terrace near the outdoor kitchen an assortment of artfully arranged hors d'oeuvres to entice the imagination and delight the palate. Complimenting these was a chilled magnum of Taittinger Comtes De Champagne Blanc De Blancs—light, fruity and, above all, elegant. It was a vintage of extraordinary finesse—perfect when paired with a course of light hors d'oeuvres served well before dinner.

Sarah had spent the afternoon near the pool on the far end of the terrace, oblivious to Franz's labors. Bruce had been beside her reading until he dozed off in the warm spring sun. Having completed her sun-worshipping session, Sarah rose from her chaise and dove into the heated pool. Emerging from its blue depths, she climbed the pool stairs, padded her face and hair dry and then wrapped herself in an oversized white terry towel. Bruce was still dreaming blissfully when she turned to go inside, but just then, Franz caught her attention with an inviting wave of his arm, beckoning her to come and view his labors.

Approaching him, Sarah caught sight of the sumptuous spread. "Dinner already? I find that 6:00 is a trifle early for dinner, especially in the southern realms of Europe."

"Yes, I would agree," Franz replied, "but 6:30 is an excellent hour for appetizers. And you just have time to change before the sunset cocktail hour begins. Although instead of cocktails, we will begin our dinner with Taittinger Comtes De Champagne. But don't worry, you'll have plenty of time to recover your appetite afterward, as the main courses—yes, there will be two—will not begin until 8:00 pm."

"Then this is intended to be an all-evening affair?"

"Yes, that is, unless you and Bruce have a more compelling dinner engagement."

She laughed. "No, I don't believe we have any other social engagements on the calendar this evening."

"Well, good. Then perhaps you would like to dress for dinner? It will be casual alfresco tonight."

Turning to leave, Sarah flashed a flirtatious smile.

As she walked away, Franz, called after her, "And if that oaf sleeping on the chaise doesn't wake up soon, leave him and we can enjoy a quiet dinner together, just the two of us." Sarah kept walking as if she had not heard his comment.

Sarah showered and slipped into a sleek black dress, draping her curves just enough to add mystique. She was determined to enjoy herself fully tonight, and she chose a simple string of natural pearls and pearl earrings. Glancing at the clock, she was surprised that it was only 6:32. She must have hurried in getting ready without realizing it. Franz had said 6:30, so she sat indoors and waited another ten minutes before emerging through the French doors of the bedroom onto the terrace facing the pool. Bruce was gone.

She glanced across to the far end of the terrace and saw him with Franz. They were talking and laughing about something, obviously enjoying themselves. She walked toward them slowly. Bruce was facing Franz, with a glass in his hand, enjoying an appetizer. He noted Franz's eyes shift from his to something off to his side. Instinctively, as he turned, he said, "There you are darling. We were just talking about you."

"Really? She feigned innocence, "I would never have guessed."

Bruce reached for a second glass of champagne and handed it to Sarah. "A toast to our guest chef of the evening." He clinked glasses with her.

Franz added, "And to a most beautiful enchantress," as he touched her glass with his. They all drank.

Bruce excused himself, "I'll just go and change for dinner. Sarah, you must try some of these fabulous appetizers Franz has prepared for us. He is a true culinary Houdini. I swear, I'd be persuaded to hire him as our personal chef, although I'd worry that if we offended him in any way, by failing to pay him sufficient compliments or something, he might assassinate us in our sleep." With that he chortled and walked off across the terrace, still holding his half-full glass of champagne.

"Would you?" asked Sarah.

"Would I what?"

"Would you … you know … " as she drew her hand across her throat in a slow, menacing, slicing motion.

"You?" responded Franz. "Never … no … not to such a beautiful neck. Now Bruce, well, that might be a different matter. I might … speaking as your chef … dispatch him. But probably less dramatically, maybe a little arsenic in his *soupe de poisson*. Then you and I could have dinner together, just the two of us!"

Sarah laughed and turned away to admire Franz's elegant *hors d'oeuvres* artistry.

"You didn't learn this from a book, I suspect."

"No, I didn't. Before entering the German army, I spent a year in culinary school."

"You trained to be a chef?"

"Yes, and not only did I train, I found it most satisfying."

"How did you go from training as a chef to becoming a … "

"A hit man? An assassin? Is that what you're wondering?"

"Yes. How did you go from training to be a chef to becoming a professional killer?"

"I was very young, living in Paris at the time. I had a girlfriend. And yes, don't look shocked, I liked women … and they, me. My girlfriend … I probably … no, I would most certainly have married her when I finished my schooling."

"So what happened?"

"She was murdered. A man, someone who she knew from her school. She was also a student. Music. She sang. She sang beautifully—a voice like an angel. She was a very pretty girl, blonde and very pretty … like you. He, the other man, became infatuated with her and began stalking her. One night, he confronted her. She rebuffed him, and in his blind rage he strangled her."

"How awful!"

"Yes, it was."

"So what did you do? I mean, how did you get from there to here … now?"

"Well, I killed him," Franz responded matter-of-factly, no trace of emotion evident in his voice."

"Just like that? I mean, no police … no …."

"No, no police, no courts. The police were investigating. He was the prime suspect. But we were all considered suspects, myself, and her other friends. She had told us that he was stalking her and that she was afraid of him but, the police could find no proof since he had an iron-clad alibi. Some friends of his lied and said that he had been playing cards with them that evening, at the time the murder had occurred."

"Well, how did you know that he wasn't with them?"

"Because he told me so. He admitted to me what he had done. He confessed!"

"Why would he … " Sarah questioned. Franz just stared at her, and she began to comprehend his meaning.

"Now you understand. He told me…before he died. I offered him a choice, and he took the quicker option. Not that it was especially quick … or merciful … just more so than it would have been."

Sarah felt a chill course through her body, like a sudden cold breeze off the water, as she contemplated what Franz meant by, "not that it was quick … or merciful." A silence hung momentarily in the air, before Sarah continued, "And the police never charged you?"

"They cannot charge you with a crime for which they have no evidence of your involvement. I have … had, at the time … friends, too, and they vouched for my whereabouts in the same way his friends had done for him."

Sarah looked at Franz … for the first time really looked at him, looked into his eyes and saw someone she had not noticed before: someone living in a world of pain.

"He had it coming, then," she said.

"Yes, he did. I merely ensured that he got what he deserved. Justice!"

"So that led you to … ?" Her voice trailed off.

"No, not directly. I didn't just wake up the next morning and decide to become a professional killer. I mean, this is not a profession one simply chooses out of a job description catalog at school. No, after that I needed a change. So I joined the German army, where I discovered that I was uniquely skilled as a marksman, a sniper, a talent for killing with a high-powered rifle. The army put it to good use in the Kommando Spezialkräfte, Germany's top special forces unit. When I left the army, I could not go back—not after all I had seen and experienced. It was simply impossible to return to my past life working in the culinary arts. So I decided to put my skills to use in the commercial marketplace."

"And you've never looked back?"

"No!"

"How do you like the appetizers?" Franz asked, without a pause.

"Amazing! They are truly exceptional!"

"Exceptional food for an exceptional woman. Smart, discerning and a rare beauty. I can understand why Bruce chose you."

"Or maybe, I … chose him," Sarah responded coyly.

Franz's gaze remained on her, but he didn't look convinced.

Silence settled over them both. Sarah took one of the small plates Franz had set out. Placing a few of the tempting delectables on it, she took her glass of champagne and walked over to the terrace wall. Sarah sat sideways on the wall, placing her plate beside her and slowly sipped her champagne. Franz stood in the outdoor kitchen, gazing at the rays of the setting sun streaming over Sarah, her red hair ablaze, her curvaceous figure silhouetted in its rosy glow.

It wasn't long before Bruce resurfaced. Refreshed by his nap in the sunshine and a shower, he became a bundle of energy and wit. He walked across the terrace to Franz, paused, and then turned to look at the view Franz was admiring.

"Gorgeous scenery," Franz offered.

"Indeed," Bruce replied. Both men smiled.

Dinner was served at precisely 8:00 pm, just as Franz had promised. He prided himself on the positive traits of his German heritage, including strong organizational abilities and dependable punctuality. He was 'precise' in everything he did—one might even say premeditated!

The dinner he had prepared was indeed extraordinary. The appetizers were followed by a gourmet mushroom soup, then a Mediterranean three-green salad with capers and mandarin orange slices garnished with sprigs of fresh dill. The first main course was fish, a seared scallop dish with Jalapeño Vinaigrette complimented by a Terre Valse Cococciola wine from Abruzzo, Italy. The second main course featured Beef Wellington with seared foie gras and duvelles, paired with a Fench Bourdeaux—St. Emilion. For dessert, Franz with a flourish unveiled a flaming caramel pear tart, served with fine Italian coffee, complimented afterward by more champagne from a second chilled magnum.

As the evening progressed, their conversation transformed from cordial to friendly, Franz openly flirting with Sarah, in a friendly, and at times humorous manner. This was a game Sarah knew and could feign well, now delighting in Franz's alleged attentions. With demur satisfaction, Sarah playfully rebuffed his advances while Bruce, amused by the charade, acted the part of a witless husband. Finally, around 11 pm, Bruce said, "I think I've had a little too much sun today, not to mention the champagne. I'm turning in."

Franz warned him, "If you leave her alone with me, I may steal her away."

Rising to leave, Bruce replied laughing, "If you can afford her, you are welcome to her, but I warn you, she is very expensive to keep." Then, he rose from the table, turned, and with a wave of his hand, strolled back into the villa and to bed.

Franz looked at Sarah, sitting aglow in the moonlight. "Damn, you'd be nice to have, but he's probably right. I probably can't afford you."

Sarah turned to look at him. "Too true," she replied.

Franz stood up. "It's been a long day. I haven't worked so hard in the kitchen since culinary school. I had forgotten how much work cooking is … and also, how rewarding, especially when it's for those who truly appreciate my efforts." He leaned over and kissed Sarah on the cheek. "Thank you for a wonderful evening." He headed across the terrace and into the guesthouse. She watched as the guesthouse lights went on, then off again a few minutes later.

Sarah lingered for several more minutes, sipping her champagne. Lights along the coast below twinkled like a crescent of retreating stars against the jet-black sea—the breeze soft against her bare shoulders, the evening still warm. She felt wonderfully relaxed and sleepy from the lavish dinner, wine, and champagne.

IMBROGLIO TRILOGY

Chapter 25:

The Pursuit Begins

Earlier on March 20th, Berlin to Mykonos

It was just after 7:30 am when the break they had been awaiting the previous day materialized. A German Federal Police investigator entered the conference room and enthusiastically announced that police in Mykonos, Greece, had reported a verified sighting of one of the suspects the prior afternoon. The man had what appeared to be a large carry-out bag and was leaving the Kalita Restaurant in Mykonos Town on the west side of the island, an area of restaurants and shops catering to tourists. The investigator stated, "One police officer made the initial sighting and, after radioing in, a second officer had quickly joined him, confirming from the photographs provided by Berlin that this was indeed one of the three suspects.

"However, the Greek police officers lost visual contact when the suspect walked through a crowded market, only catching sight of him again from a distance as he drove away. The officers reported that their line of sight was too obstructed to identify the car make or model. Their police vehicles were parked on the far side of the market; consequently, they were unable to follow before the suspect's car was long out of sight. However, they could confirm that it appeared to be a brightly-colored auto.

The officers doubled back to the restaurant, but the suspect had paid with cash, leaving no credit card trail. Upon showing the photograph to a restaurant employee, the suspect's identity was confirmed as Tom Barrington. The Greek police did add, however, and I believe that this will interest you all, as I assume we will soon be on our way to Mykonos, that Kalita is indeed a very fine restaurant!"

"That's very helpful!" Domiik bristled. "Please tell them that their prowess as travel guides is surpassed only by their effectiveness as police officers." Sardonic laughter rippled through the room.

The German investigator began again, "The Mykonos police have subsequently been ordered by the Hellenic Police (the Greek Federal Police force under authority of the Minister for Citizen Protection) to maintain surveillance if the suspects resurface, but not to attempt interception or any form of contact with them, as the Hellenic Police will be taking charge of the situation."

At a minimum, the team now knew that their suspects were on Mykonos or at least, one suspect for certain. On hearing of this new development, Marek became visibly agitated over the decision of the prior evening. "This is what I was afraid of. Now all they need do is flip on a television, check online news or open a paper, and they will immediately discover that we are on to them: their true identities as well as their presence on Mykonos. Not a very big place. They'll run, I tell you! They'll run quickly, if they have not done so already this morning, as we sit here speaking."

"I think you're overreacting," a German police investigator disagreed. "They may not yet be aware that we know they are on Mykonos, and the Hellenic Police have already begun moving reinforcements in this morning. The island will be sealed off by evening, possibly sooner."

"Sealed off?" Marek countered heatedly. "Have you ever been to Mykonos? I have and know it quite well. You can't seal it off! Do you have any idea what it is like? If I remember correctly, it is only about 100 square kilometers in area, with about a half dozen towns and villages. At this time of year, late March, with Easter nearly upon us and some of the continent's schools out on vacation, the local population of ten thousand or so will have swelled to nearly double that number. Unless the Greek authorities intend to search every house, shop, goat shed, and chicken coop on the island, plus caves and boats, our suspects could hide there for a year without being seen. And with hundreds of kilometers of serpentine coastline, they could sneak off after dark—or even in broad daylight—any time they please. There are innumerable beaches, coves, and small harbors from where a small boat can easily be launched.Who knows, maybe they will snorkel out to a submarine!"

"Well, it is what it is! We'd better get moving and get ourselves to Mykonos. We can only hope and pray that when we finally arrive, they will still be there," Domiik chafed, a tone of disgust permeating his voice at the likely consequences of the previous evening's ill-timed decision to broadcast the suspects' names and faces across all of Europe. "Mykonos has a small airport." Turning to their hosts, he asked, "Can you find someone to sort out immediate travel arrangements while we get ready to leave?" One of the German Federal Police said he would take care of it and left the room hastily.

Before long, the eclectic group of international investigators was on their way to the airport. Unfortunately, organizing the airline tickets and transportation to the airport had taken too long, resulting in the group missing the 1:15 pm Aegean Airlines direct flight to Athens, which further frustrated the Warsaw team. Their only available option was to take the 2:15 pm Swiss flight to Zurich, with a connection to Mykonos via Athens, not arriving until 10:25 pm that evening.

While waiting to board the plane at Frankfurt airport, one of the Germans mentioned that had there been a little more time to organize, they could have arranged a direct flight from Frankfurt to Mykonos on a military aircraft. Later, while the Warsaw team was sitting together in Zurich having coffee between flights, Marek reflected, "That's German efficiency: they'll arrange a direct military flight which will take only three hours versus eight, but it will take twelve hours to orchestrate!"

On the ground in Athens, while waiting for the connecting flight to Mykonos, Murray's mobile rang; he moved away from the group to take the call. As the others began boarding the plane, he returned, and pulling Marek out of line, told him that he'd been ordered to attend a high-priority meeting and would not be proceeding with them to Mykonos.

"Is the meeting about this case?" Marek asked.

"Yes," Murray answered, "I'm quite certain of it—but that's all I know."

"Stay in touch," Marek insisted. "If you discover any new information, we expect you to share it as soon as possible ... no holding anything back from the rest of us."

"I understand," Murray replied. "And I will do so within whatever boundaries may be set for me. You understand that, if I am ordered to be silent on anything, I must comply with those orders. But of course, I will pass on everything that I am at liberty to share. Hopefully, that will be the sum total of what I discover. I just don't know what to expect." Shaking hands with Marek, Murray left, and Marek rejoined the boarding line.

Upon landing in Mykonos, the group headed towards a line of waiting unmarked police cars for the short ride to their hotel, which was located in the less fashionable district of the island, and naturally far less expensive than the coastal areas dotted by luxury hotels and palatial villas. After a late (almost midnight) dinner and drinks with the Hellenic Police ranking brass, who had come to Mykonos to establish a command post in the hotel ballroom (the only room in the hotel that was large enough for this purpose), the investigative team prepared to get to work immediately. However, the police were still in the process of getting the command post staffed and operational, and insisted that no 'outsiders' would be allowed into the room until 8:00 am. And that was final! Unhappily, the investigators headed to bed, planning to reconvene first thing in the morning.

IMBROGLIO TRILOGY

Chapter 26:

Murray Summoned

Murray left the others, exited the Athens International Airport passenger terminal building and stepped into a taxi. He instructed the driver to take him to Universal Aviation Company, located at the General Aviation Terminal (GAT) of Athens Airport. Upon learning the destination, the driver who was already pulling forward, slammed hard on the brakes and protested vehemently. Angrily, he ranted, "You can see it from the main terminal. You expect me to lose my place in the taxi line to take you a kilometer? Όχι (NO)!"

Murray was in no mood to argue, especially with a taxi driver who was yelling at him in broken English and simultaneously cursing him in flamboyant Greek, all the while gesticulating wildly. Taking a U.S. $50 bill from his wallet, he thrust it forward, nearly striking the taxi driver in the face. "Ah … now you American speak good Greek … and with excellent accent too. I go!" the taxi driver responded, his eyes aglow.

The taxi sped off at breakneck speed toward the north end of the airport property. In retrospect, Murray pondered whether the next time a $20 bill might result in a saner and more comfortable ride. Just outside of Gate 12, the taxi screeched to a stop in front of the General Aviation Terminal. "Thank you for the Grand Prix race," Murray remarked as he exited.

In front of the taxi sat a string of three black Chevy Suburbans, all with darkened windows and running engines. The rear passenger door of the third vehicle opened and, hearing his name called, Murray got in. As soon as he had closed the door, the vehicles sped around the building, disappearing through Gate 12, barely slowing as the guards opened the gate. Crossing the tarmac, the three Suburbans came to an abrupt halt not far from an airplane hanger. They waited until, moments later, a private jet, white on top with a blue belly, narrow gold side stripe and the words 'UNITED STATES OF AMERICA' emblazoned in black, taxied rapidly from the runway toward where they waited.

In the Suburban's front seats, the driver and a passenger, both males, were dressed in dark blue suits and wore earpieces and mirror sunglasses. As the jet rolled toward them, the front-seat passenger told Murray to "stay put," and then got out and walked toward the plane.

Almost immediately after rolling to a stop, the plane's front door opened, deploying the stairway. Moments later, six individuals, four men, and two women, deplaned down the stairs. They proceeded directly to the first two vehicles; the man from Murray's Suburban climbed back in. Off all three vehicles sped, back through Gate 12, quickly traversing the short distance to the Attiki Odos Motorway, and then on towards Athens.

"Where exactly are we headed?" questioned Murray.

The front-seat passenger turned towards him and responded, "The U.S. Embassy on Vasilisis Sophias Avenue." A few more minutes passed as the three vehicles raced along in tight formation, when suddenly the driver hit the brakes hard, as the brake lights from the vehicle ahead flashed on, its nose dove and rear-end rose. The two men in the front seat turned towards each other and Murray noted the quizzical looks on their faces. The three vehicles, like a fast-moving train, shifted right simultaneously and headed down an exit. "Change of plans," came the voice of the front-seat passenger. "Back to the airport." The Suburbans crossed over the motorway, turned sharply onto the entrance ramp heading back in the direction from which they had come, now accelerating still faster. They reached the end of the on-ramp at the same time as a string of cars on the motorway. The Suburbans blew by them on the shoulder of the road, much to the unsuspecting motorists' surprise and chagrin.

Reaching the airport, the Suburban motorcade headed directly back to Gate 12, and on reaching it, sped through without slowing, as the security personnel had been forewarned to have the gate open for their imminent return. As the vehicles proceeded across the tarmac, Murray could see prodigious heat plumes rising from the jet's engines. "This is going to be one quick take-off," he thought to himself.

The three vehicles screeched to an abrupt halt in parallel formation facing the aircraft, leaving Murray feeling his stomach rise toward his throat. Before the vehicle's forward motion had ceased, the passenger in front instructed Murray to head for the plane. Murray jumped out, moving quickly towards the aircraft, as did the same six individuals who, only a few minutes earlier, had deplaned. Onboard, someone shouted, "Take any seat; we're taking-off immediately." Murray wondered, *What the hell has happened now?* This felt more like a clandestine extraction from hostile territory under fire than a departure from a public airport. He fumbled to find his seatbelt as the door slammed shut. The jet was already rolling.

No one spoke. The cabin was silent as the plane barreled towards the runway, not taxiing, but more like flying on the ground. Peering out the window, Murray could see a string of commercial aircraft lined up to the right. The pilot's voice boomed over the intercom, "We're cleared to jump the line, so we'll be on the runway momentarily. Fasten your seat belts securely." Murray watched as the aircraft turned towards the runway, cutting in front of the line of commercial airliners. As they turned, he could see that there was still one plane ahead of them, a jumbo with engines whining, sitting at the end of the runway awaiting final takeoff clearance.

The U.S. Government jet abruptly jerked to a stop. Murray lurched forward and then fell back in his seat. His face somewhat pale. The jumbo ahead lumbered forward, engines whining, but did not seem to be gaining speed; presently, it slowed and turned off the runway. "That's it," came the call from the flight deck. "We're on our way! Hang on!" Murray braced himself; the aircraft was rolling again and the pilot advancing the throttles hard, even as the jet executed the turn onto the runway. The engines' whine crescendoed into a scream, as the aircraft shot forward. Murray closed his eyes. He had been in two aircraft crashes in his life: one in a military helicopter and another in a light recon plane that was shot down over Iraq. He did not relish the prospect of a third such incident.

Seconds passed quickly, and much to his relief, Murray felt 'wheels up' and then a steep climb and hard bank to the right that reminded him more of flying in combat aircraft than a private jet. The cabin remained silent, other than the scream of the engines, as the jet climbed up toward its 30,000 foot cruising altitude and headed to an undisclosed destination.

IMBROGLIO TRILOGY

Chapter 27:

A Sudden Change of Plans

The plane continued climbing, banked to the west and out over the Mediterranean Sea, then began leveling off. An older man stood up and walked up the aisle to Murray. "I must apologize, Robert," he began, "for that episode in Athens. A bit of a foul-up." He held out his hand, "My name is James Donovan, with the NSA." He sat down in the empty seat next to Murray.

"We were headed for the American embassy in Athens, when information came through that required a sudden change of plans. You are probably wondering where we are going now."

"The thought had crossed my mind," Murray answered wryly.

"Sicily—the US Naval Air Station Sigonella, in Sicily. However, if all goes according to plan this time, we will remain on the ground there only briefly and then be off again."

"And then?"

"The Mediterranean, to visit an old president!" Murray looked bewildered. Donovan smiled and patted his arm, "Just wait, you'll soon understand." With that, Donovan stood up and went back down the aisle to his seat.

The balance of the short flight was uneventful and unusually quiet. Even those seated with colleagues didn't seem to have much to say. Murray was content to be left alone with his thoughts, glad for a bit of peace—some solitude and time for reflection. It was a luxury he hadn't experienced amidst the whirlwind of the past week.

A sudden jolt caused him to jerk forward and upright in his seat. Momentarily disoriented, he heard the scream of the engines again. The combination of reverse thrusters and sudden braking brought about the realization that the plane had just landed and was hurtling down the runway. The unrelenting stress and physical exhaustion had finally caught up with him. He had lapsed into a deep rem sleep. However brief, he would feel better for it now, especially as he was about to meet 'an old president'—whatever that was supposed to mean.

On the ground, the cabin remained silent, other than Donovan, who had made his way to the front of the plane while it was still taxiing to converse with the pilots. As the jet came to a rest, Donovan turned and announced, "We'll stay onboard for just a few minutes, then we'll be deplaning for the next leg of our journey." He returned to his seat. No one else moved. No one spoke. Murray concluded that, *either everyone else knows what the hell is going on here or is apparently unconcerned. Who are these people?* He wondered. *He didn't recognize them as CIA. Were they all NSA? And did they know who he was? Did it even matter?*

As they sat waiting, the pilots kept the engines running, as if in readiness for another sudden getaway, despite what the passengers had just been told. Murray glanced out the window. So this was NAS Sigonella. He had never been here before, yet knew quite a bit about its operations, having benefited from them on multiple occasions. Darkness had fallen, but on the brightly lit tarmac the relentless, 24/7 activity of moving aircraft, as well as constant vehicular traffic servicing the planes, was visible. As he recalled, Sigonella was a hub for U.S. Naval Air operations across the Mediterranean and Adriatic, as well as landlord to some forty other U.S. Military command operations, most of which served CENTCOM (United States Central Command). He remembered that the base was comprised of two parts, NAS I and NAS II, the latter being the newer portion, where most of the operational units resided. *That's where we must be sitting now,* he thought.

The jet's engines cut out, resulting in an eerie silence, but it didn't last long. He could hear the sound of other engines, and a prop wash growing louder. "Here comes your ride," the pilot announced over the speaker. "Time to go."

The copilot rose from the cockpit and opened the door a row forward and across the aisle from Murray, deploying the staircase. "Keep your heads down!" he shouted over the deafening roar invading the aircraft cabin.

"Let's go; we have no time to waste," Donovan called out from the rear of the jet. Quickly, they all moved forward and down the stairs, Murray in the lead and without a clue as to what was going on or where they were headed next.

Before them a Sikorsky MH-60 (Knighthawk) Multi-Mission Naval Helicopter was rolling to a halt. As the Knighthawk propellers finished turning, the right cabin door opened, even before it had fully stopped. An airman inside was motioning for them to come. The group quickly clambered aboard and into the seats. "Buckle up!" the airman shouted above the roar, as the giant blades began spinning again and the helicopter spun around 180 degrees, in motion once more. Having traveled a mere fifty meters from the jet on which they had just arrived, the helicopter stopped. It remained motionless for a moment before the roar of the engines wound up to a fever pitch and Murray could feel its wheels leaving the ground.

He had never been a fan of helicopters. What was that definition helicopter crews frequently joked? Something about *ten thousand highly complex and totally unrelated parts moving in unison at high speed, bent on self-destruction, furiously beating the air trying to stay aloft?* He preferred airplanes, which could at least glide downward when in trouble, as opposed to helicopters, with their associated euphemism of a so-called 'controlled crash.' He had after all, experienced first-hand, the reality of a 'controlled crash,' suffering a broken back and barely escaping with his life. Murray had no interest in reliving that experience.

As the helicopter rose and began flying in a forward direction, a crewman handed out 'float coats,' the Navy's version of life vests. "I strongly suggest that you put these on; although, it's merely a safety precaution. Nothing to worry about. Besides, it's a clear, calm night which should make for a smooth forty-minute ride." Murray raised his eyebrows and wondered. *Life vests? Little good they would do in shark-infested waters.* Nevertheless, he put one on—his thoughts focused elsewhere.

From where Murray sat, he had a mostly unobstructed view out a window. It was now completely dark below, and if he turned his head and strained, he could still catch a fleeting glimpse of NAS

Sigonella and the shimmering coastal lights of Italy. They were headed out over the Mediterranean Sea. But what point could they reach within forty minutes of eastern Sicily? Algiers, Tunis, Tripoli, Misrata … or Benghazi? … And what on earth did Donovan mean by visiting an old president?

Suddenly, Murray's mind clicked. He knew! Of course, it had to be *Harry S. Truman*. With that revelation, his mind and body relaxed. He decided to sit back and enjoy the moonlit ride on this warm, late spring evening.

Chapter 28:

The Villa

March 21st, Mykonos, Greece

Just after 6:00 am, room phones began to ring, urgently summoning the investigative team to the ballroom. An anonymous tip had been phoned in, purportedly identifying the location where the suspects were staying and saying they had been seen in a coffee shop the previous day. Police were already on the move to position their first units to secure the area. Just down the road from the villa was a café, not yet open for the day's business. Arriving at 6:30 am, police summoned the coffee shop owner to open the door. He immediately identified photographs of all three suspects, confirming that they had been in his shop for coffee and pastries the previous day. He wasn't certain of the precise time, but it had been quite early in the morning, perhaps 8:00 or 8:30, as he recalled. Where they were staying, he did not know, but he assumed it was nearby, as he thought that they had walked down the street after leaving. He did not recall seeing them with a vehicle.

This seemed to correspond with the anonymous tip they had received indicating the villa location as being within a few minutes' walk from the coffee shop. By 7:00 am, the ballroom was a beehive of activity, filled with the combination of Hellenic Police and the investigators who had arrived from Germany the previous evening. It was decided that the SWAT teams would close in first, with the others close behind them. The Greek authorities were determined that this would not be a repeat of Berlin, especially as there were neighboring villas occupied by tourists in close proximity.

The force moved out, as quietly as possible, splitting up and taking various routes so as to arrive undetected from three directions and without sirens or lights. It was 7:20 am when they departed the hotel, and with the advance units already in place, there was no apparent need to disturb the still-sleepy neighbors with a noisy ruckus of sirens and screeching tires. The operation should be executed as discretely as possible, the police commissioner from Syros had stressed.

By 7:45 am, all was ready, and the SWAT teams began their move on the villa. The property was capacious, even for Mykonos, encompassing nearly two acres and enclosed by a three-meter high privacy fence in front and a high wall along each side. The villa was situated near the very back of the property, overlooking the sea. In the front, the driveway was accessed by a tall electronically-controlled steel gate with a keypad on the right gatepost, common practice for high-end villas on Mykonos.

From outside of the compound, the view of the house was screened by a line of towering cypress trees located about four meters distance inside the fence. The curving driveway was offset to the left of the house (looking inward from the street), thus preventing a line of sight view of the house from the road.

As the Greek police did not have a helicopter available on Mykonos, nor a UAV (Unmanned Aerial Vehicle) drone, they were left blind as to what might be occurring inside the compound. The individual calling in the phone tip reported that he had delivered a package to the villa late the previous afternoon, and while waiting outside, had noticed through a window what appeared to be a cache of weapons laid out on a table in plain sight. Early that morning, he had seen photos of the three suspects on television and was certain that one of the men pictured had answered the door. He claimed to have also seen all three at a coffee shop earlier in the day.

Based upon this information regarding a weapons stash, and the absence of a line of sight view, it was decided that they would storm the villa using maximum overmatch. The plan was to use several ladders to surreptitiously breach the fence, placing men between the fence and the cypress tree line. Then, when they were all in place, the front gate would be blown, and three SUV's of heavily armed SWAT police from the mainland would speed down the driveway to the villa. The SUV's had been urgently commandeered by the police earlier that morning from a local car rental company by rousing a very unhappy branch manager from bed. At the same time as the front gate was blown, the police hidden behind the trees would move forward to surround the villa on three sides and provide covering fire if needed, while a Greek Coast Guard cutter would stand-off from the villa. The police fully expected that their suspects would not be arrested without deadly force.

With the ladders in place against the privacy fence, and following a brief delay, the order to proceed was given by the Police Commissioner. Marek, Domiik, Adrianna, and Jedrzej waited in a police communications van parked just down the street from the villa. They had been instructed by the Commissioner to remain there until the 'all-clear' signal had been given from within the villa.

The blast at the gate reverberated through the van. Marek opened the door and jumped out, heading toward the villa at a full run. A few moments passed and Domiik, Jedrzej, and Adrianna followed, with Adrianna calling to the others, "I thought we were supposed to wait for the 'all-clear' signal!" But none of them stopped.

As Marek rounded the gatepost and headed down the driveway, he heard the screeching of the SUV's tires and then a loud crash. *One of them has rear-ended another;* he thought, *just what we needed!* He hadn't run like this in days, and it felt good. Cooped up in conference rooms for the past week, his strict exercise regimen had been abandoned. He reflected with a grimace on how quickly his fitness level must have fallen—he was already beginning to feel winded! Then he remembered that the bulletproof vest he was wearing was heavy at seventeen pounds, and a bit small, constricting his chest and preventing it from expanding with deeper breaths as he ran.

Nearing the villa, he now heard the loud bangs of stun grenades being detonated. He recalled the words of the police commissioner to the SWAT teams. "We want these assassins alive, but do not endanger your own lives to capture them. If you sense danger, shoot first." His words had been understandable, especially in light of

Berlin, but not very satisfactory to the Warsaw team, who desperately needed to question the trio.

Still twenty meters from the front of the villa, Marek stopped for a moment to catch his breath. Adrianna was right on his heels. Looking back, he could see Domiik and Jedrzej approaching. Gunfire erupted from within the house. He held out his arm in front of Adrianna then pulled her down to the ground with him. "Wait—wait until its safe," he reminded himself as much as her.

Heavily armed police were moving all around the perimeter of the house. The front door was hanging ajar, with only the top of it still connected by its hinges, affording a partial view of the foyer. There was another short burst of gunfire. Domiik joined them, as did Jedrzej, exclaiming, "Damn, I hope the police aren't shooting each other in there."

Despite the exigence of the moment, Marek could not help but laugh at his colleague's comment. Images from an old, black-and-white French comedy he had seen years earlier flashed through his mind: police running through the rooms of a house shooting at each other. The others looked at him as if he were crazy. Maybe he was—cracking a bit from the stress and fatigue.

Just then, one of the SWAT team members emerged from the front door and yelled at them to move back behind the line of cypress trees. "They're breaking into a locked closet inside the villa, and it's possible that there is an explosive device inside." They made a quick retreat, as SWAT officers poured out of the villa. A bomb-sniffing dog and its police handler walked down the driveway. The handler looked like the 'Michelin Tire Man,' nearly as round as he was tall, wrapped in his bomb suit. As he and the dog entered the house, Jedrzej expressed the thoughts they were all thinking. "If he finds a bomb like Berlin's, that bulbous suit will be scant consolation."

The minutes passed slowly, as everyone waited. A large group of police had gathered near the driveway entrance gate to wait. Finally, the 'all-clear' signal was given from inside the villa. "Let's go," said Marek, and they hurried towards the villa.

At the door, one of the SWAT team members approached them, taking off his helmet. Sweat was rolling down his face in glistening trickles. "Sorry, but your prey has fled. Flown the proverbial coop."

"What about the shots we heard? Two, maybe three distinct bursts," Domiik questioned.

The man shook his head. "It was nothing! Just nervous trigger fingers spooked by imaginary ghosts. Not unusual, especially in a situation like this—a violent history which has already cost numerous officers' lives. When in doubt, shoot first, ask questions later."

Domiik sat down on the beautifully manicured lawn just a few meters from the villa's front door. "How?" It was all he could do to verbalize the rhetorical question. "How could we have missed them yet again … and what do we do next? Are they still even on Mykonos?" he asked to no one in particular. "Do we now conduct a house to house search of the entire island?"

One by one the others joined him on the lawn. Adrianna suddenly threw back her head and inhaled deeply. *Hmm, what an exquisite fragrance!* Sitting straight up she noticed for the first time a profusion of brightly colored flowers bordering the villa's front garden. *Beautiful! How can this be?* she wondered. *The police, all these people …*

and no one even noticing, much less appreciating, this lovely garden. The world has gone utterly mad.

She awakened from her thoughts to hear Marek, sitting very near her on the lawn, conversing with a SWAT officer. "No one?"

"No, not a living soul."

"But they had been here?"

"Yes, come in and you will see." The team followed him inside, into the spacious dining room located at the front of the villa, to the right of the foyer, behind which was the kitchen.

The dining room table looked like an arsenal. "What the … ?" Jedrzej observed. "There are enough guns here for an American Bonnie and Clyde style shoot-out. What were they planning? Why would they depart leaving all these weapons? What tipped them off? And when? Was it our inopportune decision to release the media blitz?"

Domiik picked up one of the three fully automatic M-16 assault rifles lying on the table, part of a collection which included six handguns, several boxes of ammunition and an assortment of surveillance equipment, including night vision.

"Don't even tell me, " Marek shook his head, "the M-16's are all stamped 'U.S. Government issue.'"

"I can't speak for the full arsenal, but this one certainly is," Domiik responded, shaking his head.

As the teams of police completed their sweep of the villa, they began to gather in the dining room. The SWAT leader spoke, "We've found something else you should see." Following him through the house to what appeared to be the master bedroom suite, he led them into a large walk-in closet. "This closet was locked when we came in.

Notice that the door appears to be wood, but in fact, it has a reinforced steel core and frame, as you can see from the edge and had, until we blew it, a very substantial combination lock. The closet was empty, except for one shelf containing an internet router and a PC. The screen was on and sequentially displaying views of the main indoor living areas as well as outside around the villa's perimeter."

A cable dangled from it and appeared to have been severed. "This my friends," the officer pointed, "would have resulted in Berlin #2. There was a cardboard box of C-4 sitting atop a plastic crate on the floor with the other end of the cable hanging from it. "You may recall that there was a short delay earlier before the command was given by the Commissioner to 'GO!' He was awaiting confirmation that we had isolated the entire island. There will be many angry people this morning, tourists, shopkeepers and the like, who will not understand why there has been no cell or internet service across the entire island since just before 8:00 am. Moments before he gave the order to proceed, all outside access to the island was cut, as well as all internet and cell phone access on the island. We were concerned with just such an eventuality as this … like Germany. We were not about to allow a repeat."

Adrianna spoke, "So, they intended to blow up the villa with only the police in it."

"That we don't know and cannot assume. There can be no doubt that the suspects, or someone else, was prepared to detonate the C-4 remotely. From where? Who? When? These are all questions with answers we do not yet know."

Marek went outside where it was quiet to call Murray.

Chapter 29:

Night Extraction

Much Earlier That Morning, on Mykonos

Shortly after 1:00 am, the three suspects quietly left the villa by car. Dressed in dark clothing and faces blackened with charcoal, they headed south towards the airport and then west, to the coast. Following the road onto the peninsula, they passed Casa Del Mar Mykonos Seaside Resort—one of the most exclusive luxury resorts on the island. Continuing on a little less than a kilometer, they entered the grounds of the island's waste treatment plant, where they could be certain they would not be seen. The driver turned off the headlights. From here they would proceed slowly by moonlight.

Before them, the roadway split. They veered left, making their way past the treatment plant buildings. At the south end of the facility, the road curved right to pass along the southern side of the facility buildings and the open top treatment tanks. However, they followed a left fork onto a single lane that dead-ended two hundred meters further on, next to the last building in the complex. They were now at the southernmost tip of the Mykonos island.

Here, they abandoned the car, keys in the ignition, after removing from the trunk a Zodiac rubber boat, electric air pump, Evinrude 25 hp outboard motor, gas can, TAC flashlight, and handheld, marine GPS. Attaching the air pump cables to the car's battery, they waited while the boat inflated. It required two trips to carry the raft, its motor and their gear along with water bottles and snacks taken from the villa, the seventy-five meters across the rocks to an embankment overlooking the water and then down to the shore below. There they loaded the raft and waited. At precisely 2:15 am, they walked the raft out into the water, climbed in and started the engine, holding it on the lowest throttle setting to minimize the engine din.

The tide was going out. The Mediterranean has a very low amplitude tide, typically maxing out at a fraction of one meter on Mykonos. Still, in a rubber boat, even a minimal tidal pull can have an effect. They maintained the engine on very low throttle, just a bit above idle until they were out of earshot of the coast. Then they increased it to the full throttle position, which still wasn't particularly fast. The moon was nearly full, and its light reflecting off the water provided enough illumination to see clearly for navigation, but also silhouetted them against the dark sea. They headed due south, out into the open waters of the Mediterranean Sea.

Turning on the GPS, they held a straight course. Their escape had been flawless. The sea was calm and the only sound to be heard was the drone of the small outboard motor. In the warm evening air, their cares seemed to retreat for the moment, until they saw a large boat moving fast across their path a little over a kilometer away. It was brightly lit, and—drawing closer—they identified it as a Greek Coast Guard cutter. Suddenly, its searchlight flashed in their direction.

IMBROGLIO TRILOGY

They killed the motor and glided to a soundless stop. Ducking down as low as they could in the bobbing black rubber boat, they remained motionless and silent. The searchlight flashed towards them a second time. Collectively, they held their breath … waiting. The sound of the cutter's engines remained constant as it passed before them and then began to diminish, as it slowly moved out of sight headed toward Mykonos.

They restarted the motor and continued on. After seventy-four minutes of running time at full throttle, they stopped and shut off the motor. This was the GPS spot. Now, they had to wait … it should be exactly thirteen more minutes.

Right on schedule, the water about two hundred meters south of them stirred. A black behemoth rose from the deep, like a primeval monster from the ancient past. As it did, the sea around them remained utterly silent, other than the rushing sound of water pouring off the rising leviathan. When the water had settled, they engaged the engine once more and began gliding slowly towards the huge, wet, black object glimmering in the moonlight.

A hatch opened, and a dim red glow could be seen emanating upward from below. They maneuvered the rubber boat toward it. Four men carrying flashlights appeared on deck and tossed down a chain ladder with hard plastic rungs. "Leave the motor running on idle and tie off to the ladder. Send the woman up first, then the two of you," came a stern command from above. In that order, the trio left their little boat.

A crewman clambered down the ladder after them. Reaching down, he turned the motor so that it would head away from the submarine, then rotated the throttle to slow and untied it. The ladder was pulled up, and a canister thrown into the rubber boat as it motored away from the sub. Seconds later, a half-meter long, brilliant orange flame shot out from the canister. They could hear the air chambers popping as the rubber boat caught fire and unceremoniously sank, dragged beneath the surface by the engine's weight.

The three were led forward to the open hatch and climbed down. They heard the hatch close hard and seal behind them. Seconds later, the dive horn sounded three short blasts.

"Welcome aboard *USSN 774*, the *USS Virginia*, fast attack nuclear sub ... and, just so you know, you are guests of the United States Navy ... and under arrest," an officer informed them.

Chapter 30:
Visiting an Old President

The Knighthawk helicopter turned south-southeast then maintained the heading for thirty minutes. Below, in the light of the full moon, Murray could see that the water's surface was smooth as a sheet of black glass. Moonlight shone across it—shimmering in the darkness. Then he saw something else, off in the distance, at first a faint glow, then a brilliant, rapidly growing expanse. A translucent river, flowing in the black sea. A ribbon of light creating a fitting pathway leading straight to the old president.

Murray discerned the change in rotor pitch instantly, which was followed by a reduction in the engines' roar. Below, the lights of ships reflecting against the dark water came into view. The bioluminescent trail of algae led straight to the fleet's center, churned up by 'the old President,' *Harry S. Truman*, a United States Nimitz class super aircraft carrier, CVN 75, launched from Newport News Ship Building in September of 1996. Together with its strike group of surface ships and submarines, it reminded Murray of a group of small islands, but these islands were all moving, silently and in perfect unison. The *Truman's* flight deck was awash with light as the helicopter turned once more to approach the carrier from its port side. Moments later, the Knighthawk's wheels touched down on the carrier's flight deck, its door slid open, and the seven passengers scrambled out.

With the admonition to keep their heads down, a deck handler guided them quickly across the busy flight deck. Entering the carrier, they were led to the midships BDS (Battle Dressing Station), at the base of the Island (the aircraft carrier's operations tower). There they were greeted by the ship's Executive Officer (XO), who welcomed them onboard, then briefed them on the location and use of the EEBD (Emergency Escape Breathing Device), in the event of a fire or smoke while onboard.

Murray had always marveled at the immense size and complexity of these floating cities, capable of projecting America's military might to any point on the globe. With a total compliment of 5,000 plus personnel on the *Truman*, combined with an additional 2,500 in the balance of the battle group, these nuclear-powered behemoths of the sea constitute the largest warships ever built by any nation. They remain operational for fifty years, requiring only one midlife refueling of their nuclear reactors.

※ ※ ※

Marek *Calls Murray*

Once onboard, Murray arranged to have his calls forwarded to the Truman. When Marek called at 10 am, he was routed to Murray onboard the aircraft carrier without his knowledge. Marek was direct. "Where are you? And what have you learned?"

Murray ignored both of Marek's questions, replying instead, "On the second occasion we met in Warsaw, I asked you if you trusted me. You may recall that this question followed my admission that we—as in, the United States Government—were aware that both the weapon and bullet were of American origin."

"Yes, I recall that."

"Now, I must ask you once again. Do you and your Warsaw team still trust me?"

There was a pause on the line. "We do."

"Marek, I'm speaking of *real* trust here. I mean blind trust. I need all of you to trust me completely."

"I can speak for the rest. We do … all of us!"

"Good, then I need you to do something for me based on that trust. I need you and the others—Domiik, Jedrzej, and Adrianna—to follow my instructions precisely. Will you do that?"

"Yes. But what are you asking?"

"You raided the Mykonos villa this morning and came up empty-handed, correct?"

"The raid was commenced just after 7:45 this morning, and, yes, we came up with nothing but some additional American weapons and more C-4, which, when the lab analysis comes back, I'm certain will also prove to have been American-sourced. But I assume that you already know that."

Murray did not respond to Marek's last comment. "All right, there's nothing more your team can do on Mykonos. You need to come here."

"And where is here?" Marek responded.

"Just trust me and come. Yes?"

A pause and then, "Okay."

"Get out of there … I mean the villa. Make some excuse that you need to return to Poland or wherever ASAP. Say that you think the suspects have already left the island. Go to the Mykonos airport, but instead of the passenger terminal, go to Euro Aviation at the charter terminal. Can you be there in three hours—say 1:00 pm?"

"We can be there."

"Good! A U.S. Navy plane will land at 1:00 pm sharp to pick you up. Don't say anything about this to anyone outside your team. Alright?"

"And where will the U.S. Navy plane be taking us?"

"Marek, you just have to trust me on this one. It will all become clear when you get here. Are you with me?"

"Yes. Okay, I'll tell the others, make our excuses and head for the airport. We'll stop at the hotel for our things on the way."

"Just be there. The Navy plane will not want to wait. Questions will be asked if they linger on the ground too long. It needs to be a quick in and out."

The call ended. Marek was mystified and wondered how he would explain this to the Greeks, much less to his own team. The villa had been cleared out by now, except for the Greek forensics team, which was combing the area for clues. He walked up to where a group of police stood talking with the Warsaw and German teams and addressed the Commissioner. "We've been recalled to Warsaw. Interpol believes that the suspects have already left the island."

"That's preposterous!" the Commissioner responded. "We have the island sealed. Impossible! They could not have escaped."

"All the same, we have been recalled immediately. However, before we leave, I do want to compliment you on your foresight in cutting off internet and cellular service to the island before the operation. I'm certain that you'll catch hell from the local politicians, after they suffer the wrath of tourists and merchants who have been inconvenienced, with no credit card verification services, etc., during the black-out. Nonetheless, you saved many lives today, and I'm certain that I speak on behalf of my Polish and German colleagues when I say that your police officers demonstrated a very high degree of professionalism in carrying out every aspect of this operation."

"Thank you," the commissioner responded. "And we will stay in close communication as our operations here continue. Don't stray too far, so that it will be easy for you to return quickly to Mykonos when we have captured these criminals. It is only a matter of time now. We will apprehend them!"

"I certainly hope you do. And quickly." Marek shook hands with the Commissioner and other leaders of the Hellenic Police, as well as with the German contingent. Domiik, Jedrzej, and Adrianna did likewise. The Poles were all a bit baffled by Marek's sudden behavior and unexplained change of plans. After all, he worked for Interpol and they for the Polish government. Interpol could not recall them ... and to Warsaw? Why? But their trust in Marek was such that they played along, even though they had no clue as to what was motivating his actions.

Marek turned to the team as the handshaking came to a polite conclusion. "Come, we must get back to our hotel right away and then to the airport." The Commissioner ordered one of his assistants to arrange a car to take them to their hotel and then on to the airport. Overhearing this, Marek thanked him for the courtesy.

Arriving at the hotel, the police driver told them he would wait for them. "No need to hurry." Inside the hotel, they headed directly to the elevators.

Once the doors closed, Marek spoke. "Come with me to my room." They each nodded in agreement. Closing the door of his room, he motioned for them to sit. He pulled up the coverlet of the yet unmade bed for additional seating. Marek remained standing, "I've just spoken to Murray."

"Yes, so we assumed," replied Domiik, an eyebrow raised.

"I cannot explain at this moment all that he told me. For now, what is important is that we have a 1:00 pm flight from the airport here. Murray didn't tell me much more … just asked me … that is … us, to trust him."

"Trust him?" Jedrzej questioned. "The fingerprints of America are all over this mess, and he asks you … us to 'just trust him?'"

"I know it sounds insane given today's events, in addition to those of the past week, but what choice do we have? We have no real leads. And … I do trust him. When he was on the phone, I had to speak for all of us without the opportunity to consult with you. Forgive me, but I did and … I agreed."

"So, where are we off to, or perhaps we shouldn't ask?" Domiik inquired.

"I don't know … and that's the truth. All I know is that a U.S. Navy plane will be picking us up at 1:00 pm sharp, and they don't want to be seen waiting around on the ground. So, if you are agreed?" All three nodded, though their eyes revealed confusion mixed with doubt and anxiety. "Get packed and let's be out of here in fifteen minutes."

A quarter of an hour later, they met downstairs to check out. This accomplished, they loaded their luggage into the police car, and the driver started for the airport. "What airline are you flying?" he asked.

"I don't know," Marek responded deceptively. The driver looked at him askance. "My office is making the arrangements for the tickets. They didn't have the details yet, so I am to phone them when we arrive at the airport. They said it would take a little while to accomplish. You know, the bureaucracy and all. Not like you or I deciding to travel for ourselves. We'd just go online and book a ticket. Right?"

"Yes, that's exactly what I'd do," the driver remarked.

"Well—you know these government functionaries! They see it as their purpose in life to make certain that we don't spend too much for the tickets. Heaven help us if we incurred the extravagance of business class, or worse yet, first class."

"Oh yes," the driver agreed. "It would create a national economic crisis if you did that." They both laughed. In the back seat, Domiik, Jedrzej, and Adrianna did not laugh.

Arriving at the terminal, Marek said, "Just drop us off in the middle there. That way when I call the office to find out what airline we're on, at least we won't be at the wrong end of the terminal." The driver chuckled good-heartedly and pulled over. Helping them with their luggage, he took special care of Adrianna's and made a point of offering her a lengthy good-bye.

As they walked into the terminal, Domiik mused, "I think the young police officer is smitten!"

"Don't even start," Adrianna retorted with a frosty stare. Turning to Marek, she asked, "What now?"

"We'll give 'lover boy' a minute or two to finish gaping at you, and, once he drives away, we'll catch a ride to Euro Aviation at the charter terminal."

❋ ❋ ❋

Hard Landing

They arrived at the Euro Aviation charter terminal just after 12:30 pm At the counter, they were informed that their plane was scheduled for an on-time arrival at 1:00 pm The woman at the desk looked them over carefully as if she knew something more than she was saying. She invited them to help themselves to the coffee, soft drinks, and refreshments which had been set out. "Have you had lunch?" she questioned. "We can have sandwiches prepared. It will only take a few minutes, and you have plenty of time before your flight departure."

Marek thought it was a good idea. "Yes, that would be very nice. Now that I think about it, we didn't have much in the way of breakfast this morning." He remembered how they had been awakened early by the phone calls. "That would be excellent. Adrianna here looks like she's ready to bite one of us. It might not be safe to be on a plane with her being so hungry."

Adrianna flashed a half smile. "You have no idea how much you have to fear from me!"

"We'd better watch our behavior," Domiik joked.

She laughed. "Yes, *boys*, you'd better!"

They headed for the complimentary beverage table. "Ravenous ladies first," Marek waved her ahead.

A very pleasing platter of sandwiches appeared a few minutes later. "This is the only way to fly!" quipped Jedrzej, "No crowded terminals, check-in and security lines or stale peanuts and pretzels. I could grow accustomed to this very quickly."

"Don't," responded, Domiik. "It won't last. Only the Americans fly in private jets, not us humble Eastern Europeans."

"That's true!" Jedrzej responded, a smile spreading across his face. "Of course, it may soon become routine for Adrianna. Murray did offer her a position in DC with … " he made an obvious show of glancing around the room secretively. "You know: *The Company!*' I'd bet money they fly on private jets all the time."

Adrianna smiled again, "I promise I'll send each of you a postcard from DC … with fondest memories."

Minutes later, the woman at the reception desk came over to them. "You can gather your belongings. Your plane has just landed and will arrive momentarily." They quickly finished their sandwiches and thanked her again as they prepared to head for the doors leading to the tarmac, but not before Jedrzej glanced at the three sandwiches remaining on the tray.

"Should we take these along with us, just in case Adrianna gets hungry again during our flight?"

"I'll be fine…I've satiated my appetite. You'll be safe with me on the plane," Adrianna's broad smile beamed.

"Better safe than sorry," Marek joked.

"Being a U.S. Government plane, I expected that we would be served a three-course dinner onboard," Domiik added.

As the U.S. Navy plane taxied toward them, Adrianna turned to Marek, "That's rather odd-looking for a naval aircraft. Are the Americans still using old propeller planes?"

"Well, it's no fighter-jet, that's for sure. And you're right; it is a bit odd looking. As to the propellers, I assume there must be some reason for still flying Navy planes that have them."

The aircraft came to a halt, but its engines remained running at a high pitch, making it seem as though they had barely throttled down. A side door opened and a naval officer exited the plane by the short doorway stair, coming toward them at a run.

The team opened the building's double doors and stepped outside. "Mr. Farkas, sir?" the officer asked.

"Yes," Marek responded.

Please follow me. And please be careful to stay in line with me and away from the props."

Once on board, they buckled in immediately as the plane was already heading for the runway. "What's our destination?" Marek shouted to the officer?

"To see the ole' man."

"What did he say?" Domiik asked Marek above the clamor.

Marek shrugged his shoulders, "I couldn't hear him."

The engines roared even louder as the plane taxied the short distance to the runway, turned, and then accelerated for take-off.

The ride was noisy but smooth. No one talked. Nearly an hour out over the Mediterranean, the engine noise ebbed as the plane began to bank. "There he is," the officer shouted above the roaring engine noise.

"There who is?" Adrianna hollered back at him.

"The ole' man. The *Harry S. Truman* of course."

Adrianna peered out the window. Below her, she could now clearly see a massive aircraft carrier, seemingly rising from the water to meet their descending aircraft. "You mean that we're going to try to land on that?"

"Of course! But not to worry, it won't be some wild, white-knuckle landing like you see in the movies. This is a Marine Corps Osprey. Heard of it?"

Adrianna shook her head, "No!"

"Phenomenal machine. It flies just like a plane, taking off and landing on airfield runways. But it can also land vertically, like a helicopter. The pilot will set it down on the carrier's flight deck smooth as silk. You'll see."

Adrianna sat up straight in her seat and yanked her seatbelt hard. She decided that, unlike Jedrzej, she definitely preferred the many inconveniences of commercial airline travel: bad meals … no meals … peanuts, pretzels, security lines and all.

The sound of the engine grew louder, then to a distinctly pitched rumble. Adrianna could feel the reverberation of prop wash beating the sides of the aircraft. She nervously watched the huge engines, located on the very end pods of the wings and looking as if they were ready to fall off at any moment, begin to rotate upward on their pillions, from horizontal to vertical, pointing skyward. Simultaneously, she sensed that the plane was rapidly descending vertically while still flying forward, creating an unnatural sensation of falling forward while remaining level. She could see the aircraft carrier's massive tower coming into view horizontally, then sliding past her vertically, as the aircraft continued its descent towards the deck. Now the tower loomed high above her, and the Osprey's descent ended abruptly, as it slammed down on the flight deck so hard that she felt the jolt all the way up her spine.

The engine roar died away to a low-pitched rumble. "Smooth as silk?" she called out to the officer as she stood. "Maybe next time, when he lands this thing for the second time in his career, he'll do it 'smooth as silk!'"

"Now be nice to our hosts, Adrianna," Marek scolded playfully. "After all, if they decide they don't like you, they could toss you overboard. It would be a long swim back to Mykonos!"

"Not to worry," she answered. "I'm a strong swimmer."

Marek eyed her up and down. "I'll bet you are!"

Chapter 31:

Surprise at Sea

Upon the arrival of Marek, Arianna, Domiik, and Jedrzej on the USS Harry S. Truman, they were ushered into a small training room. Murray was there to greet them. "You certainly have a panache for the dramatic, Murray," Marek quipped as they shook hands.

"I apologize for the cloak and dagger intrigue, but I can assure you, as you will shortly see for yourself, that it is truly necessary. Please sit down. You are guests of the United States Navy, and the Navy will do everything possible to ensure your comfort, and assist you while onboard. I suppose you wonder what I, and now you, are doing onboard a United States Navy aircraft carrier in the middle of the Mediterranean Sea?"

"You must be a mind reader," Jedrzej responded.

"Well, as I said, you are guests aboard this ship. However, you are not the only guests here. There are others. In particular, there are three others. Tom Barrington, Ryan Flynn, and Rebecca Moore are all also here, as guests of my government.

The moment passed slowly as the others processed the words Murray had so glibly spoken. "You mean to tell us that the killers identified by Herr Kohler in his photographs are also aboard?" Domiik responded in a voice exhibiting wonder, but tainted with disgust.

"Yes—"

Jedrzej interrupted him. "As guests? Here? Criminals— murderous assassins! They killed two heads of state, including, let me remind you, my own country's Prime Minister! They are also responsible for the tragic deaths of over a dozen German police officers. Just this morning they nearly blew up a villa which the four of us could have been inside … and you call them guests of your country! Murray, this time you have gone too far … this is simply way too far!"

"I understand your outrage," Murray replied, "and I would agree wholeheartedly with you. However, there is an old spy craft adage that 'the value of any piece of intelligence is dependent upon its provenance.' Remember that when we first met Herr Kohler, I was not altogether convinced about the guilt of his contract employees. If these three are to be believed—and I will not say that as yet I even fully understand their account—then there is a covert back-story to everything we think we know. For the present, all I am asking is that you hear me out … more accurately, hear them out. Put aside your anger and exercise the self-restraint necessary to hear their story without any preexisting biases stemming from what you 'think you know' regarding this case."

"And how are we supposed to do that?" Domiik asked.

"Right now … I want you to meet them … here … now."

"But we know they are guilty," Jedrzej responded indignantly. "There can be no doubt. We have their photos, video from numerous CCTV surveillance cameras from the bombing scene in Prague, their hotel … and they have also been identified by hotel staff there. And then Berlin's train station and Athen's airport CCTV. Now you say they may not be guilty—that you believe them? Why, because they are Americans? Because they are working directly for the CIA when they are not employed by Herr Kohler? No Murray, I respect you, but this is going too far! The CIA and your government, your president Michaels, cannot get away with this." His voice growing more furious as he spoke.

Domiik stepped in, "Murray, I will listen, but this had better have real substance, and not merely constitute the white-washing of an American rogue operation gone wrong. If it is, we refuse to participate in a cover-up effort with your government."

"I understand your feelings and reservations fully, and I would not … I am not … asking anything of the sort. I too want to get the bottom of this. When their story was initially related to me, I didn't believe it at first, not a word of it, until I spoke with them myself. However, now I am beginning to believe they are telling the truth, and if so, they are just as much unwitting victims of this plot as are the rest of us. But you must decide for yourselves. Will you agree just to meet them and listen with an open mind?"

Marek answered first, "Yes, I want the truth also, whatever it may be."

"Domiik?"

"I'll listen, but I make no promises beyond that."

"Adrianna, you?"

Adrianna looked at Murray thoughtfully, pondering her answer. "All right. I will."

"And you, Jedrzej? Can you put aside your anger long enough to listen … with an open mind?"

Jedrzej was silent. He was uncomfortable being cornered by this scenario, and, for the first time since meeting Murray, he disliked him intensely. He was convinced he could no longer trust the American. He gave no response. In fact, he felt sick inside. Was he being railroaded by Murray into giving his assent? This had all the earmarks of an American cover-up … and Murray seemed to be using peer pressure tactics to bully him into conforming with the others.

"All I ask is that you hear them out. Nothing more … I promise. Just listen to their story and decide. Will you just do that?"

Jedrzej sat motionless, arms folded across his chest. What could he say? The perpetrators were being treated as guests onboard and, well, if he said "no," what would happen then? His colleagues would undoubtedly proceed to interview the fugitives without him. Anyway, they were at sea. There was nowhere for him to go. "All right," he blurted back at Murray gruffly. "But not because I want to … only because I'm a virtual prisoner on board this massive ship surrounded by thousands of American military personnel. And perhaps it won't be Adrianna who will have a long swim back to Mykonos—it will be me!"

Murray smiled, attempting to break the tension. "I'm sure that even if you refuse, the U.S. Navy won't throw you overboard."

"Ahhh! But they might force me to 'walk the plank!'" Jedrzej retorted dryly, his voice and expression devoid of humor.

"Right, then. Let me take you to them."

Chapter 32:
Double Image

Murray led them down a passageway to a more spacious room, decorated with naval-themed pictures, and memorabilia. At one end of a large conference table were seated three men, and a beautiful woman with large blue eyes, a creamy complexion, and strikingly brilliant red hair.

Entering the room, Marek and the Polish investigators remained standing while the others rose from their chairs in awkward silence to greet them. Murray stepped forward and began. "This is Marek Farkas of Interpol, Lyon, and my Polish colleagues, Domiik Figurski, Agencja Bezpieczeństwa Wewnętrznego, Internal Security, Jedrzej Lorbiecki, Government Protection Bureau and last, but certainly not least, Adrianna Bartoszck, Weapon Forensics expert."

Then, turning to the others, he continued, "This is James Donovan, with the American NSA, the National Security Agency." Donovan held out his hand to Marek and the Warsaw team, who shook hands with him warily. Murray continued, "And to James's left are Rebecca Moore, Tom Barrington, and Ryan Flynn—the three American suspects you have been seeking." The Warsaw team did not extend their hands to greet the three.

"Please, be seated" Murray began again, "I know that this meeting will be uncomfortable for some of you ... well, probably for all of us, but it is critically important that we put our personal feelings aside for the moment and seek to discern the truth. Our respective countries and governments all have a great deal riding on what happens here. In fact, so does all of Europe and the United States, as our failure to discover the truth could have far greater international consequences than we have experienced thus far.

"When I told Marek, I was being summoned from Athens, that was the truth. In fact, it was the whole truth as far as I knew it at the time. I was told that I would be picked up and driven to an urgent meeting at the U.S. Embassy in Athens. However, on the way to that meeting, plans changed abruptly; we turned around and headed back to the airport. That sudden alteration of plans occurred because a U.S. submarine was rendezvousing to pick up three people in a rubber boat in the middle of the Mediterranean Sea. These three people to be precise." Murray extended his right arm in an arc toward Barrington, Flynn, and Moore.

Upon our hasty return to Athens airport, I boarded a U.S. State Department jet, along with a team from NSA headed by James Donovan, and flew to the US Naval Air Station Sigonella, in Sicily. Upon arrival, we immediately boarded a U.S. Navy helicopter which brought us here. I understand that your journey was not much different from my own.

"I would now like to introduce James Donovan. He'll provide you with the same background information which was related to me earlier today upon my arrival. James ... "

All eyes turned to Donovan. "I contacted Murray yesterday," because of a call I received from a young woman whom I know very well, Rebecca Moore," he gestured towards the woman seated next to him. "Rebecca worked for me at the NSA. That call came in yesterday, in the early morning hours, around 5 am DC time. I was rudely awakened from a very sound sleep," he added, flashing a teasing smile at Rebecca, "But I'd prefer that Rebecca told you herself, about the reason and nature of that call."

After a moment's hesitation, the red-haired woman began to speak. "What I'm about to tell you may seem ... well, bizarre ... no, not bizarre ... absurd, but it is also true. You may choose to believe it or not, but it is the truth.

"I understand that you have met Herr Kohler, our contract employer. And, as you know, we have each worked for Euro Strategic Security Services as independent contractors for one-to-two years. As Herr Kohler informed you, we received a private offer, a roughly forty-five to sixty-day personal protection assignment for an extremely wealthy Greek shipping magnate and his family, as well as for their visiting guests. We were told that once a year he blocks out a month or so in the springtime to invite each of his company's top clients for a week at a time to his seaside villa on Mykonos.

We approached our employer, Herr Kohler, and he graciously agreed to give us a leave of absence for this private contract assignment. The work we do can be extremely stressful. Rarely the glamorous life portrayed on television or in the movies, most of the time it is tedious and exhausting. The clientele can vary widely: from pleasant to rude, arrogant and obnoxious. Unfortunately, the latter is far more common than the former.

"We are security professionals and take seriously the protective services we provide. This temporary assignment was portrayed as being uncomplicated and relaxed at a spacious private villa on the Mediterranean coast and, most importantly, protecting a family, their business associates, and friends who were very low-key and amiable. To put it succinctly, a plum job! And a well-compensated one at that!

"We began the assignment earlier this month. We'd been told that we would be traveling to Greece. However, at the last minute, we were informed that there would be a several day delay. We were told the villa's owners had previously employed a contractor to perform some major remodeling updates to the property prior to their return for the planned period of guest entertainment they had scheduled. However, the contractor had fallen behind schedule in completing the renovations, and the villa was not ready….

"This did not seem unusual to us. Do construction contractors ever complete a renovation project on time? And this is Greece, where schedules for anything, in particular construction, are at best ambiguous! Remodeling a large Greek villa can take years to complete, especially with an absentee owner who is not there to ensure that completion dates are met.

"So we had some time to kill." Rebecca's face flushed, "I mean, 'time off!' The client's contact man was very apologetic, assuring us we would be paid the full fee, despite the delay. And, as an added perk to compensate for the delay, we were invited to spend the intervening time at a private chalet in Switzerland with all expenses paid. At this time of year, there is still excellent spring skiing higher-up in the Swiss Alps. Unfortunately, this chalet wasn't near any of the best ski areas. Still, a few days of paid rest in the Swiss Alps during such an unseasonably warm spring was naturally very appealing.

"So, off we went on a holiday which we all enjoyed immensely. We spent most of our time sleeping, eating, and just relaxing. The chalet was fully stocked. We could have spent a month there and not run out of anything besides fresh fruit and vegetables, which had also been amply provided for us, enough for our entire stay! Good thing too, as it was extremely remote … isolated … the nearest hamlet was a thirty-five-minute excursion down a winding mountain road. But once we were settled in the chalet, there was absolutely no reason to drive down to the village.

"Well, what began as a few days was soon extended to a week. Once again, this occurred under the pretext of uncompleted renovations. We weren't concerned. The break was just what the three of us needed. We are all good friends, and the chalet was spacious. We were perfectly content cooking meals, talking, and watching movies. It was wonderful! The chalet had an extensive film library. And each of us appreciated having some time alone. The hiking was amazing and the scenic views spectacular, with early spring wildflowers carpeting the mountainsides.

"So, that's how we passed the time until the message came to leave for Athens. Also … you must understand, the chalet was completely isolated with no TV reception or cable, and certainly no internet access. It was completely 'disconnected' from the outside world. In fact, the message to come to Mykonos was delivered by a local man who received it from a courier service in the town below and carried it up to us. He was the caretaker of the chalet. Given the total isolation, we knew nothing of the events unfolding in Prague, Warsaw, or Berlin. And, quite honestly, even if we had, we would have blocked them out! It was so refreshing to be totally 'unplugged' from everything—a privilege seldom experienced in our line of work.

"When the news arrived that the Greek project was finally ready to 'go,' we immediately packed up and headed out. There was a vehicle at the chalet, a Land Rover AWD, which was at our disposal. However, we had arrived at the chalet and were picked-up to leave by a black car service. The driver took us to Zurich airport, where we boarded a flight for Athens."

"At what time did you land in Athens?" Marek asked.

"At 3:45, Ryan responded.

"That's right; it was just shortly before 4:00 pm," Rebecca added.

"Then what?" Marek probed.

Tom answered, "We had reservations at a hotel in Rafina, so we took a taxi there. It's not far from the Athens airport. In the morning, we boarded a Golden Star Ferries for Mykonos, arriving on the island just after noon local time. A rental car had been reserved for us. We loaded up our luggage and drove to the villa. Ryan moved us in, while Rebecca perused the kitchen and checked out the amenities, and I drove into town mid-afternoon to pick up take-out from a local restaurant for a late lunch and bought some groceries at an outdoor market. We spent the evening at the villa."

Tom continued, "early the following morning; we walked to a nearby café for breakfast. Then, we returned to the villa and conducted our security survey of the house and grounds. The owners were scheduled to arrive the next evening … I believe that would be right about now.

That morning, two large boxes had arrived for us and later in the day a package addressed to the villa's owner was delivered. Opening our boxes, we found three fully automatic M-16's, several handguns and a great deal of ammunition in the first. In the other, we found night vision and a cache of surveillance equipment.

We had been told that the weapons and necessary equipment to adequately protect the client, his family, and guests would be provided, but we did find the M-16's a bit extreme for a civilian job in Greece. I mean, it's not Iraq, or a Mexican drug cartel's villa, after all! However, some clients have rather odd ideas. Maybe they watch too much TV—too many action movies, as a result they think that an assailant or kidnapper is going to attack with uzis and hand grenades. And the more they fixate on it, the more paranoid they become. We call it the 'Hollywood effect.' So, although it was overkill, having not personally met the client, we all had a good laugh and dismissed it as the overactive imagination of a fearful Greek shipping magnate.

We discovered a locked closet in the master bedroom, which is hardly a strange phenomenon, as many wealthy people store valuables in a strongroom and have safes. Some also have 'safe rooms' built into their homes. But we did become suspicious when we also found concealed video cameras hidden throughout the villa. However, there weren't any in the bedrooms or bathrooms. The surveillance cameras had only been installed in public areas and outdoors, so it wasn't any sort of voyeurism issue.

"After inspecting the villa, we concluded that the only place from which the cameras could be controlled was the locked closet.

Again, all of it seemed a bit over the top for Mykonos, but we were still okay with the assignment and planned to discuss these things with the client when he and his family arrived. We always initiate such conversations with a new client … it's part of the protocol on first-time assignments, as well as when we return to previous assignments following a hiatus.

"Late morning, we decided to do a little shopping and explore Mykonos town. Ryan and I wandered down the street while Rebecca stopped into a shop to pick up a few items. Rebecca, you should describe what happened next."

Rebecca nodded, "as I paid the clerk, I caught sight of a newspaper for sale with our pictures on the front page. I picked up the paper, quickly flipping it over, so the photos didn't show, paid for my purchases, and rejoined the others at a nearby outdoor cafe. I showed them the headline. We purchased a pay-as-you-go mobile phone and immediately headed back to the villa. On reading the newspaper article, we discovered that, while vacationing in Switzerland, we had become dangerous and wanted international fugitives. The news article stated that we were the prime suspects in the murders of two European Heads of State, as well as responsible for the ambush death of two German police SWAT Teams. We were stunned! We wondered what to do, and then I thought of James, so I immediately phoned him and asked his advice."

"And what did James Donovan of NSA tell you?" Marek asked.

"He told us that he had also seen the story the previous evening on U.S. television and had been trying ever since to reach me. Of course, he wanted to know what was I into. So, I very quickly related to him what I have just told you—the abbreviated version. He told me to sit tight; he'd get back to us shortly."

"And then ... ?"

"We did just that. A couple of hours later, he called back and told us to rent or buy a rubber boat, motor, fuel tank, dark clothing, charcoal and a list of other items ... and he'd be back to us with instructions."

"Why charcoal?" Domiik queried.

"For our faces. James said that clear skies were predicted, and a full moon as well. With my fair complexion, he worried that my face would reflect moonlight like a beacon against the dark water!

"We also found some touristy-type clothing in the villa: hats and island-style, casual clothes which we could wear, and blend in better. The guys took the car to go and buy what was needed. In town, they divided up the shopping list and split up, as by themselves they would be less easily recognized

I remained at the villa, as they felt I would draw too much attention. Then we waited for James's next call. He provided instructions and timing for a sea extraction. After Tom and Ryan returned from town, we stayed in the villa until well after midnight before making our escape. Fortunately, we slipped away undetected, although we had a close call with a Greek Coast Guard cutter and narrowly missed being spotted."

Silence invaded the room. For several seconds no one spoke.

"That is quite the story," Marek said thoughtfully, leaning back in his chair. "What do you think?" he turned to his colleagues.

"A fascinating tale," Adrianna responded dryly.

Domiik sat thinking.

Jedrzej slowly shook his head. "What about the photos of you in Prague, Warsaw, and Berlin. Were those your identical twins … or your ghosts?"

Ryan Flynn responded. "Look, I know how this must sound to you after the week you've have had chasing us around Europe, but … excuse me, where are those photos?" Murray leaned back and, reaching behind him, took a manila folder from the shelf. He pushed it over to Ryan.

"Murray showed us these photos early this morning when we arrived on the *Truman*." He opened the folder and laid the photos out individually on the tabletop. Take a close look at these. Show me one that is of us. Any one of us."

Marek, Adrianna, Domiik, and Jedrzej leaned forward to look at the photos. "There," Domiik stated forcefully, pointing to a photo of a man and a woman taken at Morrow's Boutique Hotel. "Right there!"

Rebecca asked, "So that's Ryan and me?"

"Yes, you and Ryan. Or, as we knew you, Bruce, and Sarah," Domiik pointed again to the photo.

"*Oh …* " Adrianna quickly placed her hand over her mouth, as if to pull back the single syllable she had just uttered.

"What?" asked Domiik.

"Damn, I see it," Marek added.

"See what?" Jedrzej demanded.

"Go ahead, Adrianna," Marek said softly, looking at her. "You saw it first. Tell them."

"Tell us what?" Domiik and Jedrzej were growing increasingly frustrated.

"Look at the photos!" Adrianna spoke softly and in a calm voice.

"We *are* looking at them!" Domiik's voice rose in frustration.

"No, you aren't. *Look* … I mean take a *really hard look!* What do you see?"

"I see the two of them: Sarah—Rebecca and Ryan … whatever his name … Bruce," Jedrzej insisted.

"Domiik," remember what we said about the police artist's renderings in Berlin? We said that they were artistically inventive sketches that could be anyone. Right? Now, look at these. Look at all of these photos. What do you see in these photographs that convinces you they are of Rebecca and Ryan or Tom?"

"To begin with, her bright red hair."

"Domiik," remember your little joke with Marek? With red hair and blue eyes, the sketch could be me … Adrianna. Yes, the woman in these photos has red hair, but under that ridiculous hat and dark glasses, she could be me—or anyone! And look carefully at the men. Yes, they could be Tom or Ryan … but a million other men as well. Not one of these photos provides enough clear facial definition to be identifiable as Rebecca, Ryan or Tom. Do you remember, we couldn't use them for facial recognition analysis?"

"But what about the CCTV of them leaving Door #1 at the Athen's airport? That certainly is them," Domiik stated emphatically.

"Yes, that is them without a doubt, but remember the reports of the man matching the shooter's description Leaving Door #4 and the woman departing the airport via the train bridge exit?" Marek countered.

As the truth dawned, Domiik's expression darkened. Bristling with rage, he slammed both fists down hard onto the table. "You mean that this whole thing has been one giant charade?"

"The murders were no charade. They were certainly real. There are enough mangled bodies to prove it," Murray countered.

"But what about their backgrounds?" Jedrzej argued. "You, Tom Barrington, a highly proficient U.S. Marine Corps sniper, 'credited with numerous kills.' Ryan Flynn, explosives and demolition. And you Rebecca Moore, just happen to be a Cyber Security expert. Well ... you're the one I couldn't place ... I mean, as far as your expertise, what that had to do with the assassinations."

"Are you forgetting the computer surveillance equipment and remotely detonated bombs in Berlin and Mykonos?" Adrianna reminded him.

"Oh yes, that's the fit. She's the tech geek."

"Then ... you ... are not the ... assassins?" Domiik haltingly questioned, looking bewildered, and speaking very slowly, as if to himself. He stared intently at the three seated across from him. Then, suddenly, he stood and began pacing the floor.

Murray turned to Marek, "Remember less than an hour ago when I first told you that these three were onboard, you said that this morning they had tried to blow up the villa just like they did the house outside of Berlin? Remember?"

Marek nodded his head as if lost in thought somewhere far away.

"And what time was that?"

"Ahhh ... around 8 am this morning," Marek responded.

Do you want to guess where these three were at 8 am? They were right here, aboard this aircraft carrier. Not what I'd call being in a position to blow anything up."

"What you're saying, Murray is that we've been set up … right?" asked Jedrzej.

"It would appear so if what they are saying is true. And not just us. They've been set up as well, as the would-be assassins.'"

"I don't know who I believe anymore," Jedrzej concluded, shaking his head. "And why are we sitting on this damn American aircraft carrier in the middle of the Mediterranean? Why not in Greece?"

"That was my end," Donovan offered. "Think about it. If these three are not guilty, not the assassins, yet they are Americans tied to the U.S. military and intelligence agencies; the weapons are American, the high tech bullet, the C-4 … over and over it's all tied to the U.S. If the media gets hold of this, you can just imagine the field day they would have and the political fall-out that would follow.

Getting these three out of Europe and under American jurisdiction —hidden here—where no one can find them, as you so aptly put it, was imperative. And what better place from which to collaborate to find out the truth about what is going on—and, most importantly, determine exactly *who* is behind this conspiracy? No, this was the only way!

"We couldn't take them stateside. Too many chances for a leak. As for Europe, which country? Imagine the legal and jurisdictional issues—the media and political pressures! And which government would want to be seen defending these three as innocent until proven guilty? They'd be tried, convicted and condemned by the media before the trial even started. No … better to be here. From here, we can operate with anonymity until we uncover the truth!"

"I see," said Domiik. "It does make perfect sense. But their stories *must* be carefully validated … and in detail! We cannot simply take their word for it. Switzerland, the chalet, the caretaker of the chalet, the flight to Athens … "

"Yes, yes," Murray cut him off mid-sentence. "We are already well onto that. So far, their story checks out 100%. Remember the blood on the roof at the Warsaw crime scene? What type was it?"

"Type O negative … if I recall correctly," Jedrzej replied.

"That's right. And do you remember Herr Kohler's personnel files? Tom's blood type was listed as O negative. Tom readily admits that he is O negative, but just to make certain, we tested it here onboard and confirmed that he is indeed O negative. However, immediately upon his arrival, we flew a sample of his blood back to Sigonella for a DNA match. It's not a match with the blood found in Warsaw. It's not even close! So, the real shooter, who 'bled at the scene' very likely didn't fall from the platform at all, but merely planted that blood on the rooftop along with the American origin weapon and clearly had prior knowledge of Tom's blood type. Fortunately for Tom, and for all of us, every individual's DNA is unique, and that could not be replicated with planted blood."

Murray went on, "Also, remember the bandaged head wound and limp in the CCTV video from Warsaw? Our doctors onboard carefully examined Tom and concluded there is no evidence whatsoever of any recent injury of that kind. In fact, his only discernible injury is a small fresh cut on his left hand, incurred last night during their escape from Mykonos."

"I don't get it" … Jedrzej broke in, "Then, why Berlin? What possible purpose could that have served? The bomb and senseless killing of all those German SWAT officers."

"At this point, we do not understand what or who is behind the events that have taken place thus far or what is their purpose and most critically… their end game plan. But it is becoming clear that the sinister machinations underlying this plot are far more sophisticated and wide-ranging than any of us has realized. I now believe, and James agrees with me here, that Berlin was, at least partially, a decoy … a ruse … and that the murder of those police officers was planned merely as a set-up, part of the chain of events leading to Mykonos."

Marek looked puzzled. "What are you saying? What do you mean by a set-up for Mykonos."

"We now believe that the raid on Mykonos was intended to succeed … or at least in part. Remember the telephone tip the Greek police received? The goal of that anonymous phone tip was to manipulate us into raiding the house this morning. And the real perpetrators intended that these three would perish in that raid.

Consider the scenario: early in the morning, without warning or apparent reason, they suddenly find themselves under direct attack by a large unknown force. Not understanding what is happening, and with such heavily armed forces suddenly coming against them from multiple directions, they would instinctively utilize the conveniently supplied automatic weapons to defend themselves. Do you recall telling me that there had been gunfire at the empty villa, the Greek SWAT Team adopting a 'take no chances, fire first mentality?' Once the shooting began, the C-4 would have been remotely detonated, and it would appear to the authorities—to us—as a mistake on the part of the panicked killers."

"And if they didn't fight or defend themselves, but decided to surrender? Then what?" Domiik asked.

"From what I understand of the morning's events, there would have been scant chance for them to surrender. But if they had somehow managed to do so without being shot first, the C-4 would have been immediately detonated. Rebecca told us that the house was wired with hidden video cameras. And, Marek, you confirmed during our phone conversation that there was enough C-4 in the locked closet to obliterate the entire villa.

Either way, with these three incinerated in the blast, the only real evidence regarding the assassinations would have conveniently vanished in an inferno, just as did the evidence from the Berlin house. These suspects, the weapons … the Greek SWAT police inside the villa … all gone! A replay of Berlin. And where would our investigation have led from there? *Nowhere!* It would be over. *The end!* We would still have no idea as to *who* was behind this or *why*? Or even where to begin looking. Whoever they are, they'd walk away. Free and clear."

"And now what happens to us?" Tom Barrington asked.

"We will keep you under wraps … hidden here until we can flush out the real killers," Donovan responded.

"But how?" "With a trap?" Donovan replied.

"And we … we're the bait." Rebecca added, "Aren't we?"

"Yes, you are *the BAIT!*"

Take heed lest you too quickly unmask the PRETENSE with which your enemy conceals himself and in so doing, unwittingly destroy your most cunning weapon against him.

To be continued …

Book Two of the—**IMBROGLIO Trilogy:**

The BAIT!

IMBROGLIOTRILOGY.COM

To learn more about the **IMBROGLIO TRILOGY** and upcoming books in this series, **THE BAIT!** and **REVELATIONS**, please visit www.ImbroglioTrilogy.com.

There you can interact with the author, John Di Frances and follow his blog as well as signup to receive updates on the release dates of the upcoming books, as well as other books by John. For those who signup online, we will be offering the opportunity to obtain special, author signed pre-release editions of **THE BAIT!** and **REVELATIONS** through local bookstores before they become available to the general public.

If you have enjoyed reading **PRETENSE**, we would appreciate you telling your local bookstore or if you purchased it online, posting reviews to that book seller's website. We also encourage you to spread the word about **PRETENSE** and the **IMBROGLIO TRILOGY** among your friends, work colleagues, and family by social media. And don't forget, although we live in a digitally interconnected world, person-to-person word of mouth is still the best way for you to introduce more readers to John's books. So please, tell others.

IMBROGLIO TRILOGY

Excerpt from an interview with the author.

<u>Question:</u> Why does a global corporate strategy and innovation consultant and business author suddenly begin writing fiction?

<u>John's Answer:</u> *"Because we all need a little fantasy in our life ... some make-believe. And if it includes compelling characters, a bit of intrigue, suspense, action, and a subtle touch of humor, all the better! Face it; modern life is fraught with pressure, stress, deadlines, commitments .... We all need an occasional escape from REAL LIFE!"*

I have had a lifelong desire to write suspense thriller fiction. It began in grade school when a teacher asked us to write a little story. After a paragraph or two which was probably all she expected, I realized that my vision of writing a full length novel would have to wait. The waiting was simply far more extended than I ever expected, but at least the seed was planted. Then one day late in 2016, after forty-three years of marriage, I casually mentioned to my wife Sally my long-held desire to someday write a suspense thriller. 'Her response was what are you waiting for? Go ahead, take some time off from your work and do it now.'

Writing fiction is far different from business books, and I had no idea if I could do so successfully, but that day I decided to take the plunge. I wrote one chapter and asked her to read it. She is an avid reader, but suspense thrillers are definitely not her genre. Regardless, she liked it. She was an English major in college and tends to be brutally honest, especially about literature, so I thought that if she liked it, maybe I could write fiction. I wrote the second chapter, then the third and so on. After each, she would read it and tell me if it was any good. One day, about halfway through the book, she asked if I had more chapters she could read. At that point, I knew I had a novel.

Writing part-time I finished the first draft in five weeks. However, like all of my books, it required many more months to turn that first draft into a finished book with which I was happy. **PRETENSE** is the result.

Question: And you enjoyed writing fiction?

John's Answer: I have never enjoyed any aspect of my professional life as much as writing fiction. It's far more like a vacation than work! And following **PRETENSE** will be Book Two, **The BAIT!**, already underway, and then Book Three, **REVELATIONS**, the conclusion to the **IMBROGLIO Trilogy**.

Question: Have you thought beyond the **IMBROGLIO Trilogy?** What comes next?

John's Answer: Who knows, but I have many ideas for more suspense thrillers in the future.

About the Author:

John Di Frances

A University of Wisconsin Honors graduate; John holds a degree in Business and Economics. He has served as an outside director on corporate boards of directors and has been retained as an expert witness in corporate litigation cases. John has been a faculty member of the National Contract Management Association, served as an instructor for numerous educational institutions, seminar providers, federal government agencies—including the FBI—and professional associations.

John's professional career spans decades of global strategy and open innovation consulting to corporate, nonprofit, academic, and government agency clients. He also has ten years of corporate employment including management and senior executive positions. His writing draws upon this extensive international business knowledge and life experience.

John's multifaceted career has included some highly unusual activities such as assisting clients in complex problem solving of Advanced (Black) Military Weapons Systems as well as working undercover in the Caribbean Islands to find and seize the assets of white-collar criminals. One such undercover assignment included the seizing of a $13.6 million dollar waterfront island estate and several racehorses. He has worked in cooperation with the FBI, SEC, RCMP (Royal Canadian Mounted Police), and the Swiss National Police.

However, most of his professional life has been dedicated to helping companies, nonprofits, and government agencies in the twin disciplines of Open Innovation and Strategy Development, or what John terms *Strategic Open Innovation.* He has assisted a wide range of organizations globally, from Fortune 100's to start-ups. John is the author of four business books and co-author of a fifth, with two more business books in process. Since 2000, he has also served audiences internationally, as a professional keynote speaker.

Over the course of his career, John's professional memberships have included the following organizations:

American Bar Association
Chicago Writers Association
National Speakers Association
American Christian Fiction Writers
Turnaround Management Association
Association of Certified Fraud Examiners
National Contract Management Association
American Defense Preparedness Association
Wisconsin Professional Speakers Association
National Defense Industrial Association
Association of the United States Army
Meeting Professionals International
Wisconsin Christian Fiction Writers
American Petroleum Institute
United States Naval Institute

28014945R00170

Printed in Poland
by Amazon Fulfillment
Poland Sp. z o.o., Wrocław